HOT WORK

A WOMEN IN TRADES ROMANCE®

KATE COLE

Cover by Paige Moreland @lpm_draws

Platform artwork by Erika Plum @custombyerikaplum

Published by Bryant Press

First Edition 2025

Print ISBN: 978-1-7381397-2-9

eBook ISBN: 978-1-7381397-3-6

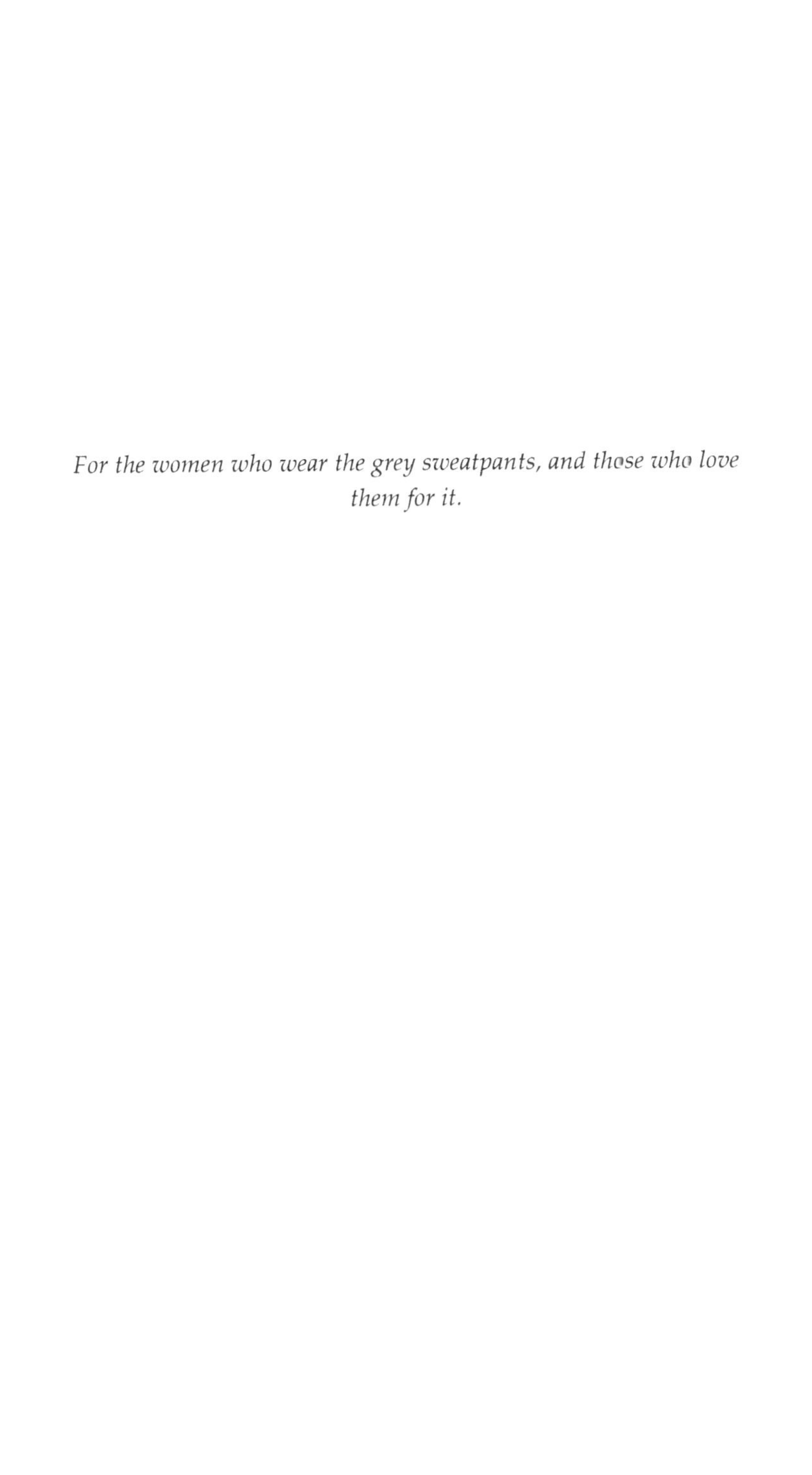

For the women who wear the grey sweatpants, and those who love them for it.

CONTENT NOTE

This book contains scenes which take place underwater and are life threatening. It also addresses topics such as post traumatic stress, and situations where mental health has been impacted by workplace incidents. Discussions around reproductive autonomy are represented on the page. *Hot Work* also contains depictions of homophobia.

OFFSHORE PLATFORM

HOT WORK

(hat w3:rk)
noun
Work that could produce a source of ignition, such as a
spark or open flame.

Examples include welding, cutting, grinding and the use of
non-explosion proof electrical equipment.

Also: work with hot divers who are ten years your junior in
very remote places.

CHAPTER 1

The basic white label on my Pelican case says "Property of Violet Thomas" in Helvetica font. Printed in thirty-two-point lettering, it's clear without being bold, easily legible, no super-fluous serifs.

Just like me.

Snapping the last latch shut, I stand to assess the situation. Pulling the ever-present elastic from my wrist, I throw my platinum locks up into a messy bun while I scrutinize my baggage.

Not my best work, but not my worst either.

I've mastered the art of packing efficiently at this point in my career. After fifteen years of routine work travel, I'm an expert minimalist. Like every other aspect of my life, my gear is reduced to the bare essentials: everything I need and not a single thing I don't.

Leaving the pile of equipment at the door, I return to my bedroom. The place is eerily quiet, my sparsely decorated apartment just barely lit by the first hints of sunrise.

I'm always restless in the hours before I leave as my mind grapples with the challenges that await. Today is no different. Here I am, awake and packed ahead of my alarm and still a full hour to go before I need to leave for the airport.

Pausing at my bedroom's threshold, I look at Charles—a large duvet-covered lump—on the left side of my bed. He sleeps so soundly, oblivious to my tosses and turns. I trip over my own sweatshirt as I approach him. It's a rumpled heap on the floor, strewn haphazardly the night before. I bend to grab it, along with three other garments tossed across the hardwood, and stash them in the laundry basket in the corner. That's when I notice Charles's own pile of clothing neatly folded on my chair.

We're as opposite as opposites come.

Charles and I have been together for three years and grown used to the routine we've developed. I'm away for long stretches of time and leave often, so each time we reunite there's a period of acclimatization as we get to know each other's quirks and habits all over again. Every time we do, we reinforce deeply entrenched patterns and parts: mine as the chaotic and creative character played by Violet Thomas, Charles Lane in the disciplined and restrained co-starring role.

He's yin to my yang.

I met Charles at a pivotal time in my life. I was thirty-seven. He was strong and secure when I was uncertain and scattered. He brought the stability I'd been seeking, and his predictability became the anchor I needed when I'd felt adrift.

I was lucky to find Charles. Even luckier that he saw a future with a tattooed and spirited tradeswoman that no one could have imagined as his romantic partner.

Charles rolls onto his back and opens his eyes like he knows I've been watching him.

"Hey," he says, running a palm across his face. He's cutest when he's like this: disheveled and natural.

"Hey yourself."

"Ready to go?" he asks, voice scratchy from sleep.

"All packed. Just need to shower."

"Have a great flight. Text me when you get there…if there's cell service." He rolls back onto his stomach and stuffs an arm up under his pillow.

I try not to be annoyed by the dismissal.

Charles doesn't have to be up for hours, and I really should let him sleep, but it'll be weeks before I see him next.

His breathing quickly resumes its rhythmic cadence.

The man likes his sleep.

I weigh my options and decide to make my move.

I quietly peel off the pyjamas I'm wearing and toss them on the floor. Scratching my naked, tattooed ribcage nervously, I stand beside the bed for a moment and reconsider. It's odd that I find myself uncertain after all this time, but when it comes to the man in front of me, I confess to always feeling just a little out of my depth.

Before I lose my nerve, I lift the duvet and slip underneath the cool cotton covers. His slim figure is warm beside me as I press the length of my body against him.

He fidgets from the disturbance.

His back still faces me as I slide my hand under his sleep shirt, seeking out the smooth muscles of his back. It's been a long time since we've done this—been skin against skin—and I'm surprised by how quickly the heat builds inside of me, eager for his touch.

When he doesn't immediately wake, I kick things up a notch. I move a hand around to his trim stomach and try, a bit awkwardly, to nip at his ear.

Charles groans and shifts.

I interpret this as interest and start to move the hand lower, inching toward the waistband of his pants.

He grabs my hand just before it slips beneath the fabric.

"What are you doing?" he asks, suddenly wide awake.

"Thought I'd say goodbye." I move to take another nibble of his ear.

He swats me away like a fly.

I try not to take it personally, but the gesture stings.

"I'm tired. I've slept terribly," he says.

He didn't seem to have had any trouble sleeping to me.

I gently coax him to his back and attempt a sultry voice. "Let me do all the work."

I plant one kiss on his lips—thinking he might just need some convincing—but his lips are hard and immovable, tightly shut and closed for business.

"It'll be two weeks before we see each other again," I explain, doing the mental math on how long it's been since the last time we exchanged more than a peck on the lips.

Too long.

I boldly move to climb on top of him, attempting to straddle his waist, but his hand catches my vine leaf-tattooed thigh and blocks me, holding me in place.

"I'm tired, Violet." This time his voice is loud and firm.

I shrink back to my spot beside him and instinctively cover myself with the sheet.

It's not the first time I've been rebuffed, but his methods aren't usually so harsh. An unexpected swell of emotion rises, and I push it back with a breath.

"Sorry, I just thought—"

"Go shower," he says abruptly, cutting me off mid-sentence. He softens the message with a light but dismissive pat to my hip.

I'm quick to leave the bed, collecting my discarded garments as I go. I head directly to the bathroom and turn on the light. The vanity mirror is unforgiving, reflecting an embarrassed and tired freckled face. My hair is wild and my green eyes glassy with tears.

Forty years old and silly boys still break my heart.

Whatever.

I shower, dress, and reorient myself to default setting.

Airplane-friendly clothing: check.

Water bottle and snack: check.

Book, phone, and charger: check.

I call myself an Uber and track it as it comes. Each minute passes slowly in the lonely silence of my living room. When the quiet gets too loud I decide to wait for my car downstairs.

I stack each item carefully—as I've done so many times before—and gently click the door closed behind me without so much as a kiss goodbye.

I try the combination lock on the equipment chest one more time, but it refuses to cooperate.

Nothing seems to be going my way today.

First the sting of rejection this morning, then my unexpected period in the airport washroom, and now this frustrating lock that feels like a kick while I'm down.

Something—most likely hormonal rage—starts to build from deep within me and threatens to explode.

Stepping back, I regain composure before attempting it again.

The lock still fails to unlatch.

Piece of shit.

I should've replaced this thing long ago. Corroded by years of exposure to water and salt, it's been giving me grief for months. Who knew it would choose today to finally give up the ghost?

The oxidized metal stares back at me like a middle finger to my Monday.

That's when I finally snap. I step back and deliver a hard kick to the equipment chest with my booted foot. The pleasure I get from the assault is interrupted by several figures emerging from the galley.

We're miles from shore on an ancient oil platform that has been plagued with faulty machinery and broken parts for years. Held together with spot welds and Bandaid repairs, it's been surviving on hard graft and hope. I've travelled all day—first by plane and then a long, choppy boat ride—to this seventies era offshore monstrosity with a condemned helipad. I'm one of six commercial divers who will put this godforsaken platform out of its misery over the next two weeks.

"Are you winning, V?"

I follow the voice calling me from across the deck and see Bruce, our team leader, convened with four other guys.

"Not sure, Bruce," I yell back, "but kicking it sure felt good!" I give another tap to the hard plastic container with my steel toe for good measure.

"Take a break from abusing the equipment and meet the new guy." Bruce gestures for me to come closer.

As I approach, I spot Nick, JT, and Steve right away, but don't recognize the other figure in the crowd. He's backlit by end-of-day sunshine, making it difficult to make him out. Raising my tattooed hand to shield the bright sun, it's enough to catch a few details: a tall, large frame with closely trimmed light hair. He's wearing oversized sunglasses that cover a good portion of his face and it's off-putting: all I can see is myself reflected back at me.

Mystery Man steps forward and fully blocks out the sun, his details come sharply into focus. "Have you tried a lubricant?"

The combination of what he's said and the striking youthful beauty—yes, beauty—of his features completely throws me.

My brain is momentarily incapacitated. "Pardon?"

"On the lock." He points over at the equipment chest. "Sometimes you just need to add some lubricant."

This time, I swear I see half a smile form with his perfect pink lips when he says it.

I attempt to assemble a sentence.

Nope, still nothing.

Bruce puts me out of my misery. "Or a good whack. Sometimes all it needs is a good whack."

I rub my forehead.

Bruce shrugs. "It'll break the corrosion up in the lock."

Okay, I really need a conversation reset.

Maybe an *everything* reset.

I shake my head.

"V, meet our new diver." Bruce turns to Mystery Man. "Filling in for Patrick while he's on paternity leave. He's coming to us from construction diving, so we're in good shape for the abandonment this week."

My eyes operate on their own accord, rebelliously scanning his wide shoulders.

Good shape, indeed.

I shake my head again.

Mystery Man steps closer and I instinctively take a step back. The angle and sharpness of his lightly stubbled jaw and the outright luminescence of his skin completely disarm me.

"Cooper Brooks." He holds out one hand and removes his sunglasses with the other.

That's when they hit me: two pools of turquoise so deep that someone could get lost in them.

Holy shit.

Whatever. I'm here to do a job and I'm immune to this kid's charisma.

"Violet Thomas." I confidently grip his large, calloused hand but drop it quickly when an unsettling buzz starts to form along my palm. I resist the urge to shake off the sensation that's left behind.

I turn to head back to the difficult lock as the other guys huddle and talk. Cooper follows me like a persistent puppy.

I walk faster.

"I should be calling you *violent* after the mean streak you just showed that equipment case." His voice trails behind me.

Oh, this guy thinks he's charming.

I pivot abruptly and rest my hands on my hips. "*Fourth Wing.*"

"Pardon?" It's his turn to look confused.

"*Fourth. Wing,*" I repeat.

"I'm sorry?" He removes those damn sunglasses again and leans in slightly. A waft of spicy and sweet scent hits my nose with his proximity. I do my best to ignore it.

"It's a book by Rebecca Yarros. Her female main character is named Violet, and her male main character likes to call her 'Violence.'"

"Are you slagging me for my lack of originality?" A smile blooms across his face, revealing perfectly symmetrical white teeth and bringing a mischievous sparkle to his eyes.

Jesus.

"Yes," I force out.

He casually twirls his sunglasses by the arm and raises a brow. "I'm hearing *try harder.*"

"I'm *saying* don't try at all." I lean back on my heels and pick at a stubborn cuticle.

"Well, *this* main male character likes a challenge."

And with that, Cooper Brooks delivers a wink that—if I were ten years younger—would have melted the gusset right out of my panties.

I, on the other hand, refuse to be fazed. I roll my eyes

and return to the locker. I hear Cooper's steps retreating behind me as he rejoins the others.

This time when I attempt the lock, it opens on the first try.

I bite back a smile as it dawns on me: *I'm in so much trouble.*

CHAPTER 2

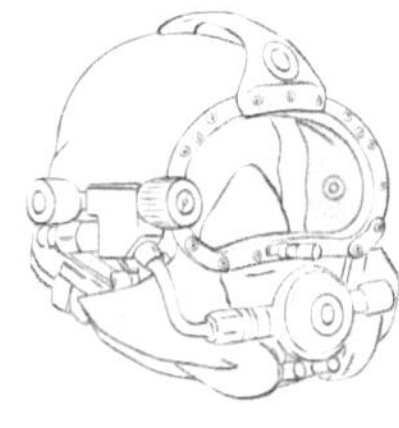

I'm the first person to the galley the next morning. Bathroom facilities onboard are rather bleak, so I've deferred the shower and instead thrown my hair into my trademark topknot. I'm pulling on my favourite worn-out hoodie as I drag myself to the table for a much-needed coffee fix.

Marsha is already there, prepping the pancakes and bacon for half a dozen hungry divers and various other offshore workers. This is unequivocally Marsha's kitchen. Unlike those of us with more niche skills who move around from rig to rig or site to site, the service crew returns to the same station every two weeks. The way the middle-aged woman competently moves in this kitchen shows everyone —without question—this is her turf.

Marsha has the patience of a saint and I cling to her— desperate for female companionship—whenever our paths cross on this platform.

We communicate in comfortable, silent nods and grateful smiles as she pours me a steaming cup, knowingly leaves a small pitcher of cream in front of me, and heads back to the griddle. She's too busy for casual conversation at this time of day.

I'd describe life on this frankenrig as a strange marriage between summer camp and prison. Not that I can complain about the amenities—at least I have private accommodations. The sleeping quarters are a communal room of bunk beds, and that's where the men sleep. With Marsha occupying the one single room and nowhere else to put me—the only woman on the crew—I've been given the VIP cabin. But don't let the VIP part of my accommodations package fool you. It's as basic as the 1970s motel room it was modelled after. Burt Reynolds would have loved it.

"Good morning, Vivacious." Cooper's voice jars me from my thoughts.

Oh lord, we're still doing this.

He looks rumpled and dozy and wears the same thing he had on yesterday—stubble just a little bit longer, T-shirt just a little more wrinkled. Of course, it only makes him look even more gorgeous.

Like he just tumbled out of bed.

Which he did.

Thoughts and prayers to my nether regions.

I'm not sure I'm ready for this kind of attractiveness yet today.

He lifts his shirt slightly when he scratches his flat stomach, revealing a glimpse of the tanned, rippled muscle as he turns to greet Marsha. "Morning. Mind if I grab a cup?"

Correction: His kind of attractiveness was *made* for early mornings.

He settles into the seat across from me and grins. "What's the matter, Villainous? Not a morning person?"

I realize I've been frowning. "Are you really going to keep doing this?"

"I have a vast vocabulary—see, two more words that start with V. I'll find one that sticks."

There's that dangerous wink again.

Clearly, *he* is a morning person. God help me—more prayers.

Marsha hurries over to the table with the carafe. I watch as her cheeks flush and she tucks her neatly trimmed greying bob behind her ear, then fusses over the placement of his mug and whether he wants cream or sugar. It feels like I've entered an alternate reality because I've simply never seen her behave like this. I'd half expected her to tell him to get his own bloody cup—like she often does to the rest of the crew—but apparently the chemicals this kid is giving off have gone straight to her brain (or, like me, other parts) because she can't seem to help him fast enough.

I call him "kid" because I suspect he's a fair bit younger than I am. It may not be an accurate assessment—age can be tricky—but he seems several years my junior. Full of youthful sass and BDE. In my mind I've placed him as a California boy. His dark tan and sun-kissed hair look like they belong on a surfboard. I could picture him with some bikini-clad blonde under palm trees.

I mean, not that I'm picturing him at all.

"Quite the platform, hey?" Cooper takes his first sip of coffee after Marsha has ensured it's precisely to his satisfaction.

"The very best in disco-era technology." I wrap my hands around my own mug, a bit nervous being alone in his company.

"This thing's a dinosaur—just call it Tyrannosaurus Rig. You could stay here all season fixing shit."

The boy is clever; I'll give him that.

"Well, thankfully they finally had enough sense to put it out of its misery."

My cell phone vibrates in my pocket. Cellular service can be spotty, so I'm quick to check it, capitalizing on a window of decent reception.

Charles: Got there ok?

I quickly type out an enthusiastic reply.

Violet: Yes! I'm so happy to hear from you.

Violet: Miss you.

Charles: I'm heading to the office soon, probably putting in extra hours this week for month end. I'll be super distracted, so good luck and I'll just talk to you when I talk to you.

My stomach becomes a clenched fist. *Harsh.*

Violet: Um, okay. Good luck with month end.

Violet: Love you.

Charles: Stay safe.

I wait a few minutes for him to say more, but nothing comes. Maybe he didn't see my last message. Maybe the cellular dropped off.

Maybe he's just a dick.

The thought sneaks out before I can stop it, but I stuff it away with my iPhone and wistful disappointment.

I focus on my coffee.

"Things alright?" Cooper asks.

I hate that my emotions are always written so plainly on my face.

"Of course. Why wouldn't they be?" I take a small sip.

"Looked like you got some bad news, that's all." He takes a drink from his own cup.

We continue on in silent sips for a few awkward seconds.

Cooper finally breaks the stalemate. "Wanna talk about it?"

I'm spared from further questions when the rest of our teammates arrive with a noisy entrance eager for their breakfast. Thankfully, all discussion turns to the weather and our work plan for the day.

We congregate next to the moon pool—our primary access point to the water below. It's customary for the team to conduct an exploratory or reconnaissance dive on the first day at a new location, no matter the project. This initial dive gives our team a chance to familiarize ourselves with the location and its unique challenges, allows us to take essential measurements required to do the job, and gives us a chance to establish a main cable line—a critical and direct line that connects the platform to the primary work area.

An abandonment, or platform decommission, is as arduous as it sounds. We've got our work cut out for us these next several days, and work planning and task sequencing is key to our success.

Team chemistry is also an intangible yet essential ingredient that can either ensure the project's success or condemn it to abject failure. The reconnaissance dive is the litmus test of any dive team's chemistry: the moment of truth when the small-but-mighty team knows whether they've got the mojo or it's a no-go.

When our hundreds of pounds of equipment are ready and it's time for our dives, I'm unprecedentedly shy about peeling off my layers to pull on my wetsuit. I don't like this new sense of insecurity. I don't know what it says about me, and I worry about what it means for the dynamic of the team. Determined to keep things business as usual, I power through slipping one foot at a time through the wetsuit's openings. I'm far from naked—I'm wearing my typical sports bra and form-fitting athletic shorts. I'd wear less at the beach. But even a single square inch of exposed skin feels a bit off to me this morning, in light of the five-alarm pheromone fire that turned up on the platform yesterday.

Shaking things off, I focus on what's in front of me, one simple task at a time. I'm making adjustments to the thick neoprene as I pull it over my hips when I catch sight of him in my periphery. I go rigid with awareness but I'm powerless to the instinct to turn my head and watch.

The golden glow of his exposed back, arms, and chest glistens in the morning sun. His name is Cooper, but maybe it should be *Copper* on account of how his tanned skin deepens in the morning sunshine. I've simply never seen anyone or anything like him. In fact, I kind of figured humans like him were just fiction: contrived godlike creatures whose symmetrical and perfectly proportioned features cannot and do not actually exist in nature. I stand corrected.

Thankfully, I regain composure and close my gaping mouth before he notices me outright ogling him. When I turn back to the rest of the team, I catch my teammate JT also watching him in utter amazement. He must feel the weight of my gaze because he turns to look at me. His brow furrows and his cheeks turn pink, caught in the act. But then he shrugs and smiles.

"*Wow.*" His lips move silently.

Wow indeed.

We both chuckle and get back to work.

I'm glancing over one last time to shamelessly sneak another peek when I catch Cooper looking back at me. I freeze. He turns away, then surprises me by turning back to take another long, bold look at what's in front of him. It's an outright examination, and I feel his eyes burn a trail down my side, along the string of leaves tattooed down my arm and crossing my ribs.

I instinctively suck in my belly, self-conscious about how I look in front of this potential underwear model, but stand a bit taller too. I'm proud—it feels good to be noticed.

"You like music, Voyeuristic?" he shouts over, mischief in his eyes.

My cheeks flush, but I dish it right back. "Depends on the music, Frat Boy."

His mouth opens in mock surprise. "You do realize that I'm about ten years past frat boy?"

I'm not sure what we're doing right now. Is this teasing? Is this flirting?

He pulls out an obnoxiously bright yellow Bluetooth speaker from his equipment case and sets it on the work-bench in front of us. I watch as he cues up his music.

"Oh god," I mutter, bracing myself for what's to come. Surely bold rap or brash hip hop. But they don't come. Instead, it's the familiar opening bars of a song we've all heard a million times before and yet haven't heard enough.

"Is this Vanilla Ice?" Steve asks with a curious expression.

"Christ, no." Cooper cringes. "I know we've just met,

but do you think that little of me already?" He picks the speaker up with his massive hands.

I chuckle and listen to the exchange.

"It's Bowie and Queen. A classic. I'm going to prioritize your musical education." Cooper turns the volume up.

We all watch in rapt fascination as he moves along to the music while getting his equipment ready.

"It's called 'Under Pressure' Steve," Nick interjects. "Get it?"

"Ah." Steve nods. "Clever bugger."

Just as we've all adjusted to the sounds coming from the bright yellow waterproof speaker and the man's unbridled enthusiasm, Cooper joins in on the singing in an unparalleled falsetto.

Who the hell is this guy?

By the time the song ends, we're all bobbing our heads to the tune and my face hurts from smiling.

Mojo for days.

CHAPTER 3

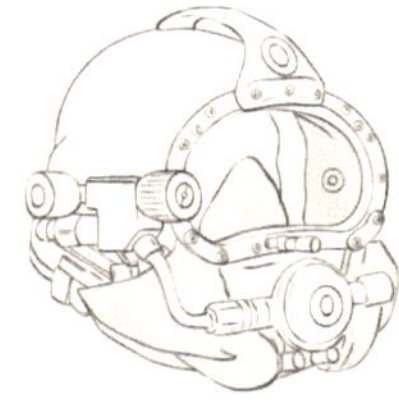

"So…Cooper." JT flashes me a self-satisfied smile. He removes his EnigmaSub ball cap and tosses it on the table, running a hand over his closely cropped head. Once settled in his chair beside me he takes his sandwich in hand.

"So. Cooper," I volley back. There are two guilty parties at this lunch table, after all.

JT's shoulders drop. "What on earth are we going to do about Cooper?"

"What are you talking about? There's nothing to be done." I sigh, resigned to our fate. It seems we're destined to endlessly drool over six feet of tanned charisma and unrelenting charm. But with all factors on the table, he's not a problem to be solved, he's a colleague. We can remain professional for the sake of the team, which—if the success of our morning has proven anything—appears to have impeccable chemistry. We can't let anything compromise that.

"Oh, there's plenty to be done…and you're just the one to do it." JT punctuates his statement with an enthusiastic bite of his dill pickle, like it's the end of the conversation.

"Why don't *you* make a move, JT? I saw your eyes the size of saucers." I feel like I'm in uncharted territory here, like I may be walking a fine line, but in my defence, he's the one who brought it up.

"I'm in a long-term relationship, V."

"So am I."

"With that dude?" He rolls his eyes. "Besides, I'm not where Cooper's interest is directed at present."

I finally take a few bites from my own plate, considering his comments. There's no way I'm Cooper's type. He's a shameless flirt who sprinkles his charm like rose petals from a flower girl basket. I'm just the token female he's been stuck working with on the offshore production platform this week. I'm nothing special.

"Firstly, *that dude* has a name." I use air quotes for emphasis. "Secondly, we need to address the elephant in the room: your interest in Cooper. I had no idea."

JT shrugs. It's really none of my business, but he and I have worked together for years. I worry about his motivations to keep this under wraps. I hope he feels he can trust me.

Then another cog in my mental machine clicks into place. I try to recall previously used pronouns but come up blank. "Wait, I'm such an idiot. Your partner Chris…it's short for Christian."

"No, Chris is Christine. I'm bi, V. I just tend to keep this quiet because of my line of work. The trades aren't always friendly about that."

My chest hurts just hearing him say that. JT and I have spent long hours in tandem looking out for each other in all types of scenarios; he's a treasured colleague and friend. The thought that he's had to keep part of himself tucked away just to feel safe breaks my heart.

JT picks up on the intensity of the moment. Ever the joker, he attempts to make it light. "But even if I wasn't, V, his kind of beauty transcends sexual orientation."

Our eyes shift to the statuesque form that's just entered the room.

No argument there.

There's a momentary pause for appreciation.

"Has *the dude* even texted you since you've arrived here?" JT's question is very poorly timed and lands just as Cooper's overflowing plate does on our table.

My cheeks grow hot, and I wince. Talking about my love life is the last thing I want to do in Cooper's presence. Ranking right up there with discussing mysterious rashes or the hair that keeps growing out of my chin.

"Can we please stop talking about the dude?" Great, now *I'm* calling him that.

"What *dude*?" Cooper chimes in.

Now we've done it.

"Just Violet's boyfriend," JT explains. I think I spot another eye roll.

Cooper takes his massive sandwich into his equally massive, tanned hands.

It's hard not to notice the size of them.

"Looks like I arrived just in time." He pulls off a generous bite.

I want to disappear into the floorboards.

My stomach turns. I push away my plate. "I prefer *partner*, actually."

"Pardon me." JT wiggles his head, mocking me.

"The *dude* you're talking about has been my partner for three years." I'm feeling a bit defensive now.

"*Partner* who still won't take the next step and move in?" JT asks.

Cooper just eats his sandwich, his head on a swivel between us, like he's watching a tennis match.

"He doesn't want to be left alone half the time." I fold my arms.

"So he's alone *all* the time? It makes no sense, V." JT pops the last bite of his sandwich into his mouth, then stands to leave.

No, no, no…

"Enjoy the rest of your lunch." He flashes a wide grin.

Damn you, JT.

Cooper and I sit in silence for a couple of minutes. Long enough to make me think I might be spared.

"What does your boyfriend do?"

So much for that.

Sitting up straight, I tuck a strand of loose silvery hair behind my ear nervously. "Charles is an…accountant."

"An accountant?" Cooper's eyebrows shoot up in disbelief.

"What's wrong with being an accountant? Too grown up for your liking?"

A pang of guilt hits the moment I've said it. I wouldn't want my age thrown in my face, and I'm sure he doesn't either. Fortunately, he doesn't seem to register the dig.

"And…*Charles*? His name is *Charles*?"

"What's wrong with *Charles*?"

"Everyone back on deck!" Bruce shouts from the galley door. They don't call him a Tool Push for nothing.

Cooper stands and collects the remains of his lunch. I think our conversation is over until he mutters—maybe more to himself than to me. "Nothing, if you're into accountants."

It's chilly slipping back into my wetsuit, but I'm quick

about it. There's not much time to waste. We have measurements to take and video surveys to do before we can start to remove the production piping and initiate the days-long abandonment process.

My friends have romantic notions of what I do. They picture me as some sea nymph creature, fluttering away with fins, my platinum locks adrift in the current. In reality, the most prominent current in my daily life is the DC that we turn on to complete our arc welding circuit. I don't even wear fins; I wear boots and walk along the floor at depths of over a hundred feet.

Waiting for Steve to surface and switch out with me, I load on over a hundred pounds of equipment. First are my cumbersome suit and boots, but that's just the beginning. My dive helmet alone weighs thirty pounds. Then I strap on a five-point harness with an integrated weight belt that has forty more pounds of lead in it. At our depths, our air is surface supply—not from tanks—but we still need a bail-out bottle as backup, and it's an additional weight.

When I connect my harness to the main line at the moon pool, any trace of my previous feminine figure has disappeared and I'm all business. Silly thoughts of boyfriends or boy toys are cast aside as I slip below the surface.

I'm both weighted and weightless as my body makes its long descent.

At these depths, I spend only forty-five minutes underwater at a time. More of our day is spent on logistics—set up and take down—than in the water. But those minutes… oh those minutes. It's just me and the vast unknown. You don't get into this business if you don't love it. The thrill and the adrenaline rush: How else could you justify the risk? It's one of the most dangerous jobs in the world. We rely entirely on our equipment and training, and sometimes I can't see more than a foot in front of me, but when your muscle memory kicks in and you're in the zone, nothing beats it.

No wonder Cooper scoffed at Charles's profession.

I complete my visual survey, take some measurements, and help collect more video. My team communicates with me via the helmet—telling me where to linger and if they want more detail.

When it's time to come to the surface, it's a slow process to avoid decompression sickness. We use our dive chart to tell us how quickly we can do it. JT is there when I reach the top, a friendly smile to accompany the burst of sunshine that makes me squint my eyes.

He's quick to help me out of my helmet and any extraneous equipment before rushing me to the decompression chamber. I've got seven minutes to get in there and strap on the oxygen before I'm at serious risk of illness. It's a race to get in, then the heavy chamber door thumps shut and I'm left alone in my pressurized tin can to binge on one hundred percent pure medical oxygen.

I settle in and let my body exhale the bubbles of nitrogen that have contaminated my system. It's oddly quiet and still after the frenzied pace of the last two hours.

I start humming "Under Pressure" and it reverberates off the metal walls around me. I giggle under my mask.

Bloody earworm.

I must be high on adrenaline.

There's not much to do in my windowless private quarters after dark. Instead of sleeping, I go in search of a kettle and conversation in the galley since Marsha should be there.

As reliable as rain, she sets me up with a peppermint tea and her quiet company as she putters in the kitchen.

I pull out my knitting at the table and start clacking at the needles. I started knitting years ago to pass the hours on planes, boats, and rigs. I generally stick to smaller projects—socks, hats, scarves, and mittens. They're portable and easy to manage on the go. Tonight, I'm working on the second sock of a new pair that's made with yarn in pretty purples and pinks—a gift for my pink-loving stone mason friend Bella who needs warm wool under her steel-toed boots when the temperatures drop.

"Oh hi, Cooper," Marsha gushes from where she stands at the counter. "Want a cup of tea too?"

I almost drop a stitch but manage to recover it.

"If it's not too much trouble." He passes over the threshold and I catch it in my periphery, as he slips both hands into the front pouch of his yellow Carhartt hoodie.

"Not any trouble at all." She rushes to grab a mug, fresh colour in her cheeks.

I roll my eyes, trying to stamp out the errant thought of how delicious that hoodie would smell.

Cooper latches onto me like a barnacle. "Lonely in your quarters, Visitorial?"

"Visi-what?"

"Cut me some slack; I'm not a hundred percent." He takes a seat across from me and weaves his long fingers together on the table.

As Marsha brings over his steaming mug, Cooper looks down at my busy hands. I wait for the smart-ass old lady remark that's surely coming. It always does. Instead, a smile forms across his face.

Cooper yawns.

"Tired, Frat Boy? Young, strapping lad like yourself…I figured you'd have endless amounts of energy."

Oh, snap. That didn't land like I intended it.

"Wouldn't you like to find out." He raises a brow—and his mug—seductively, but then burns his mouth with his first sip.

A laugh escapes me as he winces and swears.

I grin. "Karma."

His face flushes.

Oh no, sheepish Cooper is even *more* dangerous.

"But seriously," I continue, "Bruce said you're from construction diving; this work should be a piece of cake."

"Yes, from construction diving…work that nearly killed me and wrecked me for life."

"Never thought of that," I admit.

I know that type of work is notoriously tough. Hard, physical labour as structures are built and disassembled at shallower depths. Some risks of the job might be lower, but it also means longer shifts as divers can work up to three hundred minutes at a time at less than thirty feet. Companies take full advantage of keen young divers and wear them down—they never last long.

"How long did you do that?" I ask, genuinely curious.

"About five years."

I consider the math and he sees the calculations in my face.

"Thirty." He takes a smaller, more tentative sip this time. Swallows.

I flush with embarrassment. He knew I was fishing.

"Forty." It's only fair that I tell him.

His eyebrows raise. "Never would've guessed."

"Cut the crap, Cooper."

He had *to say that, right?*

"How many years have you been at it, then?" he asks.

"About fifteen." I straighten out my yarn when it gets tangled in my project bag.

"Well, hopefully I'll be useful to the team. I'm good for the grunt work, at least." His self-deprecating tone surprises me since he's been so larger-than-life and some-what full of himself up to now.

The galley grows quiet. Marsha is silently reviewing a cookbook in the kitchen, Cooper pensively fiddles with the tea bag tag attached to his handle. The only sound is the persistent clacking of my needles.

Cooper breaks the silence. "My Grandma used to knit."

Here it is, the old lady joke.

"Are you calling me old?" I pre-emptively jest.

"No, no…it's just every time I see anyone knitting, I think of her." He gives me a warm smile. "She used to knit me cozy wool socks every year for Christmas."

I'm struck by his sentimentality.

"Every time I hear that sound of the needles, I taste warm cookies and milk and smell her kitchen." He stands and takes his tea with him. "Goodnight, Vibrant."

Well, shit. If that didn't just melt my old, icy heart.

CHAPTER 4

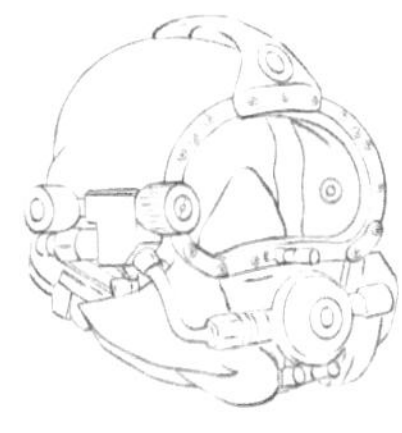

Our resident Adonis waltzes casually in for breakfast. I'm mid-omelette and seated with JT and two other rig workers who are having an animated discussion about whether banana bread should have chocolate chips in it. I have no idea why; I guess the topic of muffins came up. Their distraction affords me an opportunity to watch Cooper as he strides in and greets Marsha before giving her his lengthy breakfast order. I've never seen a man eat so much. Head office has to be losing serious money on his food budget.

I watch as he ponders whole wheat or white toast. He slips his hand up under his shirt and scratches his semi-exposed, ridiculously toned stomach. Just like he did yesterday morning. And the day before. And the one before that.

Does he seriously need to keep doing that?

Whole wheat it is. He turns toward me, worn-out Van Halen T-shirt still raised slightly at the front.

Oh lord, please let him keep doing that.

By the time Cooper makes his way over to join the

gang, they've moved on to some other generic and boring topic I also have no interest in, but I feign fascination to conceal the fact that I've been ogling him for the last few minutes.

I nod with enthusiasm and narrow my gaze inquisitively.

JT gives me a strange look, but when he spots Cooper on the approach, the jig is up. Dammit, I can't get anything past JT. "What do *you* think, V?"

Shit, I don't even know what they're talking about.

"What are you guys talking about?" *Phew.* Cooper's timing is impeccable.

JT looks a little disappointed I've not been caught out.

"Best beaches." JT takes a drink of his coffee and eyes me knowingly over the top of his cup.

"Australia, for sure," Cooper replies, settling in beside him. "What do you think?" he nods in my direction.

"I am not a beach expert."

"No?"

"I haven't been to a beach in years," I admit. I finish my last bite of breakfast and push away the plate.

"Why?" Cooper's expression reads like the very thought is preposterous.

"Charles doesn't really like the sun."

The words are out before I've thought it through. I mentally rewind the sentence and realize how ridiculous it must sound.

"This Charles guy seems like a blast." Cooper loads up his fork with eggs.

"Oh, he *is*," JT adds, sarcasm oozing from his tongue.

I flash him a warning glare.

"He's great," I reply. "He's a great guy. He's a lot of fun." I'm doing a terrible job of convincing myself, let alone the rest of the group.

My comment completely fizzles out and the group

begins to clear the way for the next round of diners that need to fuel up before their day.

I gather my plate and coffee cup and start to rise.

"Before you go…can I ask you something?" Cooper sets his slice of toast down on his plate.

I settle back in my chair.

"I have a proposition for you," Cooper begins.

My heart sets off into a sprint.

I shouldn't have had that second cup.

Instead of his usual convivial nature, he seems shy and a bit reluctant.

He certainly has my full attention.

He shifts in his seat. "That knitting stuff…do you have extra?"

"Extra?"

"Yeah, like extra yarn and stuff." Cooper takes a drink from his mug and looks down nervously at his plate.

"I have extra. Why?"

Where on earth is this going?

"I want some socks. Like my Grandma used to make me for Christmas…" he begins.

Oh, for Christ's sake.

This guy wants me to knit him some goddamn socks?

This is my biggest pet peeve about knitting. Someone— usually the most annoying person in your life—finds out you're a knitter and then drops some comment that they'd love a sweater or a large blanket with yarn from the fluffy asses of rare goats and thinks you're just waiting around for the opportunity to spend countless hours and spend hundreds of dollars on materials to knit them something.

Knitter's rage: it's a thing.

Cooper interrupts my inner boil. "I wonder if you can teach me."

Oh, god.

It's the sweetest fucking thing I've ever heard.

I feel like the wind's been knocked out of me.

"Um, yeah…sure," I reply.

His face lights up like a skein of rainbow worsted.

"Thank you. Thank you so much. I'll try to be a good student. Can we start tonight?"

"Um, yeah, sure," I repeat, stumbling slightly on the words, fumbling as I try to reconcile the brash boy I've been seeing these past few days with the soft and sensitive version that's presently in front of me.

"Great, let's meet here after dinner." He shovels another forkful into his mouth.

I stand slowly to leave, not sure what I've gotten myself into.

I get as far as the end of the table.

"Oh, and Voluptuous…I better be careful, or I might get *hot for teacher*." He points down at his Van Halen T-shirt.

Ah, yes. There he is.

"Move the camera to the left," Steve instructs from his position at the deck monitor.

Cooper is down below prepping for his first cut as we initiate the production piping removal. This platform is modest in size, but removing everything below surface and leaving behind no real visible evidence that this monstrosity was ever here will not be a simple job.

I watch him work over the monitor and listen to his choppy communication feed as he sets up the machinery.

I'm dressed and ready for my own turn when we switch out in—I check the clock—precisely thirty-eight minutes. Cooper will have just enough time to make one cut and then he will need to begin the slow, steady rise to the top.

The arms of my wetsuit are pulled off and hang around my waist, leaving my sports bra exposed to the sunshine. Working like this in the summer is such a treat. Way better than power dam repairs in January.

Cooper moves across the monitor in front of us, capably shifting the finicky laser cutter into place like he's been doing it for years.

He's not just for grunt work after all.

His slow, tedious work finishes, and he makes the gradual ascent. I ignore the little flutter I feel in my stomach when he bro-shakes my gloved hand as we trade off on the deck. I'm suppressing a smile behind my mask when I slip below the water's dark surface.

Cooper furrows his brow and bites his bottom lip in adorable and—let's face it—ridiculously hot concentration. After several rows he pauses.

"It isn't too bad, right?" He holds his work up for review.

It looks more like a fish net to me than knitting, but I don't want to break his heart.

"A solid effort."

He looks at his work, turning it in his hands and losing at least three stitches off the needle in the process.

His eyes move over to me with a raised brow. "Don't bullshit me; it's crap."

"It's your first try."

"I'm usually so good with my hands."

It's a mumbled innocent comment, and I try not to let my mind go exactly where it wants to go.

Yep. There it went.

I shake my head like an Etch A Sketch, clearing away what my imagination has just drawn. Grabbing his work, I rip it from the needles. "Let's try again."

I cast on several stitches for him, convinced that his time is better spent learning the basic garter stitch first; he can learn to cast on and cast off later.

"God, I suck," Cooper whines from across the table. He swallows a mouthful of tea and watches my hands work with the needles.

"Go easy on yourself. It takes time to master a new skill," I say.

"Knitting's a blow to the ego. I'm usually pretty good at things that require dexterity."

A flush of heat passes over my cheeks.

Don't look up, don't look up.

"Why so quiet, Valuable?"

I make the mistake of catching his eyes. He offers a devilish grin and a sly wink. He knows I've made the positively filthy connection. He mercifully lets it pass. Instead, he pulls his phone from his pocket. I see his hands move in my periphery as I nervously cast on stitches.

A few seconds later, he puts his phone in front of my face and gestures to it. "This was me when I really was a frat boy."

I'm stilled by the change in conversation. I pause mid-stitch and glance at his phone screen. I see a younger version of the infuriatingly handsome man in front of me: messy blond curls of hair flopped onto his forehead and a happy smile plastered across his face.

He's the human equivalent of a golden retriever.

I can't help but laugh.

Then I notice he's aged well. Very well, indeed.

As I'm studying the details of the photo, a notification pops up along the top of the screen. I can't make out any text, but it's from *Addison*.

"You um, have a message." I gesture to his iPhone.

He pulls it back to look. "Oh, yeah." Casually, Cooper places it screen down on the table. "I'll answer later."

I imagine this man gets a lot of…messages.

Returning to my knitting, I don't say a word.

"Aren't you going to show me yours?" he asks.

Ah yes, the old *I showed you mine, you show me yours* trick.

I eye him and weigh my options.

After a few more silent seconds, I put the knitting down and pull my phone from my pocket.

He rubs his hands together in anticipation and flashes me a grin.

I go straight to my favourites and find a photo of myself from my thirtieth birthday party and am shocked by what I see.

Wow. The change is striking.

Here goes nothing.

I hold it up for him and he takes the phone from my hand. There's an awkward moment when we make contact during the exchange, his hand brushing mine, and something charged passes between us. The moment is blessedly lost to his eagerness to see the image.

"Wow. Look at you." He expands the image to get a good look at the thirty-year-old version of Violet Thomas.

"That's me when I was your age," I explain.

The words I've selected highlight our age gap, help to reinforce a boundary, and point out our obvious differences. What remains unclear is whether I'm doing this for his benefit or mine.

The photo shows a shy expression, a long-abandoned septum piercing, and white-blonde hair with my old trademark streak of purple at the front. When he hands back my phone I examine it longingly.

"You look the same but oddly really different, if that makes sense," he says.

"I used to colour my hair like that, with violet streaks. It was my thing." I shrug. "You know, playing up the whole *violet* thing."

"It's cool. Why did you stop?"

"The maintenance was a pain, and it was time for a change-up." I pick my knitting back up and resume my cast-on.

"Change-up?"

"*Grow* up, really."

"Lots of older people colour their hair, V."

I notice he's not used a random v-word this time. I also notice I'm slightly disappointed. "I guess."

"I like the nose ring too." His tone has changed, and I look up at him reflexively; my eyes going to his before thinking better of it. I can't help but notice his turquoise pools have darkened and his face is suddenly serious. It's completely disarming. I'm both thrilled and terrified to be here alone with him in the galley after dark.

I clear my throat and finish the last cast-on stitch.

"Okay, try again." I hand back the needles.

We settle into another comfortable silence, each working away from our respective sides of the table.

"Does Vampire Accountant also knit?"

I almost spit out the mouthful of tea I've just taken.

I know I shouldn't find his criticism of my partner funny. I shouldn't be laughing at Charles's expense, but Cooper's summary judgement of him is rather spot-on.

I suppress a chortle and take another sip. "No, he's not a knitter."

"Our first day…when you got the text messages…were they from him?"

My stomach drops. Oh god, I do not want to get real right now.

I go rigid. "Why do you ask?"

There he goes, scratching his beautiful belly under his shirt again.

"Based off what JT's been saying and some of your body language, I think it might have been." He fiddles with his yarn nervously, like he knows he needs to tread lightly.

"Hmm." I don't know what else to say.

"No one should be disappointing our Valiant."

Valiant.

My traitorous heart thumps in my chest.

This is my favourite one yet.

A smile gives me away.

"Ah! You like that one!" His soft-looking lips turn up with a victorious chuckle.

I remain silent for fear of incriminating myself.

"It fits," he continues. "I've seen how fearless you are. Three days in and I still worry I might shit my pants at a hundred feet."

My cheeks grow hot from his approval. Over forty years old and I learn now that I've got a praise kink.

"It's all just muscle memory." I shrug.

"All I know is what I see. And that's a strong, calm, and competent woman who doesn't let anything faze her— present company included." He chuckles.

My chest tightens. I've never taken compliments well. I need to change the subject, fast.

"Stop trying to sweeten me up; I'm not knitting socks for you." I slip a stray hair behind my ear.

I hope I'm staying cool on the outside, because I'm most definitely not on the inside.

"I'm just stating facts. No sugar involved—yet." He raises a devilish brow.

Oh...my.

He starts to collect his things and I feel a pang of disappointment.

"I guess it's getting late." I begin stuffing needles and yarn into my bag.

We clear up in silence and make our way back to the deck. As I'm about to head off toward my cabin, he grabs my arm in the darkness. The entire side of my body charges like it's completed a circuit, and his warm hand robs me of breath. I turn to face him.

"You're a solid stunner, then and now." His voice wraps around me like a blanket. "If I had a woman like you, I'd never let her face fall like yours did."

I swallow hard.

"Goodnight, V." His hand pulls my body's heat with it as it leaves my skin, making me shiver.

Cooper saunters off toward the shared quarters.

I'm too stunned to reply.

CHAPTER 5

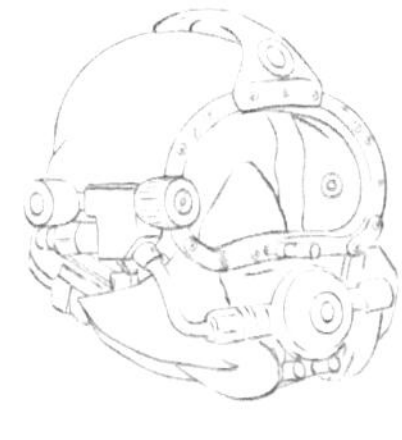

I have a hard time settling into sleep. After tossing and turning for several minutes, I decide to read a few chapters of my latest romantasy book. If dragons and shadow daddies can't help, I'm surely doomed. I'm propped up on pillows and mid-chapter when I hear a knock on my door.

This never happens, so I wait it out—it must be ambient noise coming from the platform.

Several seconds later, there's another quiet but distinct series of taps.

I reluctantly rise and open the door.

There's no peephole—on a rig designed for men by men, there's no reason for one—so I'm surprised to find Cooper leaning against the jamb.

"Cooper?" My heart sets off in a gallop.

"V…" There's a question in his voice.

I want to be the answer.

"I've noticed you haven't been using those ridiculous V-words anymore." I cross my arms, shifting my weight to my left foot. "Thank you."

He boldly crosses the threshold without even asking if he can come inside. His movements set me off balance, and my arms splay to preserve my footing.

"But there's still one V word I never used." His voice is low and rich like dark chocolate.

"It's my favourite," the man practically purrs.

With each step he takes forward I take one back until my heels hit the cabin wall. Butterflies move in my stomach as my hands brace against the paneling behind me. He cages me in. A wave of heat rolls off him and passes over me.

"Whi—which V word is that?" I stutter.

I know exactly which one he's talking about, but I want to hear him say it.

He takes up maximum space. It's most unsettling in a nipple-hardening way.

My throat tightens.

"This one." He boldly grabs my crotch with his large, hot hand.

BEEP, BEEP, BEEP.

I'm bolt upright in seconds and whack my forearm on the bedside table. The novel that's been sitting on my chest falls to the floor as the sting of my arm sets in.

What the actual fuck?

It takes a few seconds to adjust to time and place. I pick up my phone and quiet the alarm before looking at the time.

Shit, it's morning.

It was just a dream.

Relief and disappointment wash over me in equal measure.

I haven't had a dream like this in a long time; when it's so real that you wake up still feeling hands on your skin.

I try to hit reset, wipe the images from my mind, but it's

pointless. The heat of his breath lingers on my neck, his firm grip squeezes between my legs.

I cover my face with both hands.

Pushing aside the complexities of dreaming about a man who is not my romantic partner, I'm immediately confronted with the fact that I'm now going to have to work a full shift with the man who fondled me in my dreams last night.

Well, shit.

On the bright side, at least my alarm went off when it did; it could've been so much worse.

Cooper outdoes even himself for cheerful when I arrive at the moon pool.

A mischievous glint peeks from over the top of his cell phone as he thumbs the screen. When I approach, he blasts me with the obnoxious sounds of David Lee Roth. Cooper sings along as the yellow speaker wails, already mid-melody. The clever bugger sings along but changes the words.

"Gonna make her mad, so mad...singing 'Hot for Teacher.'"

Oh my god.

I rush to the air cylinder rack where he's propped his electronic ordnance and press the power button.

"Enough," I snap.

Cozy knitting sessions, silken praises, red-hot dreams... this needs to stop. Now.

I glance over at Cooper and he's chuckling as he preps his gear, clearly very pleased with himself.

"You play DJ, then." He holds up his phone in a peace offering.

"I will." I reach for it, but he holds firm for just a few seconds—long enough to catch me with those turquoise torture devices. It's completely irrational, but I'd swear he's looking right into my soul, or plucking the erotic fantasies from my mind. Heat rushes up my neck, but before it has a chance to reach my cheeks, I clutch the phone and twist away.

With my back turned, I'm safe to peruse tracks with his atypically excellent cell reception.

Something tells me the world just cooperates with Cooper, aligning in front of him before each of his confident steps.

As I search Apple Music for one of my go-to work playlists, a text bubble pops on screen. This one's from *Grace* and has three pink hearts in it. I release a low groan.

I really did not need to see that.

Thankfully, it disappears quickly from view, and I cue up *Reapers* by Muse. Some metal will help restore the balance and reset the morning. There's nothing even remotely suggestive about it.

I've always liked heavy metal. Today it washes over me like a tonic, instantly dropping my shoulders and clearing the platform deck of any lingering sinful thoughts.

I sigh. All is right with the world.

As the bass drum comes in to join the guitar, I chance a look in Cooper's direction. He has another mischievous grin and is nodding.

He raises a brow. "Should've known you'd like it hard."

Well, so much for that.

The sun is low in the sky by the time the crew is clearing up for the day. Buzzing comes from my equipment bag and I'm quick to check my phone's messages before the cell service dips again.

> Charles: What time does your flight come in? We're joining Todd and April for dinner on Saturday.

His message annoys me enough to cause a physical reaction. After two weeks away from home, I will want nothing except a long hot shower, my warm bed, and silence. I'm not sure why Charles inevitably chooses the nights I arrive home for social functions and quality couple time. When I'm about to leave, he seems to close himself off to me. When I get home and need time to decompress, he's all in. Three years into this relationship, how can we be so out of sync?

I consider my reply.

It will be at least twenty-four hours before I'm fit for human interaction after arriving home, but I don't have it in me to fight.

For three years Charles has been my anchor, but the reassuring weight of him now feels like he's holding me down.

> Violet: Sure, should work. I land at 5.

I sigh in resignation.

> Charles: Everything going okay? Miss you.

His words should fill me with warmth: they're ones I've been waiting to hear. Instead, they leave me cold. Something makes me pack away my phone, leaving him hanging like he's done to me so many times.

I'm so distracted by the exchange—what I've left unsaid and what it all means—that I don't hear someone coming up alongside me. Lost in analysis, I spin on my heels fast enough that the hanging arms of my wetsuit whip out around me, and I walk into a wall of warm muscle.

I freeze in place as hot, calloused hands grab my upper arms to stabilize me. At this distance—basically *no* distance—I see the fine blond hairs that cover his smooth, tanned chest. I don't need to look up to know who's in front of me, to see whose prize pecs my hands are spread across. If not for the copper tan, his scent would have told me: the faintly familiar mix of sweetness and spice that's drifted across the galley table every night this week, intensified now from his body heat and our proximity.

I don't dare look up, so instead I look down.

Big mistake.

I catch sight of the defined transverse abdominis muscles that taper into a pronounced v and disappear behind the lower half of his wetsuit.

To this point, it's all been fun and games between us— childish teasing and jests—but the way he feels against my hands is no joke. The smooth, hard muscle sends a burst of heat between my legs, travelling up my body like ripples on a pond, hardening my nipples on its way to flush my cheeks.

And it all feels so intuitive after this morning's inconvenient dream.

We stand frozen like this for what seems an eternity before Cooper clears his throat.

Realization hits like the shock of a cold plunge. My eyes snap up to his as I move to step away. His expression is implacable, but he bridges the gap before slowly wrapping each of his enormous hands around my wrists.

I'm a tall five feet nine inches and strong enough to handle the hundred-plus pounds of our equipment, but his massive frame and fingers make my stomach flutter with newfound fragility.

A loud clang of nearby equipment finally pulls me from my fog and I'm instantly horrified. I've just spent god knows how long (seconds? minutes? hours?) feeling up my colleague on the platform deck.

"Oh my god, I'm so sorry." I rip my arms from his hold.

I flee the scene, grabbing my bag as I go.

It only dawns on me once I'm safely around the corner that he hadn't pulled away either.

CHAPTER 6

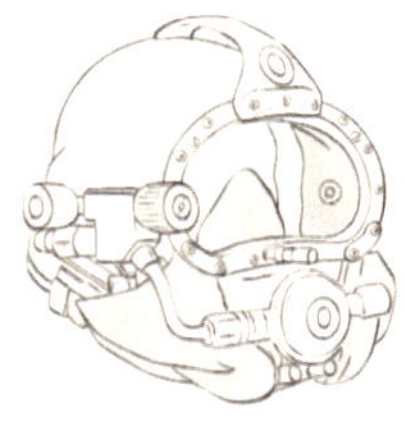

I toss my knitting bag and drop onto the bed in an exasperated huff. I've travelled to the door and back at least half a dozen times second-, triple-, and more-guessing whether I should head out for our nightly knitting lesson.

After ten days, it's become routine. Never stated, but understood that we meet back at the table once bellies are full, loungewear is on, and yes—admittedly—others have settled in for the night.

It's never been expressed that these sessions are only ours, but I'd be fooling myself if I didn't admit that being the centre of Cooper's attention—a once-terrifying prospect—has come to thrill me. Let's face it, I've done nothing to encourage group participation.

I lean my forearms on my knees and take a deep breath. If I *don't* go, it will seem obvious that our run-in on the deck has changed things.

Enter awkward.

Exit work mojo.

But if I *do* go, knowing how the feel of his skin under my fingers affected me, what does that say about me?

What does it say about my relationship with Charles?

I consider the options.

"Fuck it." I stand and grab my project bag.

I lurk at the doorway to the galley like an absolute weirdo. Where the hell is the confident, fearless, self-assured Violet I used to know?

Probably back on the deck with the remains of my dignity.

Standing there tentatively, one foot in the room and one foot out, I watch sun-kissed Cooper scroll through his impeccably-cell-serviced phone with one hand while his cozy hoodie pocket holds the other.

Marsha spots me as she rushes over to the table to deliver his usual peppermint tea.

"Want some tea, Violet?" she asks.

The stalker is outed. My cheeks flush. "Sure Marsh, thanks."

Cooper sits up straighter and casts his phone aside. "Hey!" His enthusiasm is palpable.

I wince.

Oh god, don't be nice to me, I'm a fucking pervert.

"Hey." I approach the table stiffly and avoid his gaze.

"I was hoping you'd come."

Did he have to use those exact words?

As I ease into my usual spot in front of him, Marsha brings my tea.

"Thank you."

"No problem, V." She pats my shoulder, then heads back to the kitchen.

I pull my own project out of my bag then pass Cooper

his yarn and circular needle. He snaps them up and sets them in front of himself on the table. It's such an unexpected picture: this handsome man with his massive hands, holding knitting needles. I can't help but chuckle.

"What?" he asks.

"Nothing." I need to avoid conversation as much as possible tonight. "You know what you're doing now?"

"I think so." He resumes the stockinette stitch in the round that he started a couple of days ago. I gave up teaching him cast-on or rib stitch and ended up knitting his sock cuffs for him after repeated failed attempts. With the first sock started, he now just has to knit a long tube in seemingly endless rounds on the circular needle. When he's finally got a sock that's long enough, I can shape and cast off the toe. There's no way I'm teaching him how to turn a heel.

We fall into a quiet domesticity, punctuated with a few curse words when Cooper almost drops the odd stitch. I'm happy to not talk for a while.

"So," Cooper breaks the silence. "Right before you felt me up on the platform earlier—"

"That was an accident," I interrupt. I grow rigid, shoulders reaching for my ears. Heat spreads over my scalp.

"Relax." Cooper laughs. "I'm just teasing."

I sit back and my shoulders begin to settle where they should be.

"Right before we *collided*"—he pauses for emphasis—"you had a sour look on your face."

He leaves his sentence there.

I take a sip of my hot tea, stalling, then inhale a deep breath. "I'm being cornered into a social situation when I get back on Saturday."

"Oh?" he asks.

"It's just that...it's the last thing I want the first night home. What I want to do is lock myself in my apartment and burrow under the covers—"

"And just be quiet," Cooper finishes my sentence.

I stare at him speechless for several beats, eyes catching on a small scar next to his eyebrow.

"Yes?" My word lilts up at the end. Not quite asking, but more like, *How did you know?*

When I realize I'm still examining his face, I look down at my knitting.

"People don't get it," he offers. "How much noise there is. They think we're in the middle of nowhere, frolicking in the peaceful sea. They don't think of the crew, the machines, the helicopters, the planes. It's a constant drone."

"Right?"

Even now, the hum of the machinery is a background to our chatter.

"I like to order in food and just pretend the world doesn't exist." He takes a generous drink of his tea. "You know…the first night back."

I sigh. It sounds amazing. My mind drifts to pad Thai and high thread counts.

"Is this a stitch and bitch?" JT hollers from the doorway, bringing me back to now.

Oh shit.

The lid on our little evening meetups is officially blown.

The smirk on JT's face is just a warning. I brace myself for what's about to come.

"JT, come have a seat." Cooper shifts to his right to make room on the bench beside him.

JT complies, settling in and boldly grabbing my teacup to sniff. "Mint?"

"I'm sure Marsha won't mind grabbing you a cup." Cooper begins to wave her over, but JT intervenes.

"That won't be necessary. I'm not much of a tea drinker."

"I've had too much of it myself. I'll be right back." Cooper rises and heads off toward the washroom.

I grimace.

JT wastes zero time.

"Well, well, well…what do we have here?"

"Don't." I set down my knitting and sigh, then grab my tea to busy my hands again.

"You little stockinette seductress."

"First of all, what you see here is innocent," I reply. "Secondly, how on earth do you know about stockinette stitch?"

"My mother is a knitter. Nice distraction tactic, but it won't work."

I take a long drink of Mint Medley, avoiding JT's judgemental gaze.

"Teaching our boy how to knit, are we?" His smirk turns into a full-on grin. "Provoking him with your purls?"

"Stop it."

"Kneading him with your knits?"

"JT!"

"Garter stitch has always sounded so suggestive to me." He snickers at his own joke. "Don't even get me started on *fingering*…"

"You perv. Stop it. There's nothing more than collegiality going on here," I explain.

"You've never offered to teach *me* how to knit."

"You're already a master at needling," I retort. "And I didn't offer—he asked."

"Of course he did."

"What's that supposed to mean?" I lean on my elbows and study his raised brow.

"Cooper's no moron. He knows a fine woman when he sees one."

"Dude, thanks…but no."

"No?"

"No."

"I see your little exchanges on the deck. He's endlessly flirting with you." He mirrors my pose.

"Gimme a break, he flirts with everyone." I refuse to let him make me blush. "He's got women ten, fifteen, twenty years my junior who are hitting up his phone and probably falling at his feet," I add. "He's not noticing the old lady with the saggy bits."

"Are you kidding me right now?" JT's face turns indignant.

I settle back in my seat, struck by the shift in his tone.

"With your silvery strands and emerald eyes? You're stunning, Violet Thomas. Do you hear me?"

"Aww shucks, *Byron*." I pick my knitting up, trying to ignore the heat of my cheeks. "Why do people keep using that word?" I mutter more to myself than him.

"Interesting…has someone else called you stunning lately, V?" Brightness returns to his eyes.

"Why are you even here, JT?"

"Steve has gas. Not all of us are blessed with private accommodations, Princess."

I lean in toward him. "Well, something has to compensate for the millennia of sexual oppression."

"Zing," JT remarks.

As if on cue, Cooper's abandoned cell phone awakens on the table beside us, a pop-up banner illuminating the screen. We're both too nosey not to read the text from *Erica* that's clearly there to see. *"Nighty night, charmer."*

I flash a smug grin at JT. "See?"

"Yeah, yeah." He shrugs. "By the way, couldn't help but notice that Charles didn't come up in your defence just now."

His comment hits its mark just as Cooper rejoins the table.

I feel instantly cold…and guilty.

Thankfully, Cooper's return spares me from further discussion.

CHAPTER 7

"The barometric pressure is dropping faster than formal wear during Covid, and the Doppler looks a mess." Bruce uses his Sharpie to point to the large storm tracking across his laptop screen.

Nick has the weather service website up using the one ancient hard-wired internet connection we have on deck. My eyes pan the wide expanse of sky above us and see four grey clouds merge into one. It's moving in fast.

"How bad is this going to get?" Steve rakes a hand through his hair. He tends to get a titch seasick when the waves kick up.

JT shrugs. "It's only a little storm." The man got trapped on a rig during a category five hurricane once, so nothing really fazes him anymore.

The same scene plays out every time bad weather rolls in: Nick pulls up the Dopp, Steve panics, JT talks him off the proverbial ledge.

"How much time do we have?" I ask, trying to calculate

how much equipment will need to be locked down and tucked away before the winds really pick up.

"Doppler is saying four hours." Nick hits play on the tracker, and we all watch in silence as a collection of large, colourful masses creep toward our blue location dot. They converge and mutate into an alarming shade of red at our geographical pin precisely four hours from now.

Shit. Not much time.

The rainbow of colours on the screen tells me, in no uncertain terms, that this is going to suck.

We're heading home the day after tomorrow. Looks like our disco dive is going out with a hustle.

"We better get busy then." I push away from the makeshift work surface and begin to collect my own equipment first.

"Wait." Cooper's brows are furrowed. "Why aren't we evacuating?"

The question is fair. Under usual circumstances, offshore platforms evacuate in high winds for safety reasons.

Bruce follows my lead and starts to collect his gear too. "The helipad is condemned, so the only way on or off this godforsaken thing is by boat. Even if the boat left shore now, it won't get here in time. Waters wouldn't be safe to navigate by the time it made it here anyway. We're better off battening down the hatches and staying put."

Cooper's cool and confident composure begins to crack as the weight of Bruce's words sinks in. He's used to working at shallow depth—close to shore, easy to get to the mainland if the situation warrants it.

I feel sorry for the guy. He's about to experience his first real run-in with the sea. People think these platforms are fixed to the ocean floor, but this sucker is a semi-submersible—it's only anchored. This rig flexes and moves as required; it would snap against the strength of the current otherwise. Cooper is about to experience waves and water at epic proportions. I decide it's best to distract him.

"Cooper, we need to lock down everything or it will be lost to sea. Follow our lead."

We spend the next two hours tying down and stashing away everything we possibly can while nature transforms to charcoal grey, turning the daytime sky dark as night.

I place the last of my personal items into my cabin cupboard and latch it. Nerves flutter in my stomach, anxiety spiking with each sudden shift of the floor.

Hanging on tight to fastened furnishings, I navigate the room and consider where and how I want to ride out this storm.

My travel flashlight has been proactively zipped into my athletic jacket, and I've had the foresight to change into moisture-wicking wear. At least I'll have light when (not if) the power goes out and I'll dry quickly when (again, not if) rain or sea water gets in. My cell phone—as useless as it is—stays plugged into the outlet while we still have power. It precariously slides back and forth along the bedside table with every list of the structure.

I'm putting my hair up into its usual bun when the cabin turns dark.

There it goes.

I reach for my phone, unplug it, and switch it out for my flashlight. When converted to a lantern, the Maglite has enough brightness to illuminate the interior of the cabin.

An eerie silence follows: machinery that's been a constant background noise for the past twelve days now silent, far-off sounds of wind and waves just a warning in the distance. The notorious calm before the storm.

My nerves cause a shiver. I get under the covers—shoes on and all—and somehow drift off to sleep.

"Violet!"

BANG, BANG, BANG.

I'm jarred from my sleep. It takes me a moment to remember the time and place.

"V!"

BANG, BANG, BANG, BANG, BANG.

I'm not sure how I've slept through it—all the noise of the storm suddenly floods my senses. There's a constant rush of water, whistling of wind, creaking of metal.

"V!" A voice shouts even louder from behind the door. The howling wind prevents me from making out who it is.

The wind against the cabin door makes it difficult to open, but with effort I crack it several inches. I worry I might be dreaming again when I find Cooper leaning against the frame. He's in exactly the same place and posture I'd discovered him in my dreams just mornings ago.

I stare at him for several seconds as rain—now coming sideways—pelts him across the face.

"Can I please come in?" he shouts over the rumble of thunder.

"Oh god, sorry," I say as everything finally registers. I open the door wide enough to allow his entry but attempt to keep out the rain.

He stumbles across the threshold, dripping wet, his

trademark light grey hoodie now dark from rain, faded jeans a deep indigo blue.

I don't get much time to study him before we're both nearly knocked off our feet by a sudden shift of the cabin. I grab hold of the bed frame, Cooper clings to a wall.

"Jesus Christ!" he exclaims. "This is insane."

I chuckle. "It's been worse."

"I'm paying closer attention to the fine print in my contracts from now on."

Another tilt of the floor sends us scrambling.

"What the hell are you even doing here?" I ask, once the room rights itself. "Just walking across the deck right now is incredibly dangerous. A terrible idea," I scold.

"You're all alone in here." He gestures over to me, but another shift of the cabin has him returning his hand to the wall.

His intentions dawn on me as I watch a single drop of water slide along his angled jaw and fall from his chin.

"Oh Christ, you think I'm some damsel in distress? I don't need rescuing, Cooper." If I didn't need both hands for balance, I might be tempted to shove him out the door— safety risks be damned.

"I know you don't need rescuing, Violet. You're the most capable person I've ever met. But no one should be alone right now. If you hurt yourself in here, no one would know for hours."

The man makes a fair point.

"No one has ever given a shit about this before," I note.

"And we'll address that ethical issue later, but you're not riding this out by yourself on my watch."

"I'll come to the group cabin…or you could send JT over," I suggest.

We cannot be alone like this.

"Steve's already thrown up all over himself *and* JT—you don't want to do that."

"Shit," I mutter.

I rack my brain for other options but come up empty.

"This looks bad, Cooper."

"What do you mean *this looks bad*?"

"The two of us by ourselves in here!" I shout.

"But JT's okay?" His wet brow furrows.

"Everyone knows JT and I are friends. You're the new guy. Aren't you worried about what others are going to think?"

"I don't give a single ounce of shit about what others are going to think. You're unsafe in here by yourself."

Ah, yes. The boldness of male youth.

Where has my boldness gone? Oh wait, I just found it under forty years of lived bullshit and double standards.

The woman's reputation always takes the hit.

A crack of thunder and an accompanying wave settles the argument. We're both knocked clear off our feet and tossed to the floor. My cheekbone hits the abrasive carpet with a painful thud. When I open my eyes, I'm staring down the dark corner of the bedside table. It's a sobering moment and a scary near miss. He's right: no one should be alone right now.

Looks like we'll be dealing with the consequences later.

CHAPTER 8

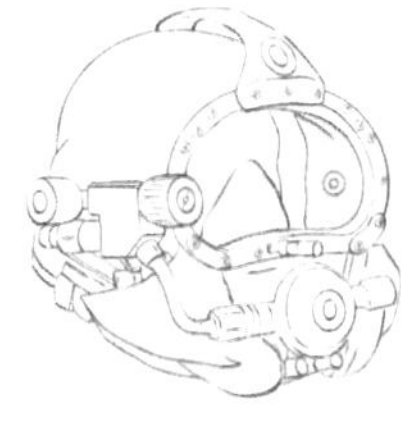

"Are you okay?" Cooper asks from his side of the cabin. I can't see much beyond the bedside table because the Maglite has been thrown across the room, right along with us.

My cheek stings with carpet burn and face aches from the impact, but I'm okay.

Thankfully.

Fortunately.

"Yeah, I'm okay." I manage to get myself up on all fours to recover the flashlight, then shine it on Cooper's wet frame.

He joins me on hands and knees. "We need to get on the bed."

This is getting less appropriate by the minute.

"No." I shake my head.

"V, it's the safest place for us." He gestures to the built-in bed, clearly designed for one. "Where are the restraints? We have them in shared quarters." He pulls himself up to stand on his knees.

Fuck. Okay.

Just like on old ships, semi-submersible platforms come equipped with human restraints. Much like a seatbelt keeps you safe in a moving vehicle, restraints on an oil rig keep people secure in their cabin beds when the seas get rough. We don't need them often, but they're potentially lifesaving when we do.

My stomach turns. I have an iron stomach—I never get seasick.

What is this? Nerves?

I ignore it and crawl to the under-bed drawer in search of cabin belts. "I'll look."

In my peripheral vision I see Cooper attempt twice to get to his feet. He finally manages it, bracing himself against the wall.

Casting aside coveralls and other protective equipment, I dig deep in search of something I haven't seen or used in years.

Out of the corner of my eye I *think* I see Cooper reaching for his belt, but I keep digging.

Three pairs of safety glasses—toss.

A single leather work glove—toss.

His hands move to his fly.

My head snaps in his direction. "What the hell are you doing?"

Cooper freezes, thumbs inside the waistband of his pants.

"I'm taking my clothes off."

"What the fuck, Cooper?"

"I'm soaked through, V. I can't get on like this." Another gesture towards the bed.

The single bed.

The *tiny* single bed.

Fuck.

"This is wrong on so many levels," I mutter.

"It's not just me I'm thinking about; I'm sparing you too. Unless you wanna get wet?"

I glare at him.

His hand covers a smirk. "Sorry, pun not intended."

"Just keep your underwear on," I retort.

"Of course I will. Jesus."

I go back to my hunt. "Just…get it over with."

Cooper peels off his wet jeans and hoodie in my periphery. I try to ignore the flash of bronzed skin and black boxer briefs behind me.

It's no big deal. No worse than a bathing suit, right?

"Never been instructed to do that before," he quips.

"Cooper," I warn.

"Sorry, couldn't resist."

Reaching into the farthest corner of the drawer, my hand finally hits nylon webbing. Bingo.

I pull out a long, thin strap with attached slide buckles for tightening. Pretty basic engineering.

I go back in search of another, but my hand hits the back of the compartment. Nothing.

Panic sets in.

I pull out every single item, checking again.

Nothing.

No. No. No.

Another crack of thunder sounds, sending a chill down my spine. The cabin shifts again, pitching me forward while Cooper lands back on his knees.

"Oh god," I whimper.

Cooper crawls up alongside me. "What's wrong?"

"There's only one strap." My words come out in a whisper.

"I can't hear you," he says loudly.

"There's only one strap!" I repeat.

A maniacal laugh leaves me, along with my breath. The wind knocked right out of me. Another horrified giggle escapes—like laughing at a funeral.

I've read enough romance books to know all the tropes. This one wasn't on my radar.

"Whatever. We'll make do." He pulls himself to his feet, grabbing the strap from the floor beside me.

I swallow hard.

"Get on the bed, V."

God, hearing him say that.

I call up every we're-just-colleagues, I'm-in-a-relationship, and he's-like-a-brother-to-me feeling I can but come up empty. One glance at his toned stomach as he flops down in the bed in front of me and I'm having the least sisterly, colleaguey feelings on Earth.

My hands twitch. I'm doomed never to unfeel those beautiful pecs again.

His body occupies easily three-quarters of the bed. I don't even know where my five-foot-nine-inch frame is supposed to go.

"Would you at least shift over? You're hogging the entire thing."

He squeezes up against the cabin wall. I climb on and lie on my side, back towards him.

If I'm going to survive with my dignity intact, this will have to be my approach.

"We both need to be in the same position. You're going to have to lie on your back for the strap to work," he says.

"Lie on your side too and it'll work just fine," I counter.

In the next second, it feels like he's on top of me as he reaches around to fasten the belt to its corresponding loophole on the side of the bed frame. Heat comes off him in waves. I hold my breath to avoid inhaling his incredible sweet and spicy scent. The cabin lists and his body presses into mine—Cooper's front to my back.

Oh, for fuck sakes.

"Give me the stupid thing," I snap.

I take over and get the belt properly seated in the slide buckle but leave it loose for Cooper to attach it on his side. I capitulate and settle on my back.

"Here." I shove the other end at him. I'm eager for him to return to his side of the bed. Maybe his side of the platform. Most conveniently, his side of the planet.

He doesn't seem to notice my abruptness and takes it in hand, repeating the same process: looping through the frame, seating the strap, pulling it taut.

The cabin continues to rock, thunder continues to sound, and metal equipment continues to creak ominously. But all I seem to hear are the little voices in my head telling me this is a terrible idea.

"You need to tighten your side." Cooper points to the strap.

I grab hold of it and pull, but it's awkward as hell and I can't get any leverage with the strap along my right thigh and needing to use my left hand to pull it straight. I try a second time, but still no luck.

"Here, I can do it."

I don't get a chance to argue. I watch, seemingly in slow motion, as abdominals flex while Cooper twists to face me. Before I know what's happening, he's grabbing my right leg in one massive, hot hand and pulling at the strap with the other. It takes a moment to register where his large thumb rests along the inside of my thigh.

Maybe we both realize it at the same time, because at that very second—exactly when it clicks for me—he looks up with an inscrutable expression. He continues to tighten the strap, but as he works on it with his right hand, I'm convinced his left hand grips my leg just a little bit firmer. Just a little bit higher. Just a little bit…

He sweeps his thumb along the inner seam of my

athletic leggings, and I swear I hear the rusty gears of my sex drive whir to life. Long out of service and virtually forgotten, but based on the chemical reaction his touch has initiated, my body still knows exactly what to do.

Another lurch of the cabin pitches us closer together and that warm thumb presses another fraction. Thunder and churning water are an accompaniment to the sound of my rapidly beating heart, drumming in my ears.

A charge travels up the inner line of my leg like a lit fuse, until it reaches the apex with a rush of heat and a lingering pulse. With one more subtle swipe of his thumb, it turns to an ache. A strained silence passes between us as his eyes catch on my lips. I draw in air—slow and deep through the nose—when I realize I've been holding my breath. A rush of heat floods my injured cheek when Cooper finally lifts his hand, making my face throb.

His voice is deeper than usual when he finally speaks. "Can you do me?"

Oh god, can I?

His return to the other side of the bed jostles enough sense into me that I remember all that's happening around us. I take a few more fortifying breaths before I turn to face Cooper.

Lying on top of the covers, he's all toned strength and tanned skin. The light catches the peaks of muscle, and shadows fall in the valleys of his abdominals. I avert my gaze so I can't see how his wide, strong shoulders taper to his trim waist.

Lord, help me.

Grabbing hold of his leg with one hand, I clutch the strap with the other. My hand lands on the hem of his boxer briefs, which are still damp from rain. I take a firm hold of the nylon webbing and pull hard and quick.

He shifts in the bed.

"Stay still, let me tighten this thing," I demand.

"I *am* still," he counters.

I hold his leg harder, gripping the strap firmer, biting down on my bottom lip as I tug. He flexes his quad muscle under my hand in response.

"That's good," he snaps. He wraps his fingers around one of my wrists, stopping me from repeating the movement. I glance over at him when he does and notice that he's using the other hand as a shield for his crotch.

"I'll be careful," I reassure him. I brace myself for another tug.

"I need you to stop." His voice is loud and decisive.

That's when I spot it: the obvious bulge that his hand is trying—and epically failing—to hide.

"Oh. Ohhhhhhhh." I immediately settle back, releasing both the strap and his leg.

I lie back down beside him, making every effort to avoid touching him with any part of my body. I cover my face with my hands—part horrified, and part honoured that I could elicit such a response from a man like Cooper. A man ten years my junior. A man so completely out of my league.

From the corner of my eye I watch Cooper cover himself with both hands. I have no idea what to say, so I let the sounds of the storm be our soundtrack.

Several minutes of silence pass between us, punctuated by thunder crashes and metal groans, until a gentle quake next to me breaks my reverie.

I turn to look at Cooper and his face is covered in a wide grin. He's laughing.

"What's so funny?" I ask.

"Are you kidding me?" He turns to look at me with a smirk.

I examine my surroundings with fresh eyes and see the utter ridiculousness before me: Cooper's wet boxers, power out, only one strap, accidental erection. A cackle spills out before I can think better of it and in the next moment, we're both laughing at our shared predicament.

The horrifying sounds of nature's fury should terrify us. Instead, we ride out the storm in a fit of uncontrollable giggles, promising never to tell a single soul about it.

CHAPTER 9

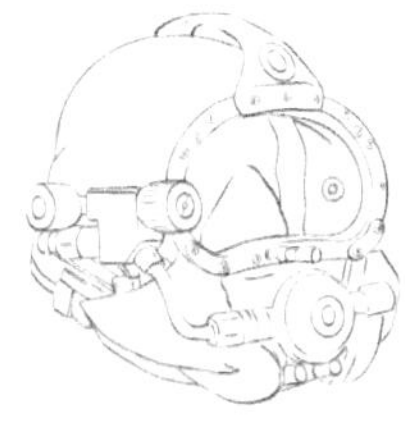

Tick, tick, tick, tick, tick.

The relentless ticking of the minimalist mantle clock is the only sound surrounding the six of us seated around April and Todd's sparsely decorated dining room table on Saturday night.

Todd clears his throat. "Would someone please pass the salt?"

Cutlery drops on several plates and three people reach for the same shaker.

Silence returns once the salt has been applied.

I know I wanted quiet, but this metropolitan mausoleum also known as "East City Condos" is a major downer.

I'd kill for some ambient machinery noise right now.

I shuffle uncomfortably in my seat, Charles reaches out to still my thigh. "You're shaking your leg," he whispers. After days of movement, the stillness is off-putting. It takes a couple of days to settle into it.

"Sorry." I take another bite of bland rice, then stir the dressing into my mixed greens.

April finally—mercifully—speaks. "You just got back today, Violet?"

"Yep." I take a generous drink from my wine glass. After two prohibition weeks on the platform, the alcoholic burn of the dry white is admittedly nice. I need it. Being in the company of Charles's friends always makes me feel like a fish out of water—pun intended. These are white-collar professionals who golf on the weekends and whose idea of manual labour is taking out the trash on Tuesday.

Forty-eight hours ago, I was being tossed around an oil platform. Today, I'm tossing salad in an upscale hipster condo. It's a bit of a trip.

"That's a nice wine, isn't it?" Todd asks from the head of the table. He's always looking for validation.

"Delicious, thank you." I nod for good measure.

I scratch nervously near the hem of my cotton sundress. After days of athletic wear, this airy thing feels awkward. I nervously play with the sleeves of my light purple cardigan, pulling them up to my elbows at first, then pulling them back down when I remember my tattoos.

I've never been embarrassed by them; in fact I'm proud of each beautiful leaf. But I know they make Charles uncomfortable in certain crowds—present company included.

I tuck my hair behind my ear and inadvertently touch my cheek.

I wince.

Ouch. My eye.

I've done the best I can to cover it with makeup, but the shadow of a bruise is still obvious. I've shown up to dinner with a body full of ink and a black eye. Oops.

My mind goes right back to the cabin and the night of the storm. The comedy of my situation with Cooper. The juxtaposition with my current setting forces out a giggle.

"What's funny?" Charles asks quietly. His eyes shift around the table.

"Sorry." I'm not sure why I keep apologizing.

"So, I hear you're an underwater welder?" April's friend Katie chimes in.

Katie and her partner Christopher have joined us tonight for dinner.

Katie and Christopher.

Not Kate. Not Chris.

Katie and Christopher.

I was clearly instructed upon introduction.

"I'm a commercial diver. Welding is just one of the many things I do." I'm not sure why I'm bothering to clarify. It doesn't matter and it just keeps the conversation going.

"What a job," Todd adds.

I'm not sure what his tone is implying, exactly.

"It's very challenging." I nod again. Seems I'm doing my very best bobblehead impression tonight.

"I never really imagined a *woman* doing that job," Katie comments.

Oh no. Did she really just go there?

"Well, there are a few of us." I slug back a generous gulp of wine, then put a polite smile on my face.

"If it's not just welding, what else do you do?" Katie continues, sipping from her own glass.

I take another bracing drink. "Well, there's welding and cutting. Disassembling and removing pipe—which was most of the work we just did at this last platform. Then there's monitoring and flow rate testing and sometimes we do things to improve flow rates."

"Doesn't it bother you that you're contributing to oil and gas dependency?" This is the first time I've heard Christopher speak tonight.

"In all honesty? Sometimes, yes. But we also do abandonments, which remove old oil and gas platforms and return the environment back to how it's intended. If we do it right, there's no evidence a platform was ever there when we're done with it. It's extremely satisfying."

"But you work for these companies?" Katie prods.

"Well, yes. They own the platforms," I explain.

"That…doesn't bother you?"

I can tell that Katie has a lot of opinions.

I don't bother to point out that her brand-new SUV—the one she and Christopher were just raving about before dinner—runs on gas and oil.

Charles remains silent, focused on his meal. I'm feeling a bit adrift right now, treading water against the current, wishing he'd throw me a lifeline.

"Those things are dangerous, aren't they?" Christopher asks. "I mean, just look at your eye." He gestures over to me with a wince.

Ah yes, my eye. An unsightly mark on the evening.

I gently touch my cheekbone.

"It's one of the most dangerous professions, yes," I confirm. No sense arguing. "But we take precautions, keep things as safe as possible."

"And spills…have you seen *Deepwater Horizon*?" Katie looks around the table, seeking out affirmation.

Charles is still silent.

"One of the best parts of my job is to make sure that the equipment and infrastructure is in good working condition, and repairing it if it isn't." I push my plate away. My appetite is gone anyway. "That prevents those types of incidents from occurring."

I don't know why I bother to try to change people's minds, but for some reason I always do.

"I just don't think I could do it."

And…that's enough.

At this point in my life, my jar of fucks has been significantly depleted: I've only got so many left to give and I need to use them sparingly. This woman isn't getting a single one.

"Listen, *Kate*." I pause for full effect. "Our gas and oil dependency—for fancy SUVs like the one you just parked outside—isn't going to end overnight. I'm glad I'm part of the industry right now; doing positive things like platform abandonments or conversions to artificial reefs to support marine life. I'm glad I can actually *do* things to make them safer and more environmentally responsible until our reliance on them is a thing of the past."

April, Todd, Katie, and Christopher exchange glances. I avoid looking at Charles.

A fork scrapes against a plate.

Tick, tick, tick, tick, tick.

"Did you really have to do that?" The second we're out the door, Charles is on me.

"Excuse me?" I say it loud and slow. "I had to defend myself because clearly *no one else* was going to help me out in there." I gesture to the building behind us.

"Give me a break, Violet." Charles buttons his sport coat and starts walking towards his car—that coincidentally also runs on gas—and shakes his head. "You're a grown woman, you don't need my help."

I follow on his heels. "Maybe I don't *need* it, but it sure would be nice to have it from time to time."

"What are you talking about?" Charles spins around to face me.

"Every time we're with your friends, this happens." I

put my hands on my hips, trying to make myself larger against his tall, lean frame.

It's true. In the three years that Charles and I have been together, I can list dozens of times I've gone home feeling small, feeling less than. Judged for being a trade worker among capital-P Professionals. But I'm professional too, hired for highly technical skills and competencies that are never recognized or valued. I'm sick to death of being seen as just the labour.

"Stop being dramatic." He turns away dismissively and takes a few more steps.

He pauses when he realizes I'm not following.

"Oh yes, there's your go-to defence. *It's all in my head.*" I pull off my cardigan. Maybe because of my building heat, maybe in an act of tattoo-revealing defiance.

He retraces his steps to stand in front of me.

"There is no grand conspiracy here, Violet. Just you being standoffish with my friends. As usual."

"Please don't gaslight me."

"Oh, for fuck's sake. *Gaslight?*" Charles runs his hands through his hair, leaving his normally impeccable coif standing on end.

He's frustrated? I'm the one who should be frustrated.

"We're supposed to be partners, Charles. We're supposed to have each other's backs."

"I don't know how to win with you. I don't know how to pull you out of this insecure mindset you're determined to cling to." His hands move to his hips.

The words sting, but he's not wrong. I know I'm endlessly seeking validation from him. Wishing he'd see me, that I was more to him than a convenient date on his arm.

"I'm not going to coddle you like some child, Violet. For Christ's sake. You literally dive headfirst into danger every single day; I shouldn't have to hold your hand."

My stomach turns. Isn't that the very thing that couples are supposed to do?

"If I had a woman like you, I'd never let her face fall."

The summer night air suddenly feels cold.

Charles emits a groan and runs a hand across his face. "Why are you so much *work*?"

And there it is.

Six monosyllabic words and we're irretrievably broken.

When it comes, I'm surprised by how easily the sentence leaves my mouth.

"We're done."

The release I feel as I finally let go is profound. I allow the reality of my decision take me like a current and engulf me. Instead of feeling fear or sadness, I'm awash with relief.

Three years of working against the tide...I can finally stop swimming.

We drive to my place in silence, and when he drops me at the door I don't look back.

CHAPTER 10

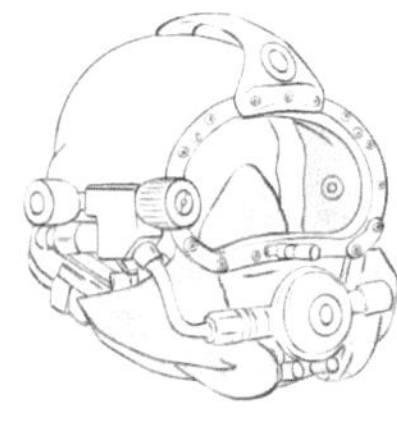

I burrow deeper under the covers and pull the sheets over my face. I've longed for this morning for two weeks: waking in my own bed, nowhere I need to be, no damp wetsuit to pull over my hips, and silence. Sweet silence.

Somehow the lustre I expected to find on the moment just isn't there.

I finally pull myself from my bed, doing my best to channel my inner Anne of Green Gables—a fresh day with no mistakes and all that shit—but it's a struggle. I don't regret what's transpired these past twelve-or-so hours, but I also don't feel good about it.

Three years into a relationship and the only item of his left behind is a toothbrush.

That should've been a sign. Flashing neon in all caps saying "THIS ISN'T GOING WHERE YOU THINK IT IS."

As I get off the toilet, I contemplate a swirl of the bamboo-handled tool in the bowl before I flush, but I toss it into the trash instead.

A nagging feeling persists while I run through my

morning rituals. I can't place it initially, and I ponder it while I take my first sips of coffee. It's not sadness or even remorse. There's a hint of shame in it.

Then it registers: failure.

I'm forty years old and starting—romantically—from square one.

I've always been a bit of a loner. It comes with the job. I'm gone two weeks out of four, which makes it tricky to form and develop friendships, and I spend a lot of time alone either in transit or private accommodations. Some would find it isolating. I usually find it peaceful.

I'm introverted, so I'm comfortable in my own company. But today it feels different. It feels like I've built a life that's hollow and incomplete. It's not the breakup with Charles that's making me sad, it's that something—or someone—is missing.

After a quick breakfast of toast (bread from the freezer) and too many cups of coffee (black, with no milk in the house), I consider the day ahead.

I could hit the gym with Bella, or grab more coffee with Greta, but for some reason, it's JT's number that I decide to dial.

"Miss me already?" he quips after two rings.

"I broke up with Charles."

Silence.

"Don't tease me, V. My heart can't take it," he finally says.

"No teasing. We're done. That's literally what I told him less than…" I check my watch. "Twelve hours ago."

"Holy shit. End of an era." He shuffles papers on his end of the line. "How are you holding up?"

I empty the dregs of the coffee carafe into my mug and consider the question. How *am* I holding up?

"I'm actually fine." I take a drink and punctuate it with a sigh. "We both know it's been a slow-moving freight train heading straight off a cliff." My shoulders drop with the confession.

"Nice that you can admit it, but it doesn't make it any easier."

"Yeah."

I thought I'd be left with a bigger sense of loss. Instead, there's just a feeling of wasted time. It was a casual swipe right that brought us together, but a conscious choice was made to stay. For three years a blind eye was repeatedly turned with each minor indiscretion. I chalked them up to pesky habits, claiming "no one's perfect"—god knows I'm certainly not. But negligence isn't a left-up toilet seat, forgotten birthdays aren't empty milk cartons.

"Well, we all know one person who will be extremely happy about this development." JT titters.

"He's not going to find out...you're not going to tell him."

"Why on earth not?!" JT's increased volume forces me to pull my phone from my ear.

"Because I don't need this crap where I work, JT."

"Yeah, yeah...don't shit where you eat and all that jazz. Bore-ing."

"Give me a break. You *do* know this isn't *actually* a thing, right? He's a relentless and universal flirt. As we speak, Cooper's probably flirting at the butcher for extra links of sausage."

"He could definitely flirt me into giving him some sausage," he mutters.

"JT!"

"Oh, quit it with the mock horror. What happened to the V I used to know? Bold and bossy with her septum pierc-ing, tossing her violet-coloured tresses around the deck, making the new guys shit—or do other things—in their pants?"

Where *has* she gone?

Lately it feels like I'm out of sync with the world, one beat behind the rest of the music. Maybe I've also lost faith that I'll ever catch the rhythm, or am I afraid to try a new tune?

I'm old enough to know everything that could possibly go wrong if I do, and still young enough to fear that it will.

"Clandestine meetings in the galley after dark..." JT continues. "No one else invited..." He chuckles.

"It's just knitting."

"Girl, you and I both know it has nothing to do with knitting."

My traitorous stomach flops with his assertion before logic has a chance to head it off at the pass.

"Gotta go, V. Are you okay though? Seriously."

"I'm fine. Thanks. Go. I'll be okay."

"Do what my mom does—go buy some expensive hand-dyed yarn collected by vestal virgins on the blue moon or something. She calls it fibre therapy." I hear background noise, like he's just stepped outside.

We say our goodbyes and I linger at the kitchen counter.

It makes sense that I'd find a man like Cooper attractive —anyone would want to bask in his light. But is it possible that a man like him would feel the same with someone like me: older, seasoned, out of fucks?

Wise, experienced...fearless, a voice counters from somewhere inside me.

A little light ignites in my heart. The kind that feels dangerously close to hope.

I swallow my last cold gulp of coffee.

Fuck, if that doesn't scare the shit out of me...

The store's door jingles as I enter. My local yarn shop is busy, even for a weekend, so Geraldine and Robyn—the store owners—don't notice me as I weave through the crowd.

I know exactly where I'm headed. The same section I'm always drawn to: the sock yarn.

A rainbow of colours faces me along the wall. A collection of muted, naturally-dyed earth tones set against bright Day-Glos and other synthetic hues that look more like candy than craft supplies.

I look for my favourites—the self-striping skeins. They're the most fun to knit. I just work in the round from a single wound-up cake and the sock transitions for me, from one colour to the next, like magic. They're like the Rice Krispies squares of knitting: they look impressive but are dead easy. Not to mention convenient in airport terminals, airplanes, helicopters, Uber rides, late nights alone on oil platforms, or the countless other places I've been known to pull out the needles.

After sight, touch is the next sense that calls. My hands skim over the soft, plush wool blends as I contemplate my next creation. Yes, there are so many beautiful colours to choose from, but just as many types of fibre to explore. Cashmere, linen, bamboo, or merino, mixed with synthetics for strength and stretch. I could lose myself in project ideas for days.

I'm halfway down the wall when I spot it: fingering weight in variegated turquoise. The similarity of the colour is uncanny. I ignore the little beat-skip that happens when I recognize the likeness.

Walking straight to the twisted skeins, I pull one from the shelf, feeling the soft plies against my fingers. I check the label: 80% merino, 10% cashmere, 10% nylon. It's ridiculously decadent and expensive—more what I'd choose for a shawl or scarf. It's not the type of yarn I'd typically use for the feet.

I take one long smell of the squishy, soft yarn and enjoy its distinct hits of lanolin and pasture. Fibre arts aromatherapy.

I move to put it back on the shelf, but something makes me pause.

I simply can't.

I throw it into my basket and head for the cash register.

CHAPTER 11

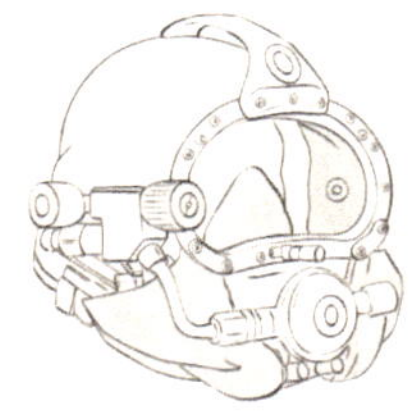

Our arrival is a chaotic shuffle as our crew offloads to the platform and the previous group—enthusiastic to leave—climbs in and is lost to the noisy and violent turn of the helicopter's propeller.

This platform is fancy. Brand new, with state-of-the-art technology, an immaculate helipad, and every modern convenience any soul could possibly need. The mood amongst the crew is rightly buoyant.

Eager to select their bunks, most of the crew scatter from the pad, dragging wheelie cases and other gear behind them. I'm delayed when my pelican case's wheel jams on some debris. I bend to deal with it, but when I reach to fix it the entire large case lifts in front of me. It gets effortlessly tapped against the concrete pad and then handed back.

"That should help," a phantom voice says above me.

I slowly stand and face Cooper. Alone for the first time in two weeks.

"Hi." He hits me with double barrels of cyan and it goes straight to my chest.

Conditions are overcast, so there are no sunglasses to protect his eyes—or my senses—from their full effect.

I had days to prepare, and I still wasn't ready for it. This man should come with a warning label: CHARISMATIC AF.

"Thanks." I attempt a calming breath, but unfortunately inhale the lingering cloud of helicopter exhaust, forcing out a cough.

I glance over my shoulder, to ensure that no one else has seen Cooper assist me. The last thing I need is him ruining my street cred with the crew.

I don't need anyone helping me with my bags, for chrissakes.

But damn, that was nice.

When I turn back to face him, a hint of pink colours his cheeks, which is a comfort. I'm not the only one who's nervous. This is our first real conversation since the...um...incident.

"I guess we're likely to have a few more...ah...safety features on this platform?" Cooper's smile turns to a cheeky grin.

I chuckle. "Yeah...about that—"

"It's all good. I found the whole thing a very uplifting experience."

I groan over his dad joke. "You're such a pill."

"An intoxicating buzz?" His mouth curves up in a suggestive smirk.

"More like a disorienting trip," I counter.

Nothing like the sedative effect of Charles, that's for damn sure.

"Even better." He raises a brow.

I turn and head in the direction of our accommodations, determined to put this dangerous discussion to an end, but Cooper follows alongside.

"Private bunks, Wi-Fi, and I hear there's even a gym."

Cooper lists the amenities and adjusts the duffle on his shoulder.

I push away the mental image of Cooper sweating it out on a treadmill and try to get us back to the topic of work.

"Such a shame though, this one's just maintenance and inspection." I chance a peek over my shoulder in the interest of maintaining camaraderie. It's most definitely not because he's just bent over to pick up something he's dropped, providing a perfect view of his perfectly round and firm... "I love a good abandonment. Every time we do one, it feels like a solar or wind farm somewhere gets its wings."

"Yeah, this work can lead to a crisis of conscience, if you let it." Cooper sidesteps a pylon and bumps elbows with me. That side of my body immediately hums.

"Hey, guys." JT comes up beside me. He has a habit of sneaking up like this. His elbow jostles the other half of me on approach, and I note the difference: the effect of *his* physical contact is practically indiscernible.

"A theatre. This one has a *theatre*." JT is giddy with excitement.

"Sweet," Cooper says. "Hey V, you shouldn't have any trouble texting Charles this time."

My face grows hot, though my inner temperature drops.

I look at JT and shoot him a warning glare that miraculously keeps him silent. I'm not sure why I'm so determined to keep my breakup quiet, but it's instinctively a no-go zone.

"Hey Coop, come check out the side-scan sonar!" Steve hollers up from the lower level.

It's nice how quickly Cooper's become one of the team. In many ways he's a better fit than Patrick—the diver he's subbing for.

"Coming." Cooper jogs ahead, effortlessly hauling hundreds of pounds of equipment.

"How are you doing?" JT asks the moment Cooper is out of earshot.

"I'm good." I'm surprised to find that I actually mean it. Who knew it would be this easy to walk away after investing three years with someone?

"Good. But remind me…why aren't we telling Cooper again?"

"There's no reason to tell anyone; it's none of anyone's business." I pick up my pace, putting distance between me and this conversation.

"You know what I think?" JT asks, right on my trail.

"No. But knowing you, you're about to tell me."

"I think it's safer to pretend you're off limits."

"Safer?" I stop and spin to face him.

JT stands solidly in front of me. "Those years with Charles really did a number on you. Killed your trust in others, but what's worse, killed your trust in yourself."

My stomach sinks to the metal deck.

I start to walk away, shaking my head. "I just want to find my cabin, JT."

I'm not ready for the post-mortem analysis. It's too heavy, too serious, too soon.

"Just promise me one thing!" JT shouts as I take a hard right towards accommodations, dragging my case behind me.

"What?" I pivot. A resigned sigh escapes me.

"Just because one gamble didn't pay, don't be afraid to deal yourself in again."

"Yeah, yeah." I roll my eyes and turn.

"And Violet…"

I stop short but refuse to face him.

"Remember you're the queen, not some joker."

Drawing in a laboured breath, I feel the tendrils of three years of disappointment and doubt wrap around me.

Not so easy to walk away from Charles after all.

I decide to have a quick workout in the platform gym after dinner, to blow off some steam and get my head back into work mode. Five kilometers on the treadmill and a short weight training circuit (texted to me in real time from my badass friend Bella) certainly do the trick.

I'm a content but clammy mess when I get to the shower facilities, eager to wash off the day of travel as well as the gym sweat. I've grabbed a change of clothes and my toiletries and made my way to a private single stall shower room on the far end of the fourth level, where I can clean up in privacy and not feel like I'm in the middle of traffic on a busy offshore platform full of men.

I push the heavy door closed behind me and attempt to latch the lock.

The deadbolt turns, but the latch doesn't set.

I turn it again and test the door. It opens easily.

Shit.

Maybe there's a reason why no one seems to be using this washroom.

I feel a rare pang of envy for my coworkers. If I was simply a man among other men, I wouldn't feel vulnerable getting naked behind an unlockable door.

I give it one more try but still have no luck.

I weigh my options.

I could walk to the other side of the platform to the busier, multi-stall shower, or I can take my chances here. I examine my surroundings. There's a sizable metal barrier that separates the shower from the rest of the room and offers plenty of privacy. Even if someone accidentally walked in, they'd only see shoulders and feet.

I decide to go for it this time, and make a mental note to tell Bruce about the issue.

I make quick work of the shower—not lingering under the hot stream nearly as long as I'd like—and get dressed amongst the cold puddles in the tiled stall, just to be safe.

I take my time drying my hair and pretend I'm not fussing over my appearance. I'm definitely *not* adding more moisturizer than usual along my laugh lines. Certainly *not* applying scented lotion to smell nice. The lip balm I've put on? That's purely to prevent chapping from the high winds here on the rig.

I stop off at my cabin and contemplate my next move. The evening knitting sessions that became habit on the last platform don't necessarily translate to this one, but somehow it doesn't feel right to just stay put.

I eye the worn-out Dead Kennedys T-shirt I'm wearing in the reflection of the cabin mirror. It's a long-time favourite and has become my signature look. Maybe it's time for a change. Time for something a little more…youthful. But would it be too obvious?

I hesitate, then grab a mauve backless yoga top that I'm pretending I didn't pack with a certain younger diver in mind. I let the silky, smooth fabric run through my fingers.

It's just an athletic top. It's not a big deal.

I peel off my old T-shirt and expose my plain black sports bra. I slide the butter-soft, long-sleeved, open-backed garment over my head and assess the results.

Better.

I've left my long hair loose but second-guess the move on my way out the door. It's too much. I throw it up in my customary messy topknot instead.

As soon as I arrive at the cafeteria, I question my decision to come. The large space is comfortable and well appointed, but also busy and loud. I'm instantly nostalgic for our rusty galley that only accommodated twelve.

Passing a few other platform workers seated at a table playing cards, I find an empty one in the corner. I pull out my latest sock project and start increasing at the toe.

"V." I look a few tables over and find Cooper, JT, and Steve huddled in conversation. The room was so packed I hadn't spotted them. "Come over here." JT throws an encouraging wave.

I collect my things and move to join them.

"Sit next to me." Cooper pats the chair beside himself.

My eyes go straight to JT, who flashes a satisfied grin.

I pull out the appointed chair and take a seat.

"Whatcha workin' on, V?" Steve asks as I get out my project to start again.

"Another pair of socks." I start to knit in the round.

"No stitching tonight for me, I'm just here for the bitching." Cooper takes a long drink from a water bottle in front of him.

I wasn't sure if his new hobby was public information; I guess this answers that question.

"Young Cooper's back is bothering him tonight, V." JT settles in his chair. I know him well enough to read between the lines and what he's suggesting. His devious look is saying, *"Maybe you can make it better."*

I ignore him and tug the tail of yarn from my project bag.

Steve and JT strike up a new conversation on their side of the table.

"Sore back?" I ask Cooper.

"Must've been the plane. Go figure, I'm the youngest one here and in the worst shape."

"What are you talking about? You're in *great* shape." The words spill out before I've considered them.

A beautiful smile passes over Cooper's face. His lips part to reveal those toothpaste-ad-worthy teeth. "You think so?"

I walked right into that one.

My immediate instinct is to distract him. I reach into my knitting bag and grab at the small, squishy folds at the bottom.

"These are for you." I hand them to him under the table like contraband—eager to get them out of my hands.

They're striped socks knit in that delicious colour-fade yarn of turquoise and blues. I don't mention that they're a perfect match to his eyes.

"Oh my god, Violet. You *made* these? For me?"

"Would you please keep your voice down. And don't call me *Violet*—it's weird." I look around, pretending I didn't just love the sound of my full name on his full lips.

I check over my shoulder, making sure no one is watching what's going down on our side of the table.

"I know exactly how much time these things take—how much work this is." He lays each sock out across his lap and runs a hand across the perfectly executed heels. "Thank you. I'll treasure them."

"It was nothing." I shrug. "A few Netflix shows. Don't make a fuss."

"I *will* fuss. A handmade gift like this is something to be treasured." He folds them.

I silently beg him *not* to put them on the table.

"Stop saying *treasure*." I cross my legs nervously. "Drink your water."

He places them right on the table and unscrews the cap before taking a generous gulp.

My eyes turn to JT and Steve, hoping they won't notice.

"How did you know my size?" Cooper runs a thumb along the soft wool.

Don't draw attention, Cooper.

"I peeked at your boots. My dad is the same size, but they might not fit perfectly."

"Are you kidding me? They're perfect. The size will be

perfect. The yarn is perfect..." He's turned to look at me and I watch his Adam's apple bob on his tanned throat as he swallows.

There it is again. The rush of emotion in his eyes that sets my heart into a gallop. I take a deep breath and try not to stitch together the next words I wish for him to speak: *You're* perfect.

"What's that?" JT's voice brings me back to the table.

We shift away from each other, and Cooper holds up the socks in celebration. "Look what V made for me."

Thankfully Steve is distracted by something on his phone, but the look on JT's face tells me I'm going to be paying for this for a while.

"How nice." A smirk passes over JT's face just as his phone rings.

I take a full breath as he mercifully stands to answer it.

"Hey, Chris." He walks to the opposite side of the room to talk, but directs one parting look in my direction that tells me this isn't over.

"I'm hitting the sack. Night, kids." Steve makes for the door. I don't bother to remind Steve that I'm older than he is.

Another noisy group enters the space as Steve exits, adding to the din.

"I can't believe I'm saying this, but I think I miss tyran-nosaurus rig." Cooper plays with the lid of his water bottle.

I laugh that he's sharing my nostalgia for that hideous platform. A new lightness meets his eyes as he flashes one of his megawatt smiles.

"Yeah, but we put that sucker to bed. Maybe I shouldn't say it, but it feels good when we take one out of service like that." I look down at the needles in front of me.

"Your secret's safe with me. You know...I have one of my own." His eyes shift to the nearby tables. I find myself inching toward him.

Unexpectedly, he turns toward me and rests a hand against the back of my chair, boldly entering my personal space.

His stubbled cheek just glances off mine as he leans in to share what he has to say.

A hum reverberates across my chest as his low voice murmurs against my ear. "I drive an electric vehicle."

When his hot breath hits my pulse point, all the hairs on my body stand on end.

Never has clean energy been such a turn-on.

He withdraws and I swallow the boulder that's lodged itself in my throat. I take a slow, steady breath through my nose, attempting to maintain composure.

Unfortunately (or fortunately?) I draw in his delicious scent. This time there's a hint of patchouli, or some other earthy element, mixed with his usual sweet spice. It's heady and heat-inducing.

As he pulls away, the hand that's been resting on the chair behind me brushes my exposed back. Fingers skimming spine. A shiver passes through me, hardening the peaks of my breasts through my sports bra.

My eyes snap to his, searching for signs of intent.

Does he know what he's doing to me?

Is it doing the same thing to him?

Those trademark turquoise pools are heavy-lidded with seduction.

He knows exactly what he's doing.

A few beats pass as we take each other in.

Finally, I clear my throat. "How very…environmentally responsible of you." The words come out strained and breathy.

"Maybe that can be another of our little secrets?" he asks.

We seem to be accumulating them.

I sit up straighter and manage to compose myself. "I

imagined you as more of a backwards baseball cap, over-sized exhaust kinda guy."

Slotting him back into the clichéd player category is safe and reassuring.

"Actually, I don't own a car—it's an electric motorcycle."

Several muscles clench of their own accord.

My eyes squeeze shut for a few seconds as I attempt to expunge the mental image of Cooper's muscular thighs wrapped around a chrome-coated sex machine.

Sweet Jesus. What is wrong with me?

What is it about this guy? Like the current, he draws me out, but then his power sends me flailing for shore.

"It's funny…" Cooper shifts back in his seat. "We've never talked about where we're from."

The large expanse of the room begins to close in on me.

It's the most basic of information, but it feels like too much, too fast.

An explosion of noisy laughter erupts from the centre of the cafeteria. It provides me with the perfect cover to collect my thoughts and belongings while Cooper's head is turned.

I slip out the door just as JT returns to the table.

CHAPTER 12

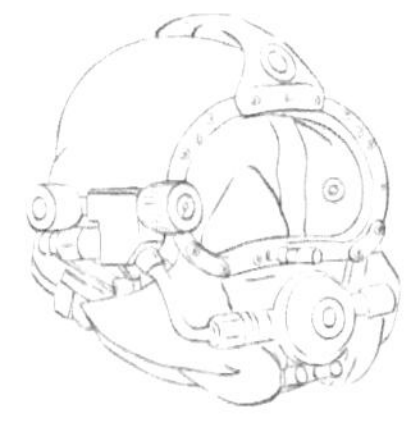

"The bottom echo is too pronounced. We're gonna have to make some adjustments to the settings." Lauren points to the darker lines on the screen and then consults her work journal.

Lauren seems unhappy. I, on the other hand, couldn't be more thrilled.

It's a great day on the rig.

The core service staff don't travel along with us, they stay at their home rigs, so I had to leave Marsha behind. But with Lauren joining us as a side scan sonar specialist, I've got a fellow female to work with this time around. Correction: I have a badass woman in STEM alongside me to geek out on tech and show these men how it's done.

I can't do much to help, so I make myself useful passing Lauren her water bottle to make sure she doesn't wilt in the summer sun. She takes a generous swig.

"Oh, Lauren." I wipe some sweat from my brow. "Just a heads up. The lock on the private fourth-level washroom is broken. I've let them know." The least I can do is spare my fellow female.

"Oh, yeah, I noticed that this morning. Pain in the ass."

"Bruce takes these things pretty seriously, so I'm sure they'll fix it quickly." I look over to where he's standing with Steve and Nick. I'm lucky to work with such a great group of guys. They care enough to make sure I have what I need, without the obnoxious tendency that some have to act like protective big brothers. I'm just one of the team.

"We want to capture the targets, but we don't want such pronounced lines and shadows. We'll play with the recorder gain settings a bit to balance the intensity." Lauren returns to her work, bending over the display.

Cooper is at depth. He's monitoring the equipment while the equipment monitors the floor. And he's deep. So deep, he's got a helium blend to make it easier to breathe today, and he's had to go down slow and steady to prevent high pressure nervous syndrome. Our tasks here today might just be monitoring and inspection—which presents fewer obvious risks than cutting and welding at depth— but it still comes with the ever-present life safety hazards associated with doing one of the most dangerous jobs on Earth.

And he's fucking hot.

Competence kink is most definitely a thing.

Watching this man by remote camera as he moves around over a hundred feet deep like he's down there shopping for groceries is doing wonders for my mood. He's dozens of meters away and completely unrecognizable if not for his distinctive yellow gloves that—every so often— enter the frame. Yet he's still completely disarming.

Yellow must be his favourite colour.

I'm more comfortable watching him from this distance. I can keep my cool a lot easier without his intoxicating pheromone cloud enveloping me.

"Okay, I think we've got it." Lauren squints at the monitor and nods. "Yep, perfect acoustic shadows."

I watch as the display begins to generate, from one side

to the other, back and forth. A perfect picture emerges of where the platform piping meets the sandy floor.

Lauren stands fully stretching her tall, willowy frame. She pulls an elastic from her wrist and gathers her long, dark hair into a high ponytail.

I glance over at Nick, who's developed heart-eyes while watching her.

Competence kink, indeed.

"Okay, Coop, time to head up," Bruce instructs from his microphone.

A muffled reply resonates over the deck. "'Kay."

The sound of his voice, even from over a hundred feet away, makes my heart race.

Cooper begins his slow ascent. I start to strap on my equipment, zipping up my suit and preparing to switch out. I try to focus on the task at hand, but my mind drifts when I remember the feel of his fingers along my back.

I literally shake it off.

Keep your head on straight.

I need to be smart and safe. No distractions.

Just the thought of the risks is enough to startle me sober.

When we switch out, my head's one hundred percent back in the game, and I show the rest of them how it's done.

I follow the light until I break the surface, reaching for Steve's reliable hand. We're buddies for today's dives, helping each other into and out of the moon pool and safety checking each other's equipment.

I clasp it, but it doesn't feel right. It's different.

And it practically pulls me from the water.

I'm temporarily blinded by the brightness of the sun but scramble onto the deck. I concentrate first on getting my footing. Once I'm stable, large hands start to disconnect my helmet.

Through water droplets I process the picture in front of me.

It's Cooper.

Deep in concentration, he unfastens and removes my helmet.

There's a rush of air, and I take a satisfying, deep breath. "Where's Steve?"

"He had a bathroom emergency." Cooper's brow is knit in concentration as he works on my neck dam.

We're on the clock to get me into the chamber, so he doesn't stop.

His competent hands work, finding the fasteners and clips, getting pieces of equipment off as fast as he can. There's a tug to the left, a push to the right.

I can't seem to move, watching in rapt fascination as his muscles flex and fingers grip. First he's at my shoulders, then he's reaching around back. I feel his hot breath on my neck as he bends to grip my bail-out bottle, smell the mint of his chewing gum.

I numbly stand, transfixed by what's happening around me.

"You okay?" Cooper asks, meeting my eyes.

My throat tightens. "Yeah."

"Let's get you into the chamber."

His voice is laced with protectiveness.

I don't need him. I don't need *any* man.

But dammit, I love how he's taking care of me right now.

He returns to the task, grabbing hold of my wetsuit's yoke where it meets my neck. He grips the top of my zipper and pulls. The zing generated as it rolls down its track goes straight to my crotch. I try to squeeze my thighs together to stop it, but there are two layers of neoprene in the way.

My chest feels tight.

I glance down at him when he untangles the surface supply cable lines wrapped around my legs. His hands find my hips as he directs me away from the pile of cord. One firm pull forward and my pelvis lurches toward him.

Oh my god. Don't do that.

A dozen illicit thoughts flood my mind as he shifts me into place, like I'm a plaything in his massive. capable hands.

Please do that again.

There's a familiar, involuntary rush of warmth that's found me since the storm: neural pathways set to elicit this response. My body can't seem to unlearn it.

I correct my posture but somehow end up inches from his tanned throat. I watch as his chewing stops, and he swallows.

Our eyes meet as he grips the nylon webbing around my hips and pulls me toward him. He unclips the buckle above my belly button and my weight belt drops. My centre of gravity shifts as the pounds fall away from me.

The noisy platform seems to fall away too, as I imagine the feel of his full, pink lips where his hands are.

"Sorry guys, nature called." Steve's voice brings me back to the moment. "Let's get her in."

Cooper steps away and starts collecting my gear.

Steve clears the path and leads me over.

Thank god for the oxygen, because by the time I get to the decompression chamber, I can barely breathe.

CHAPTER 13

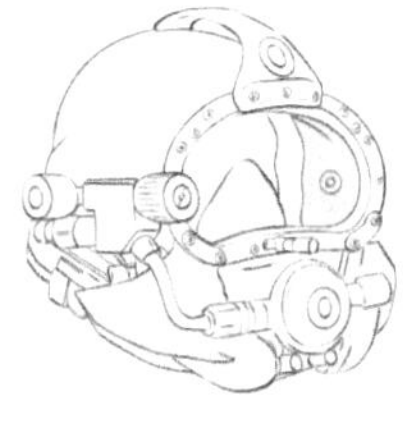

"You sure left in a hurry last night." JT is seated at the cafeteria table across from me, one brow raised inquisitively, plate already empty in front of him.

"I was tired; it was a long day." I move a few peas around on my plate with my fork.

"Cooper literally what-the-fucked when you bailed."

"That's a verb now?" I'm channeling my inner Bella Avery and deflecting with humour. She'd be so proud.

Truth be told, I'm not exactly sure why I panicked, why I ran. Some sort of self-preservation instinct seemed to kick in and I needed to shut things down.

"So, how have things been since you two...you know...*rode* out the storm together?" He rests his elbows on the table and flashes a sly grin.

JT and his goddamn double entendres.

Clever bugger.

"Hey, absolutely nothing happened that night. I was still with Charles." My heart may not have been in it anymore, but I am a woman of principle.

"Terribly inconvenient." He sighs as if my scruples are boring him, then takes a long drink of water. "I wonder where our golden boy *is* tonight." JT surveys the room, but I already know Cooper's not here. My body is on constant high alert, on the lookout for bronze skin and beautiful eyes.

I'm relieved he's not here. I need to put some distance between us. The forced proximity aspect of working on the platform with the world's answer to my sexual prayers is messing with my head.

Terribly inconvenient is right. Today's events clearly established that I have an incredibly inconvenient and inappropriate next-level attraction to a flirtatious co-worker ten years my junior.

I've got to put on my big-girl panties, quick.

I can live with this.

I can *work* with this.

What I can't do is let a man who undoubtedly sprinkles his universal charm around like fairy dust call into question my professionalism. I certainly can't let this troublesome infatuation interfere with my work. Our colleagues can never know about this. Cooper especially can never know about this.

After three years deprived of affection, Cooper's attention feels like the first hit of oxygen after a deep dive. I need to resist the temptation to clutch at the first available ass—

…I mean *mask*.

Even if it's a beautiful one.

Shit.

"I need a shower." I push away my own plate, appetite officially blown by the notion that I might be a cougar. Standing to collect my dishes, I nod to JT. "G'night."

"You're not coming back?" He looks slightly offended.

"No, I'm tired. Didn't sleep well last night."

"Interesting." JT straight-up snickers. "Something keeping you up at night, V?"

Probably the ghost of lingering fingers on my spine...or thumb along my thigh...or chest muscles against my palms.

"Maybe that can be one of our little secrets?"

Lord, help me.

I blow out a breath. Of course JT doesn't miss it. He furrows his brow. "V?"

"See you in the morning." I head toward my cabin before he can ask more questions.

My steel-toed boots feel heavy as I make my way across the large structure and climb the steps to the private bathroom. They're part of our kit of personal protective equipment that's mandatory whenever we're crossing the work area. I'm eager to get to the PPE-free zone and just chill.

It's been a day.

I climb up to the fourth level, my footsteps barely audible over the ambient noise on the rig. Exhaustion fully hits me once I reach the door. I can hardly wait to shower off the day, then curl up with my knitting and audiobook before drifting off to sleep.

And I'd better sleep tonight, dammit.

I adjust the bag of toiletries and change of clothes in my arms before I give the heavy bathroom door a generous shove with my hip. On autopilot, I step inside and let the door fall behind me.

And stop short.

I freeze in place when I hear the shower running.

Fucking broken lock.

I low-key panic and take a step back, hoping to slip out before the occupant notices me.

But then I recognize what's in front of me. *Who* is in front of me.

My eyes pinball between golden locks darkened by the shower's flow, the back of broad, bronze shoulders peeking above the grey metal wall, water cascading over tanned skin and falling in mesmerizing drops at exposed feet.

Sweet Jesus.

Two inches of powder-coated steel is all that separates me from naked Cooper Brooks.

My heart jumps to my throat. I need to get out of here before he turns around, but my feet don't seem to be working.

His hand inches up the wall, long fingers spreading against the tile. My eyes—wide in surprise—pan down to where his feet take a wider stance.

My cheeks flush.

I shouldn't be watching, but I can't seem to peel my eyes away.

It's the sexiest thing I've ever seen in my life.

My eyes snap up when I hear the first moan.

"Oh god…"

Wait…what?

"Fuck…" His hand reaches higher on the wall.

A cold panic hits me, accompanied by a rush of heat.

Oh my god.

My eyes move to his right shoulder, spotting a rhythmic rise and fall.

I shrink back as the scene unfolds before me. Another groan, another reach.

A pulse starts between my legs, met by a heavy ache.

"Fuck…"

I'm paralyzed by a heady mix of fear and fantasy.

"Fuck, V."

Did he just say…?

"God…V…" He releases a low, erotic groan.

My stomach drops, but in the next instant, hope rises in me like bubbles.

Then I remember where I am: where I'm not supposed to be.

I backtrack, slowly and silently until my hand finds the door behind me. My heart pounds like crashing waves as I run—not walk—all the way to my cabin across the rig.

CHAPTER 14

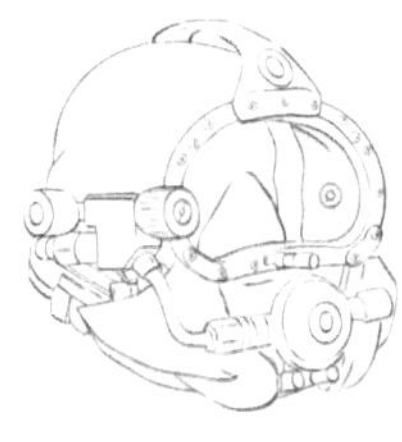

What if he'd heard me?

What if he'd turned and seen me there?

What if I had joined him?

That sinful thought creeps in.

My chest still rises and falls as I'm laid out on the bed—a trail of PPE and toiletries leading to where I'm spread-eagle on my back. I clutch the bedspread for dear life. It feels like I've taken to water in January; my lungs won't cooperate fully.

Half a dozen emotions battle it out inside me.

Mostly, there's guilt.

I invaded his personal space. I witnessed an incredibly private act when he believed he was alone. I feel terrible about it.

And terribly turned on.

Fuck.

Yes, there's that.

I let go of the covers and shift into fetal position. I calculate what's transpired and what it all means. Multiple permutations that leave me without a solution.

Up to now, I'd believed I was nothing special: the token female body on the platform who filled a gap, a diversion of sorts who is merely the subject of his gaze while on the road—the recipient of his universal charm. I certainly didn't think I was someone he had a true interest in.

My heart still pounds in my ears, the echo of my exit made in haste.

What if I'm reading into this? Maybe I've got it all wrong.

Maybe he knows a beautiful bombshell named Bea, or there's a hot Fiona back home he calls Fi?

But I didn't get it wrong. I know what I heard.

I replay the distinct articulation of the letter V on his lips and my heart sets back off on a sprint.

Heat floods every inch of my body.

It sounded like raw sex when he said it.

It feels like raw sex remembering it now.

My mind replays the intimate moments on the deck today, to when equipment fell away to lightness and I was literally worked on by his hands.

I think of how he unfastened the buckle, the warmth and pressure I'd felt from his fingers. I could've sworn I'd seen the same heat in his eyes, but with every draw of oxygen in the chamber afterward, I'd rewritten the story in my mind: revisionist history about a forty-year-old diver who couldn't possibly hold the eye or interest of a man like Cooper Brooks. Who couldn't possibly be enough.

Could I?

The surge of adrenaline that hit me in the bathroom has begun to dissipate and my body temperature plummets. Eager to get into warm pajamas, I finally stand to peel off the layers of clothing, abandoning the idea of a shower, my filthy body in good company with my filthy mind.

I brush my teeth and wash up at the cabin sink before turning out the lights and trying to sleep.

It's futile.

Tossing and turning in my small bed, the shower scene plays on a loop in my mind.

At least a dozen times I contemplate touching myself.

Who would blame me?

Being subjected to Cooper's charms and all that I've seen today is more than most red-blooded women—and many men—could stand without taking matters literally into their own hands.

Each time I talk myself out of it, I remember the sound of my name echoing off the tile.

"Fuck, V."

The sound was sumptuous like velvet.

But it doesn't feel…right.

For the first time in a very long time, I don't know what to do. As an introverted only child to divorced parents, I'm used to just…dealing. I get by on my own. But something about this situation—this man—has me completely out of my depth.

I reach for my cell phone in the darkness and wake the screen. It's barely past nine thirty; no wonder I can't sleep. Without thinking too much about it, I fire off a text.

Violet: You up?

Greta: Has someone stolen your phone? Is this a hostage situation?

Greta. Ever the jokester.

She's an electrician, practically the unicorn of women in trades. We met years ago when I was brought in to do some welding on a project where her team was doing the electrical. Women on a work site can't help but be drawn together. We're sisters in arms, battling the patriarchy one sexist asshole at a time.

I know I'm not the best about texting, but come on…

Violet: Smart ass.

Greta: Aren't you on a rig right now?

Violet: Yes

Greta: Cool. You never text from the road.
Everything okay?

I pull myself up to a seated position. Do I really *never* text from the road?

Shit, maybe I don't.

Violet: In my defence, there's usually shitty cell reception, but this one is fancy and has all the bells and whistles.

Greta: Speaking of bells...I think Bella is hooking up with her boss.

Holy shit.

Violet: LARRY??

Greta: Oh no, sorry. I mean her "client"

I rest my hand on my chest.

Phew. That would've been weird.

Greta: Sorry, did I give you a heart attack?

Violet: Mild one, yes.

I take a drink from the water bottle that's next to my bed, then settle back.

Larry, Bella's sweetheart of a supervisor, has fiery red hair but an even temper. Some lucky woman will snap him up, but I could never imagine that being her.

Violet: I know Larry's as sweet as a ginger cookie (and I suspect as spicy too) but he's like a brother to her.

Greta: Yeah, that would be gross.

There's a brief pause in our exchange.

Do I want to tell Greta? Where do I even start?

I set my phone down on the bed and stretch out my tight neck. For the past hour my shoulders have been perched around my ears. I take a deep breath. I need to relax.

I pull the elastic from my hair and tousle my loose locks.

I settle again with my phone and decide to dive in.

Violet: I broke up with Charles.

I watch the bobbing bubble for several seconds, as Greta drafts her response.

> Greta: I'm not sure how to say this, so I'm just gonna say it. THANK GOD.

I chuckle.

I love these girls. They always give it to me straight.

> Violet: Yeah, yeah.

> Greta: No offense.

> Violet: None taken. I get it.

> Greta: How are you holding up?

How *am* I holding up?

That's when I realize I've not thought about Charles even once today.

I've been too busy fantasizing about someone else.

> Violet: Charles who?

The bubble dances again.

> Greta: So that's not why you're texting?

Why *am* I texting?

Do I tell her?

I start to draft a response but delete it twice.

I hesitate, thinking about what to say.

> Violet: I couldn't sleep.

I'm not lying, I'm just not telling the whole truth.

Is it wrong that I want to keep Cooper my little secret? That I want to guard what's transpired as something sacred between just him and me?

> Greta: Well settle in for a bedtime story…let
> me tell you about the smoking hot dude
> who's ringing Bella's bells.

I chuckle and settle into a horizontal position.

We text and share some laughs and I enjoy the feeling of sisterhood, a rare treat for me—Violet Thomas—who can't even keep a houseplant alive because I'm always on the road.

"Well, don't you look fresh as a daisy," JT says to someone over my shoulder.

I take another generous drink of my coffee before glancing behind me just as Cooper is approaching our table.

The bugger does look fresh.

Freshly showered.

Freshly shaved.

Freshly…

I might drown today, due to three consecutive nights of improper sleep, but Cooper's bright-eyed, bushy-tailed, and bubbly in a superbly fitting vintage Metallica T-shirt.

Argh!

His attractiveness is relentless.

Cooper eases himself into the seat next to me with his daily heaping of eggs and bacon. "Yeah, I slept like a baby."

"I'm sure you did," I mumble.

"Pardon?" Cooper asks, eyebrow raised.

"Nothing." I take a bite of my cold toast and sigh.

I'm cranky. It's undoubtedly my unique combination of lack of sleep and sexual angst. For some reason, my feelings have flipped over from frustration to anger in the few short seconds that Cooper's sexually sated ass has been parked beside me.

I'm going to have to get over my feelings of guilt and just deal with the matter at hand—*by* hand.

Masturbation for the sake of team morale.

Who would've thought?

"Morning." Steve approaches with his own tray and drops it on the table with a clatter. He settles in next to JT and pulls out his phone.

There's a rare moment of relative quiet in the cafeteria as everyone settles into their breakfast and waits for their caffeine to kick in.

A strange *rat-a-tat-tat* sound hits me from where Steve is thumbing out some text on his cell phone.

Rat-a-tat-tat.

Tat-tat-tat.

TAT-A-TAT.

"Jesus Christ, Steve. Stop that." The words fall out of my mouth.

Three sets of eyes snap to me.

"Stop what?" Steve asks.

"That annoying sound." I gesture to the iPhone in his hands.

Steve looks around at the others quizzically. "The… keyboard sounds?"

"It's fucking annoying." I drop my toast on the plate in front of me. "Leaving the keyboard sounds turned up on your cell phone is the audio equivalent of manspreading. Turn that shit off."

The three men sit up straighter in their chairs, eyebrows raised in shock.

"What bit your ass?" Steve asks, clearly offended.

"Or maybe *NOT* bitten your ass…" JT mutters.

I full-on kick him under the table.

"Ouch." JT reaches down to protect his shins.

"Violet gets mad?" Cooper asks, clearly directing the question at Steve and JT.

JT chuckles. "Oh, Violet most definitely gets mad."

"Stop talking about me like I'm not here. It just pisses me off more."

"I've never seen you like this before." Cooper's eyes brighten, like he's amused by my discontent.

I release a low growl.

His eyes widen.

Shit. Did that sound a little sexual?

"Hey Coop, did you bring your laptop?" Steve thankfully changes the topic of conversation.

Lauren approaches the table with her own breakfast, and I sigh with relief. I signal to her to sit beside me. Some estrogen will save me.

"Yeah, why?" Cooper shovels a generous forkful of scrambled egg into his mouth.

It should be as obnoxious as a teenage boy, the way he scarfs back his food at every meal. Instead, I think about where those calories could go.

Fuck.

"Morning, all," Lauren greets the table.

Everyone mumbles their replies.

Steve continues. "I forgot my charging cord at home and I wanna video call with my parents for their anniversary tonight. You've got a MacBook, right?" Steve takes a bite from a slice of bacon.

"Oh, yeah, no problem. Just come by my cabin later." Cooper takes a drink from his coffee mug. "You know where to find me?"

"Level four?" Steve asks.

"I'm level three…cabin six," Cooper corrects him.

"Thanks, man." Steve returns to his texting, this time with the volume low.

"More side scan today, Lauren?" I try to bring her into the conversation.

"Nope, all done. I'll just analyze the data and work on reports." She takes a sip of her tea. "What about you guys?"

"Bruce said we're repairing some damage at shallow depth today, so just a little welding—nothing too major." I shrug.

Funny how running electricity through water is just business as usual for us.

My phone vibrates in my hoodie pocket. I reach for it and see a text from JT.

I glance over to him at the table, but he's already in conversation with Cooper.

JT: Notice he said his cabin number loud
enough for EVERYONE to hear?

Here we go again.

JT, the sexual enabler.

Violet: Don't.

I quickly type out the text and stuff my phone back into my pocket, focusing on my breakfast tray.

It buzzes again.

I should ignore it.

Of course I take it out and read again.

JT: ...except I didn't hear it quite the way
he said it...I heard something else...

He's baiting me. I need to put this thing on do-not-disturb.

It hums right in my hand.

Looks like I'm not getting a choice.

JT: I heard "level three, cabin sex."

I stuff the phone back into my pocket and throw an unamused look his way. He pretends not to notice, but I know he's suppressing a smile.

"Okay, folks! Ready?" Bruce yells over at us from the cafeteria door.

Eager for a distraction, I finish the last gulps of my coffee and head off to work. Bruce's words are enough to silence the group, who all stand and collect their dishes. But they don't silence my thoughts about restless nights and the comforts I'd find in cabin sex…*shit*…I mean cabin six.

CHAPTER 15

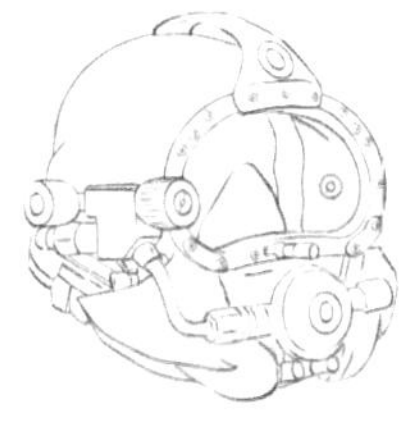

"She did it last time." JT jabs his index finger in my direction.

"Did not. *You* did." I point back.

Bruce, Nick, Steve, and Cooper watch us with interest, heads on a swivel.

JT's face flushes pink. He spins on his feet to face them.

"You always pick her." This time he's jabbing that finger at Bruce. "I'm calling it…this is reverse discrimination."

"Oh, give me a break." I rest my hands on my hips, rolling my eyes so hard it actually kind of hurts.

I shake my head at the ridiculousness of it all. We're not fighting over who *has* to submerge themselves into the dark depths and run a current of electricity that could kill them. Nope. We're fighting over who *gets* to.

Commercial divers are a special breed.

"Neither of you are doing it," Bruce spits out, his patience likely worn thin.

We both groan. I shoot daggers at JT. He throws them right back at me.

"Cooper is going to do it." Bruce gestures over to our youngest team member.

"Yes!" Cooper raises a celebratory fist.

Lucky bastard.

Steve returns to his task of preparing the equipment. He's an annoying little shit sometimes, but he's an expert welder. The dude can run a line of weld with medical precision. There was never any question that Steve would be doing some of the work today, it was just a matter of figuring out who'd be joining him.

Steve inspects the fireproof gloves attached to the micro habitat and I think I hear JT whimper. I sigh longingly myself. It's a system that isolates the portion of the metalwork requiring repair so water can be extracted, and the weld can be carried out in dry conditions. It's incredibly cool. We've moved to this methodology because it's safer than the Hail Mary pass of running the current through water, and it produces a better weld because the cooler water temperatures can't chill the mend too quickly and compromise the repair.

Bruce approaches Cooper and Steve with a handful of reference photos and sonographs. "Okay, so we've got a fatigue crack on the K node of the support structure in the ten o'clock position. Not as tricky as the twelve o'clock we did a few months ago, but we'll need to be careful setting up the micro." He points to the small but clear line in the image.

Cooper scratches his forehead and furrows his brow. I can tell he's nervous.

I'm excited for Cooper. He's ten years behind where I am and needs to build his résumé and improve his skills. I don't mind stepping back and watching it all topside if Cooper's the one who gets to make the dive.

The repair is at relatively shallow depth, so it requires a cage. As the name suggests, it's a metal basket that the divers and equipment are loaded into and then lowered to the work location. The micro habitat apparatus, despite how it sounds, is heavy and needs to be hoisted into the water by boom crane.

Nothing we do is ever done in a hurry. Every step is taken deliberately, every piece of equipment triple-checked, not a single shortcut taken. Dive safety standards require the due diligence, and our lives quite simply depend on it.

By the time we're lowering the cage, the sun is higher in the sky and Lauren has joined the team on her break from report writing to watch the show. We've collected a few other spectators from the rig crew. We don't weld all the time—and certainly not with this equipment—so when we do, it tends to garner attention.

Once Steve and Cooper slip below the surface, our eyes shift to the monitor to watch things unfold.

"What's all the excitement about?" Lauren takes a drink from her water bottle and gestures to the extra bodies on the deck.

"The guys are gonna weld," I explain, moving a few pieces of equipment to help tidy the deck. "Fancy gadgets that throw fire always impress the dudes."

"Ah." Lauren nods. "Fair enough."

I glance over at the monitor. Four hands are setting up the habitat. I spot two yellow gloves in the frame and smile.

Lauren surveys the crowd. "Cooper's down there?"

"Yeah, he and Steve." I grab a granola bar from my bag and unwrap it. "If you're going to watch, get comfortable. They'll assemble the micro habitat first, then they have to purge the water and prep the work area before they make it hot."

One of Lauren's eyebrows raises. "I'm sorry, did you just say *make it hot*?"

I chuckle. "Yes, make it hot." I take another bite and

chew for a few seconds before I speak. "Close the circuit," I continue. "You know…apply the weld."

"Oh." Lauren's face breaks into a grin. "Wait…a *micro habitat*? That sounds fucking cool." Her eyebrow raises again, this time followed by a waggle.

Should have known that Lauren would geek out on the tech.

"We've been using this technique since it was developed in 2020." I rinse the oats from my teeth with a mouthful of water. "Micro habitats for hyperbaric welding…the best in sub-sea technology and the best way to get a class-A weld."

Lauren's eyes grow wide. Like I've just opened to the centrefold of a *Playgirl* magazine.

I start to giggle. "Grab a good seat—you won't want to miss the fireworks."

It's so quiet as Steve and Cooper focus that I can hear their rhythmic breathing over the monitor as they weld.

Sparks fly behind a Lexan viewing window as the two work from opposite sides of the micro, laying down a trail of metal solder as they converge.

The cameras from their helmets show the perspectives from where they stand. Steve still works from the cage, but Cooper's had to climb the rig's support structure to get the right angle.

His back is going to hurt tomorrow.

I stand up straight, eyes shifting to the others in the crowd who are also watching the monitor. I'm surprised by the thought that's popped into my head. I'm a little self-conscious about the inside knowledge I have of his body—

all the aches and pains he's shared with me those nights alone in the galley.

I rub the back of my neck nervously and refocus on the display in front of me.

The next line Cooper lays spills out like morse code.

Shit. He's too tight.

"*Breathe, Cooper,*" I whisper.

I watch the monitor attentively as he returns to the beginning, attempting the repair again. More dots and dashes.

I grimace.

"Fuck," Cooper swears over the comms line.

Instinct takes me towards Bruce's mic.

"Relax your grip, Cooper. Let the arc do the work."

I hear his loud sigh over the speaker.

He takes a few seconds to regroup, then leans in to attempt it again.

After a few dramatic seconds, the bubbles on the screen clear and reveal an absolutely perfect line of weld. The man has nailed it. My hands come together by instinct and I have to stop myself from clapping. I awkwardly clasp them instead, twisting to see if anyone's noticed, taking a relieved breath when I see that no one has.

"Looks great, Coop," Bruce speaks into the comms mic.

Cooper signals one confident yellow thumb-up in front of his camera.

Frat boy's a fucking steel surgeon.

"Someone's a fast learner," JT mutters beside me. He's arrived out of nowhere.

I look over and catch his coy wink.

Little shit.

In spite of him, my heart grows in my chest. It's pure joy to see Cooper succeed—to see the good guy win.

I convince myself it's nothing more than team camaraderie and group pride that I'm experiencing. I'd be just as happy for JT if he'd learned a new skill…right?

But in the next instant, an entirely new thought comes to mind: I wonder what else this man could do with those hands?

Hands…tile…*"Fuck, V."*

Shit. My stomach drops and I low-key panic. I can't think about this here.

I put one foot in front of the other until I'm next to Bruce.

I need a distraction.

"Bruce, I can start the clean-up," I suggest. I grab a few random tools that are lying out on our temporary workbench.

Bruce watches me, puzzled. "A bit premature, V."

He looks back at the monitor where Steve and Cooper have disconnected the habitat and Cooper is still poised on the structure. "Coop, just come to surface. Steve can manage the rest."

"'Kay," Cooper replies through his helmet mic.

He carefully unwinds his umbilical from where it's become wrapped around the rig, and begins his slow ascent using the main cable line as a guide.

Well, shit. Now those hands are about to join me topside.

Get yourself together, woman.

They've been working at less than twenty meters, so it doesn't take long for Cooper's helmet to appear at the moon pool opening. JT is quick to assist and get him to his feet.

I try to keep my attention on the monitor, where Steve is wrapping up. He signals the crew to hoist the habitat to the surface, and it slips out of view.

"I'm ready," Steve directs from below.

Bruce gestures to the crew who are on hand to help with the cage hoist. "Let's raise him."

The platform that's been relatively sedate suddenly bustles with activity. JT works to help Cooper remove his equipment, one team reels in the habitat from its cable, a second begins to raise Steve's cage.

With the increase in activity, conversation resumes and I'm relieved by the return to the natural tempo of the deck. I follow behind JT, collecting Cooper's gear and setting it all aside for inspection and drying.

"Why isn't the cage moving?" Bruce's voice cuts through the bustle.

Most continue their activities, but I turn to watch him, struck by his concern. His tanned and weathered face is strained.

I hear some muffled comments from the direction of the hoist.

"Try again," Bruce says.

Something tweaks in my belly. In the years I've worked with Bruce I've rarely seen a look of concern pass over his face. "Cool as a cucumber" is how I'd typically describe him. He's had a long career, first as a Navy diver, then a commercial diver in the private sector. With him as tool push and supervisor, we're in extremely capable hands.

He doesn't look so cool right now.

I walk over to stand next to him and look at the monitor that he's studying closely.

"It's stuck," Steve's choppy voice indicates from the speaker.

"What do you mean, *stuck*?" Bruce asks. "Show me."

Steve pans over to the far-left corner of the cage with his helmet cam. The three-inch-thick cage frame is caught under the rig's complex structure.

Static sounds come from Steve's microphone. "The weld

location was awkward as fuck; we shifted a bit doing the work. I'm caught up under the frame."

Well, shit.

"Okay…all good." Bruce folds his arms. "We've been here before, Steve."

Bruce's voice remains constant. As always, reassuringly calm.

He hesitates, one brow raised in concentration. I'm trying to follow his lead and not panic—staying cool in front of the rest of the team, like nothing out of the ordinary is going down twenty meters deep.

"Brace yourself, Steve. We're going to give things a good tug." Bruce gestures to the two rig workers who are managing the hoist and they make the attempt.

"Whoa." Steve's camera judders and my stomach flips for him.

"Shit," Bruce mumbles.

Bruce swearing? That's a first.

"Everything okay?" I ask.

I know full well it's not.

Bruce ignores my question.

"My umbilical is caught," Steve says from below. "I'm caught up."

Well, there goes the idea of him abandoning ship.

"How bad?" Bruce asks.

A small crowd of frowns has begun to form around the monitor.

Stress on an offshore platform tends to be contagious.

"Right at the pinch point. Fuck." The growing sense of panic in Steve's voice is apparent.

I lean in and try to see what Steve is seeing. The yellow and blue of his umbilical—the crucial communication lines and surface air supply—are pinched precisely where the metal of the cage abuts the structure.

This isn't good.

"Let's give it one more try," Bruce suggests.

"I don't know, Bruce." I point to the monitor. "We might damage the line."

"My air is fucked up." Steve's voice is strained.

Too late.

"Bail out!" I bark at Bruce.

"Steve, can you swap out? Connect to your secondary." Bruce's voice is calm and firm.

The image on the screen trembles again. Bubbles pass in front of Steve's camera, reminding me of the precious air that's on his back.

"I'm trying," he says.

"Come on, Steve," I mutter, crossing my arms and covering my mouth with my tattooed hand.

A few endless seconds pass.

"I can't reach!" Steve's in full panic mode. "I'm all tangled up—I have no movement. I'm fucked."

My heart leaps to my throat. In all the years I've been a diver, I've never lost a teammate and I refuse to lose one today.

Fifteen percent fatality rate can kiss my goddam ass.

"I'm going down." I pull up my wetsuit and grab the first pieces of my equipment.

"No." Cooper steps up to me and runs his hands through his hair. "I'll go."

"Cooper, you can't go back down. You'll exceed your dive limit," Bruce commands.

Cooper angrily tosses his weight belt on the deck.

JT doesn't skip a beat. As my long-time dive partner, he knows what to do.

Without saying a word, he begins helping me with my harness and bail-out bottle, getting me geared up in record time.

"Violet's coming, Steve," I hear Bruce say behind me.

The monitor remains eerily silent.

Don't die on me, Steve.

JT adjusts my air supply line and our eyes meet for a second.

"Be careful, V." JT's voice is quiet. It's a message just for me.

His voice betrays an emotion I've never seen on him before.

Is it fear?

A new wave of affection for him washes over me.

"I will." I squeeze his arm under my diving glove.

"I know you will." JT nods, tapping my helmet once it's fastened. He tethers a set of shears to my vest and flips on my helmet camera.

"V!" Cooper shouts to me, just as I'm turning to face the moon pool.

I stop and glance over my shoulder, seeing his wide eyes through the window of my dive helmet. I nod and turn, jumping into the dark water below.

CHAPTER 16

I let gravity take me, dropping like a literal stone thanks to the lead-weighted belt around my waist.

Stay safe.

Be sure.

Don't let emotions set you adrift.

I talk to myself as I let the cable line pass through my closed hand. Attached to the work area, it's my direct connection to Steve and I'm clinging to it for dear life.

With each foot I drop, anxiety builds, but when I finally spot him and see his yellow Kirby Morgan helmet is still upright, I'm awash with relief.

When he spots me, he shakes his fiberglass-covered head.

"You're a sight for sore eyes." He butts his helmet against mine in a rare display of co-worker affection.

I'm thankful his mic still works, since his electrical is also caught up in the pinch point. Being able to communicate is going to make this much easier.

"Let's get you switched over." I gesture for him to turn,

trying to get access to his equipment. He can barely move because his umbilical is so taut.

"Jesus, Steve. What a mess."

"Tell me about it." Bubbles trickle from his mask's whisker wings as he exhales.

Bruce's impatient voice is loud through my helmet's headphones. "What's the situation?"

"Just about to swap him out," I say. "Gimme a minute."

The last thing I need is a distraction from topside.

Since Steve can't even raise his arms fully, I make the swap for him. It's just a simple valve switch, but if you can't lift your hands to do it, it might as well be splitting the atom.

A few seconds pass after I've turned the last valve. I wait with bated breath to see that it's working properly.

"That's much better," Steve finally says.

I take my own first full breath since leaving the platform.

Thank god.

"Let's get you disconnected." I try to examine the connection point—hoping to remove the umbilical properly—but I can't get proper access with how badly he's tangled.

I reason that the line will need to be cut where it's been pinched anyway, since it's been compromised by damage. I should just cut the line instead.

"Bruce, can we turn off Steve's power?" I reach for the shears on my harness. "I need to cut him free."

"Just tell me when." Bruce's voice is clear from the headphones in my helmet.

"Steve, I need to cut your communication." I stand so close our helmets touch, just to make sure he understands me.

Our eyes connect through two sheets of glass. His search mine.

"It's the only way to get you up quickly," I continue. "We won't be able to talk after I do."

He nods his helmet slowly. "Okay, boss."

Wrinkles form around his eyes, his nasal mask obscuring the smile that I'd find there.

His deference warms my heart.

I grab hold of his equipment for emphasis. "You're not going to be connected to anything while you ascend. Hang on to that fucking cable line like it's your mother's hand, you hear me?"

He nods again.

"Stay right with me."

Another nod.

"Anything you want to say before I cut?"

There's a long pause.

His eyes search mine again.

"Thank you, V," he chokes out.

Dammit, he's going to make me cry.

I knock his helmet with my hand, as hard as the water resistance will let me. "Stop that sentimental shit. Now, do we have this?"

"Yes," he answers softly.

"I said…" I lean into him. "Do we *have* this?"

"YES." His voice is strong and sure this time.

"Bruce…kill it," I order.

"You got it," he replies.

There's a moment of silence as I await Bruce's confirmation.

"Done," I hear over my headphones.

I pull Steve's umbilical towards me, wrapping my gloved hand around all three cables. I grasp the shears in my right hand and start to cut.

The first one I sever is the pneumo hose. It's the connection that indicates the diver's depth to the team above. It cuts through easily. The second I cut is the diver communication line. It's as tough as a two-dollar steak and I have to depress the shears several times before it finally gives way. The reduced dexterity of my gloved hand isn't helping.

Finally, I cut the surface supply breathing line. Bubbles erupt the instant the shears break through, obscuring our vision. This is why I cut it last.

Once Steve is free, I drop the tethered shears and grab him by his harness, eager to get his attention. He nods and watches me closely. I gesture upward with my thumb, and we make our way to the main cable.

"We're coming up," I tell Bruce.

"Okay, we're watching," Bruce replies. Knowing he's there—that the entire team is waiting for us—is reassuring.

I motion for Steve to go first so I can keep watch as he rises to the surface.

The adrenaline is starting to crash, and the effects of that, combined with the heaviness of my weight belt, make my ascension more difficult than usual.

The light of the moon pool opening is particularly majestic today, and it casts a heavenly glow around Steve's form above me as we approach.

The sense of relief I feel as Steve awkwardly flops against the deck is unprecedented. He's always been an absolute ass, but he's *our* ass. I don't want to even consider the loss we all would have felt had things turned out differently today.

It's all hands on deck to get Steve's helmet and heavy equipment off, while I rest at the surface, half of me focused on clutching the deck, the other just catching my breath.

I watch from the water, witnessing the celebratory moment as the team pulls Steve's helmet and checks to make sure he's alright. Seeing his happiness as the others ruffle his overgrown blond locks and try to bro-hug him from his prone position on the deck is one I'll never forget.

"Jesus, V." JT's muffled voice breaks my reverie. He reaches down. "Let's get you out."

I look up and find his wide smile. I'm not sure how many minutes passed as I watched from the water.

He helps me up and time seems to slow as JT and Cooper work together to get my cumbersome equipment off. I stand, uselessly watching, seemingly in zero command of my body.

"She's pale," Nick notes from somewhere behind me.

"Blood pressure drop," Bruce replies, suddenly beside me. "It's the adrenaline crash."

I pull down the top of my wetsuit and shiver from a sudden dip in body temperature.

"Let's get them into the chamber," JT suggests.

We're herded across the deck to the decompression chamber where our pure medical oxygen awaits. JT opens the heavy metal door and Steve climbs inside.

"Wait, V."

I turn, stopping mid-stride.

Cooper holds up his hoodie. "Put this on."

I stand there motionless and numb, brain and body still not cooperating.

"Here…" He bunches up the grey fabric and exposes the neck hole before stepping forward to loop it over my head.

Soft cotton and soothing scent surround me.

I slip my arms through the generous sleeves and don't even try to hide it as I inhale a deep breath through my nose, closing my eyes with the draw of earthy and spicy smell.

When I open them, Cooper is watching.

Fine lines I've never noticed before frame his eyes, defying his youth.

An inscrutable expression crosses his face. Not happy, not sad. More like I'm a puzzle he's trying to solve.

"You're incredible." He pulls my hair from where it's

tucked inside of the sweatshirt and sets it back down over the fabric, smoothing it with one large, warm hand for good measure.

I'm speechless.

"Go." He nudges my arm and gestures toward the chamber.

I turn and climb inside, taking a seat on the bench. Grabbing my mask, I take a slow, deep breath and watch as Cooper's beautiful smile disappears behind the heavy door in front of me.

CHAPTER 17

You only live once.

Seize the day.

Tomorrow is never guaranteed.

There are a million ways to say it, but it all comes down to the same key message: Bang the hottie when the opportunity presents itself.

There really is nothing like a wee brush with mortality to put things into perspective. Lying on my back in my lonely cabin bed the next morning, counting ceiling tiles and mulling over the events of the last twenty-four hours, it leads to some interesting reflection.

Age difference and work relationship be damned. It's abundantly clear that we're attracted to each other. The only question remaining is: What are we going to do about it?

Cooper thinks I'm still with Charles. He's not going to make a move.

So that leaves me.

Why shouldn't I be the one who makes the play?

I'm a strong, capable, and confident woman. In his words, a "solid stunner." There's absolutely no reason why

I shouldn't march over to Cooper's cabin right this moment and act on the chemical instincts that are working overtime to put us together.

Zero apologies for it, too.

I've been letting a sense of professionalism hold me back, but if I'm being honest with myself, I can't work with him right now without undressing him with my mind anyway.

I know this, Cooper knows this, JT knows this. Let's face it, the entire team probably knows this.

Depriving myself of exploring every bloody inch of that man has been like skipping the sin and going straight to proverbial hell. If I'm going to suffer the punishment of awkward and tense moments on the platform, I should at least be guilty of doing something.

Turning onto my side, I pull my covers higher.

I reach for my phone and check the time.

It's 5:30 a.m.

Plenty of time to get to level three, cabin six.

Releasing a long breath, I put my phone down.

I need to really be sure.

And I need to shave my legs.

If I'm going to do this, I'm doing it right.

Pulling back the covers, I rise and walk to my suitcase. I check my toiletry bag and come up empty.

Shit.

To be fair, I haven't packed a razor for work in at least a decade. Why on earth would I?

It's bad enough that I'd be turning up to his cabin in tired old workwear—the least I can do is a little primp and preen.

I crawl back into bed and consider my options.

I could pilfer one from the AED cabinet, but that seems morally questionable. (The need to shave a chest during an urgent lifesaving sitch and whatnot.)

But then I remember the freshly shaven face that greets me every morning at the breakfast table and a perfect plan takes shape.

"Good morning, JT." I slide into the seat beside him.

He puts down his cup of coffee and flashes me with a bright smile. "There's our hero."

"Cut the crap." I adjust my tray and add salt and pepper to my eggs. "I did nothing you wouldn't have done. Nothing *anyone* here wouldn't have done."

"Yes, but you actually *did* it. So let's just celebrate it like you would've celebrated us." JT takes the salt and sprinkles it over his plate.

"Whatever."

I'm quick to change the topic, and eager to get one particular conversation out of the way before anyone joins us.

I survey the room—the coast seems clear.

"Hey JT…" I hesitate, not sure how to ask. Worried my reluctance will only make matters worse, I decide to dive right in. "Do you happen to have an extra razor?"

I sip my hot coffee, covering as much as my face with the mug as possible. I watch as it takes less than a count of three for it to register.

His eyes widen in surprise. "Holy fuck, you're going to do it."

Well, that was smooth, Violet.

"I don't know what you're talking about; I forgot mine at home." I'm going for casual. I'm getting more three-piece suit.

"Don't bullshit me right now. If you're doing this, I need to come along for the ride."

"JT!"

"Not literally. Jesus, V." His eyes sparkle with vicarious joy. "You *are* doing it."

The sound of two trays hitting the table saves me.

"Good morning," Bruce says. Looks like he's making a rare appearance at our table. He's usually up and has eaten long before we do. He settles in beside me.

"Hope you slept okay." He directs his comment to me. As a former military diver, he knows all too well how scenarios can take over the mind. How the alternative endings can play out and haunt you until the happy one we all got might as well have been a tragedy.

"I'm good," I reassure him.

Steve slides in opposite me. "Morning, V."

His voice is soft, movements gentle.

"Hey. You good?" I notice my own voice is a bit softer than usual too.

He scratches at a gouge in the plastic tray in front of him. "V," he begins.

Four sets of eyes shift from his hand to his face, hanging on his pregnant pause.

"I don't even know what to say," Steve finally continues.

And I get it. We all do.

What words does one choose to thank someone for saving their life?

We sit together for a moment in silence and mutual gratitude.

I reach over and steal his blueberry muffin. "We're even." I wink.

Steve lets out a long breath and we share a chuckle. JT reaches to mess his hair.

And just like that, everything returns to normal. As normal as it ever gets for a group of people who willingly jump feet-first into dark depths to run a current of electricity through water that could kill them.

Like a silly little schoolgirl, I wear his hoodie whenever I can over the next twenty-four hours.

Our paths don't cross on the platform the next day because Cooper's been lent to the regular crew to perform repair welds topside. It's a good opportunity for him to practice working in a fall-arrest system and to get a feel for surface work. Steve and I, on the other hand, are put directly back into the water. Bruce—ever conscious of the temptation to avoid after a near miss like we just had—uses a gentle but determined approach.

For me, it's like riding a bike and goes well. I worry about Steve though. He's definitely not his adventurous self. He's tentative and timid as he performs his usual tasks. It's hard to watch. Even tougher to know when to push and when to back off. We'll encourage, but let Steve take the lead.

Once back at my cabin, I touch the soft, grey fabric of Cooper's sweatshirt, lingering at the frayed edges of the cuff. Like the patina on an irreplaceable artifact, it's been worn soft with age. I sniff and snort it with the attention an eighties rocker would've given lines of cocaine.

I slide it over my head, letting the cotton cool my skin.

Yep, my addiction is firmly set.

I'm glad we haven't seen each other. It means I've not had to return it to him just yet.

It also gives me time to catch my breath.

I examine my face in the mirror, seeing the fine lines next to my eyes, the freckles scattered across my cheeks.

Some say they're cute, but it's all sun damage from years of working on the deck. My own patina from a life spent outdoors and maybe some sunblock neglect.

I pull the hoodie's long sleeves over my hands and cross my arms in front of me.

What if I've got it all wrong?

Taps on the door surprise me.

My stomach twists.

Shit. What if it's Cooper?

I pull the sweatshirt off and toss it on the bed. I glance into the mirror again, fixing my hair and checking my teeth.

A cold sweat sets in.

I'm not ready for this.

I take a deep breath before opening the door.

My entire body settles the moment I see who it is.

"Expecting someone else?" JT saunters in past me, not waiting for an invitation.

I'm instantly struck by my feelings of disappointment. I let the door click shut as my heart resumes its normal rhythm.

"I brought you something." JT reaches into this own hoodie pocket and pulls out a navy-blue plastic razor.

I reach for it, but he pulls it back.

Of course he does.

"I'm giving you this on one condition."

"I'm not going to share every bloody detail, JT."

There's no sense denying what's going on here anymore.

"Christ, I'm not that nosey," he replies.

I roll my eyes.

"Okay, well, maybe I am. But I'm not going to insert myself like that." He chuckles. "Shit, that's an unfortunate pun."

I roll my eyes.

He hands over the razor. "I want you to promise me one thing."

I raise a brow.

"I want you to march over to level three, cabin six like the life-saving badass bitch that you are and unapologetically take every life-affirming sexual gift that Adonis is willing to give you." He waggles his brows. "Maybe twice —if time permits."

My heart swells with affection for this man.

I pull the disposable razor from his hand.

"Deal."

CHAPTER 18

Stepping into the small shower stall, I turn the control to max hot. The lock on the door is finally fixed, but the hot water seems to take forever to kick in.

One problem at a time.

I look around myself in the tight space, holding my five items and at a complete loss as to where to put them.

The shower is equipped with one tiny shelf—about four inches by four inches—clearly designed for men who use the same bottle of product to shampoo their hair, wash their bodies, and clean their engine blocks.

I'm still struggling with bottles when the water overcorrects to scalding. I jump back, naked ass hitting the cold powder-coated steel, and shift things to one arm so I can adjust the temperature.

Once I can tolerate stepping into the water, I manage to fit my shampoo, conditioner, face cleanser, and razor on the tiny shelf—thanks to travel-sized containers. I opt to hold the soap.

I settle under the stream and carry out strategic switch-outs of products from the shelf, maximizing the use of space, and dropping the razor half a dozen times in the process.

When it becomes clear I can't use the soap while holding the razor, I end up gripping the razor with my teeth, working up the lather into a makeshift shaving cream in my hands.

I bend at the waist to coat my right, vine-leaf-covered leg and knock my head on the shower wall.

Shit.

I rub the crown of my head where it stings.

The narrow stall was clearly not designed for this.

I try again, twisting awkwardly and somehow manage to knock every miniature product off the miniature shelf.

Sonofa…

No wonder I never do this.

Somehow, I manage to get the right leg soaped up, despite the effort it takes to work against the spray of water that—no matter my angle—I can't seem to get away from.

I grab the cheap, disposable razor JT gave me and scrape the blade against my skin.

I'm going to have one hell of a razor burn tomorrow.

Whatever. It's worth it.

I persevere and repeat everything with the left.

It's a herculean effort, and after a long day of physical work I'm exhausted once I'm done.

Yep, and I'm planning to turn up ready to romp at cabin six within the hour.

I pause under the shower's spray, taking a few extra minutes to get my proverbial shit together.

Running a hand over the taut skin of my belly, my mind —like my heart—races.

It's been three years since I've been here: about to put myself out there. If all goes according to plan, I'm about to learn everything there is to learn about another person. And maybe a few things about myself, too.

Looking down at my body, I try to judge it fairly. I see skin that never seems to tan, despite long hours spent in the sun. Pale skin that's decorated with fine and delicate leaves, carefully traced by an artist's needle.

I'm not built like my friend Bella, but I'm strong and fit, firm and toned. Despite best efforts, I can't *not* see the extra few pounds and the softer curves the last ten years have brought me.

More curves and pounds than what Cooper surely sees on the women he undoubtedly spends time with—women who are a dozen years younger than me.

I squeeze my eyes shut and run my face under the stream. Willing myself to wash away the nerves and self-doubt. After a minute, my shaky hand reaches to turn off the water.

Here we go.

It's hard to look sexy in multiple layers of PPE, but dammit, I'm trying.

I've moisturized from head to tattooed foot, tousled my wavy blond locks, trussed myself into a non-athletic bra for the first time in days, and applied cherry Chapstick. It's the best I can manage with limited supplies.

I'm nervous.

I push those feelings down and take another look in the mirror, hoping my attempt at girl-next-door meets safety chic hits the mark.

I apply another layer of lip balm and take a slow, steady breath.

Trying to conjure the feelings of empowerment that JT

evoked just an hour ago, I mentally chant my new mantra: *life-saving badass bitch.*

I'm almost believing it by the time I grab the door handle to head to Cooper's cabin. At the last second, I reach for his hoodie.

It's always good to have a cover story.

My inner chorus has been distilled down to *badass* by the time I make it to level three. Each syllable silently spoken in time with my heavy, steel-toed steps.

I count out the cabin numbers as I pass them: *three, four, five…six.*

I hesitate in front of the grey metal door in a slight panic, my risk-averse self kicking into default setting.

What if this is a terrible mistake?

Recalculating the events of the last few days, I arrive at the same solution I had yesterday, last night, and this morning.

I *think* he wants me; I *know* I want him. Life is exceedingly short, and we hang onto it every day literally by just a slippery cord. In a job that's got an unbelievably high fatality rate, I've learned to be rightly cautious and careful. But maybe I've been playing it a little too safe out of the water too.

I take in one more generous breath, stand up tall, and knock.

CHAPTER 19

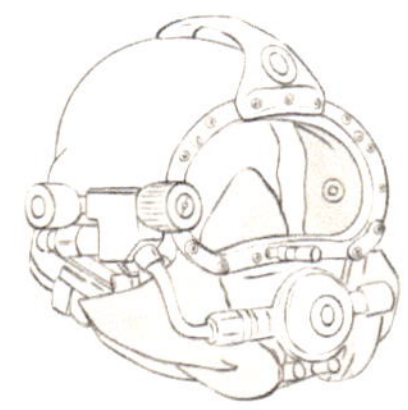

The seconds before the door opens seem to last a lifetime. I fiddle with the fabric in my fingers until the handle turns and Cooper is there.

"Hi," I blurt out, eager to break the silence.

My voice is shaky and unsure as I study his handsome features, the worn grey T-shirt, jeans low-slung on his hips.

My breath hitches.

It seems cliché even to think it, but it's true: he literally takes my breath away.

God, what this man does to me.

Now that I'm resigned to my attraction, the effect he has on my senses is heightened.

My adrenaline surges. It feels like I'm cresting a wave, zero control and barreling towards the great unknown. My stomach flips.

There's no going back now. Acting on this thing between us is something I simply must do—he's the bail-out bottle on my back, the oxygen mask after a dive.

No, it's less utilitarian than that.

Like when you've got your heart set on the crème brûlée at a restaurant and they come back with chocolate cake instead…even the most delicious alternative will never, ever do.

I take another full breath as Cooper shuffles his tanned (brûléed?), bare feet in silence, his body wedged against the door.

He's oddly stiff, not his usual gregarious self.

A few more beats pass. A wide-eyed fear crosses his face.

I mean, I knew he'd be surprised to see me, but that's not what this is.

"Vi-olet," he finally says, his mouth stumbling over my name.

Okay, V. Time to be bold.

I rest one hand against the door jamb. "Are you going to invite me in?"

Channelling my best seductress, I attempt a sly grin. When I try to toss my hair back, it only jostles my hardhat, and it shifts atop my head.

I fix it, awkwardly, knocking my face in the process.

My cheeks heat.

This is not playing out as I'd imagined.

Christ, I wish I'd had a shot of something strong before doing this. The perils of life aboard a dry platform. Water for miles, but not a drop of alcohol to drink.

In my periphery, I catch movement. My eyes shift to behind Cooper.

Long, lithe legs spread out from where someone's perched on his bed. I recognize the pink steel-toed boots immediately.

Lauren.

It's an out-of-body experience as what I'm seeing registers. Like a flick of a switch, my body turns ice cold as my brain pieces it all together.

Lauren stands and approaches. "Oh hey, V." She drinks from her water bottle casually, like she's right at home here in cabin six.

My stomach turns and my chest tightens.

Oh my god, oh my god.

Panic fully sets in.

I glance up at Cooper, hoping he's not been watching my face as understanding dawned on me.

No such luck.

His brow furrows. The look he's giving me is the same pained one he gave when he accidentally took an air cylinder in the balls on deck three days ago.

Is it pity?

Please, no.

My face shifts from warm to hot under his gaze. I'm a mix of horror and dread.

Get out, my instincts tell me.

I step back.

"V." Cooper steps forward. "It's—"

I shove the sweatshirt at his chest. "Here's your hoodie."

I don't stick around long enough to hear what else he has to say.

CHAPTER 20

I shaved my legs for this guy.

Knitted him goddamned socks.

I feel like a country music song, and it fits, since it would seem I've been played like a fiddle.

If not for the stomach-churning embarrassment colouring the edges, I would be seeing straight-up red.

I haven't been this angry in a long time. The unvarnished truth is, I never cared enough about Charles to let him get to me even during our worst arguments.

Hot rage boils in my gut, but it's not directed at Cooper.

I'm angry with myself.

That I let myself be played like this. That I fell for his charms.

I'm old enough to know better.

I turn to my side, my early morning cabin eerily silent on account of its state-of-the-art sound insulation. The silence is uncomfortable, but the thought of running into Cooper and Lauren in the cafeteria? Even worse.

The image of Lauren's face plays across closed eyelid

screens. I tighten my eyes, squeezing the vision away, desperate to unsee what can't be unseen.

Something tugs at my heart.

I guess I'm still young enough to care.

I skip breakfast, which is always a terrible idea when you rely on your body to carry you through demanding physical work. I'll have to get by on the handful of protein and granola bars stashed in my equipment case. I just couldn't bring myself to sit at the same table as the others. I'll have to eventually, but I can't do it yet.

I get to the deck before the rest of the team—even beating Bruce to the moon pool, which is a first. I keep myself busy, inspecting the gauges on the air cylinders that are racked up and ready to go for the day. They'll have already been fully checked by the dive safety officer and probably the equipment manager too, but it's a way to keep my brain and body occupied. With all that happened with Steve this week, I admit it also gives me peace of mind.

"Violet!" Bruce shouts from an upper level.

I look up to where he stands, arms resting on the metal railing.

"Come to the office." He steps away from the platform edge and disappears down the walkway.

My brow furrows. What's this about?

I reluctantly make for the office upstairs, bracing myself for what's to come.

"There you are." JT's smile greets me in the office. He raises a brow and grins, but his face falls when he registers mine. "What's wrong?"

Well, that rules out poker.

"Nothing. Nothing's wrong." I head to the farthest corner of the room and occupy myself with an ancient dog-eared National Geographic magazine that's on the counter.

JT follows me but doesn't speak. He's always been good about giving me the time and space I need.

Unfortunately, I don't get much of either. Windows frame the room, so I know the moment that Cooper approaches.

Let's face it, I probably would've known it anyway. As always, I'm hyper-aware of his presence; it seems my body hasn't gotten the message that he's not meant for me.

Cooper steps across the threshold and his eyes lock on mine like a shame-seeking missile. Those blue beacons guiding me in before I think better of it.

I turn away, pretending to be captivated by the team servicing equipment two levels down.

"What's going on?" JT whispers to me at the counter.

"I don't want to talk about it." I hope it's enough to shut the conversation down.

JT turns his back to Cooper. "Things didn't go...well... last night?" he continues.

My chest tightens.

"Didn't *go* at all." I turn back round to face the group, crossing my arms. Upon further consideration, I refuse to let Cooper see me flounder.

God, my emotions are bobbing like a hazard buoy this morning.

I'm cut off at the knees the instant Lauren enters the room in all her smart, kind, capable beauty.

Argh.

This would be so much easier if she weren't such a lovely person.

Lauren tucks in behind Steve and avoids looking in my direction.

It hits like a gut punch.

Great. She can't even look at me now. I've ruined my relationship with the one female I've managed to work with this month. I've completely shit the bed.

The office seems to shrink once the three of us are in here, but we've selected equidistant and separate zones, and so far are maintaining a tolerable distance.

Power through, power through, I tell myself.

Cooper breaks the arrangement, throwing a proverbial middle finger to my comfort and need for space. With just a few steps, he closes our distance.

My heart pounds.

No, no, no…

As he approaches, he tucks his hardhat under his arm and runs a hand through his silky golden locks. "Violet, can we talk?"

I find a chipped floor tile to analyze closely.

Violet. My entire name. Pity factor must be high.

"Good morning, Cooper." I flash a fake smile, but my eyes fail to reach his.

He leans in closer, as if his proximity wasn't painful already, and the wonderful scent of him stings my senses. He reaches for my arm but reconsiders and pulls back to scratch his jaw instead.

I glance over at JT, who gives me a concerned look.

More pity.

My eyes pan to Lauren. She quickly looks away, finding her phone suddenly fascinating.

As if on cue, clouds roll in, darkening the summer sky.

I need this to be over.

Just as I'm about to explode from awkward embarrassment, Bruce bursts through the door with dramatic move-ments. All attention thankfully shifts his direction.

"Hurricane warning, folks." He rubs his hands together. "Everyone's going home."

Thank.

Fucking.

God.

CHAPTER 21

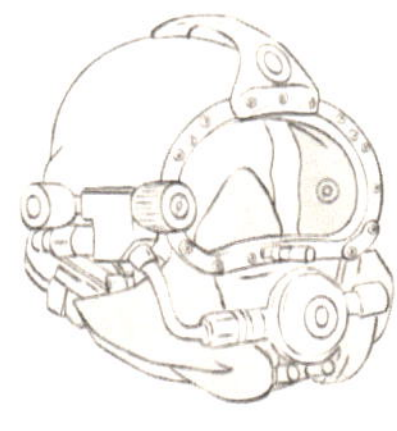

I'm three calicos shy of cat lady status.

When I wake alone—as per usual—in my admittedly decadent and comfortable bed, that's where my mind goes.

I sigh and pull up my spotless white organic cotton duvet and nestle deeper into the cocoon of coverings.

Am I destined to live out my entire life alone?

What's worse is that I can't even *have* cats because of this ridiculous career I've built for myself. This absentee lifestyle is not conducive to pets.

Just give me my domestic shorthairs and let me grow old alone in peace.

Alone.

It's how my life has been.

First, as an only child, where I practically self-parented, then cursed with a string of meaningless short-term relationships that somehow spanned decades until I found myself alone again in a long-term but counterfeit coupling with Charles.

I thought things would be different by now.

It feels like my job is the only thing I've managed to get right. I've made a reputation for myself as a skilled and safe diver, known for my flawless execution of repairs and getting things done in extraordinary conditions. And I'm compensated well for it.

I turn and feel the coolness of the sheets against my skin.

Another deep sigh.

High thread counts only go so far when you're always in bed alone.

"I said I don't want fish for dinner!" The admittedly cute toddler in the shopping cart ahead of me shouts... loudly.

I watch the woman with him—presumably his mother—set a large package of fresh salmon on the conveyor belt.

She gives him an affectionate pat on his wavy, blond head.

Yes, definitely his mother.

She says something in his ear.

"It is *not* delicious. It is *disgusting*," he states, kicking it up a decibel.

He's very articulate. Excellent annunciation. Projects well. I give him an A-plus for vocabulary alone.

His mother wisely ignores him and pushes the cart ahead to the bagging area. The persistent beep of the scanner sounds as the cashier processes their items.

My small basket of items grows heavy in my hands as I await space on the conveyor belt.

It always seems like a bit of a culture shock entering back into the land of the living after two weeks away.

Machine noise is exchanged with human noise. Life-threatening work duties make way for mundane domestic duties. From oxygen lines to food lines. It's hard to wrap your head around it sometimes.

As the mother in front of me runs her credit card through the machine, Blond Toddler enters full-on meltdown mode. I glance around and spot several sour faces, but instead of annoyance, it's sympathy that washes over me. I look at the woman's furrowed brow as she urgently gathers her bags and loads them into the cart.

I set my basket in front of the cashier and quickly join her at her cart, helping her to load the numerous bags into the back.

"Thanks so much," she says.

It occurs to me that maybe she didn't want some stranger handling her groceries. But when I glance over at her I see a tired and grateful expression.

Forget commercial diving, *motherhood* is the hardest job on earth.

"Happy to help," I reply.

As she wheels her cart toward the door, Blond Toddler twists around her to catch a final glimpse of me. I smile at his inquisitive face.

As the cart disappears through sliding doors, he sticks his tongue out at me.

I feel my phone buzz. Pulling it from my back pocket, I see I've got a new message. As if on cue, it's my own mother texting me.

Mom: I know you're busy at work, but what was the name of that book series you recommended to me last month?

This is rather typical of her: jumping right in with both feet. I haven't heard from her in days, but she's never been one for niceties. That's okay. The minor aspects of polite social behaviour are kind of lost on me anyway; I'm just as direct. It would seem that—as my old nana would've said—I didn't get my propensity for literally diving into things from licking the grass.

Violet: I'm not at work. We were sent home early because of a hurricane warning.

"That's forty-eight forty." The cashier gestures to the card machine when I pull my credit card from my pocket.

I complete the transaction.

As I'm saying, *"Thank you,"* my phone buzzes again.

Grabbing the single bag of groceries, I make my way to the exit, glancing at my phone.

Mom: Oh okay. Book please. I'm at the shop.

Yep. There's that trademark Margo Thomas directness.

"Oh no, I'm fine Mom…out of harm's way…thanks for asking," I mutter to myself as I step outside.

I don't even have time to reply and the phone goes off again.

Mom: The No Souls trilogy, I think you said??

Violet: ALL Souls, Mom.

Mom: Thank you, hun. Talk later.

Violet: You're welcome.

I wish I had one of those chatty, warm and fuzzy relationships that so many women I know have with their mothers. Like my friends Bella and Greta seem to have. But then I suppose it would only make being away so often more difficult.

My phone buzzes again, but this time it's an incoming call.

"Hello?"

"Hello, Violet, this is Dr. Andrews' office calling with a reminder of your appointment next week."

This must be my day for no-nonsense females. Dr. Andrews' front desk person is notoriously ruthless, particularly about making appointment changes. I'm in a bit of a bold mood today though, so I decide to test my luck.

"Actually...I have some unexpected free time the next couple of days...would there happen to be any openings for me to move the appointment up?"

I might as well keep myself occupied and my mind off a certain bronzed boy who's inconveniently lodged himself front and centre.

"Well..." She hesitates. "We just had a cancellation...but you probably don't want an appointment within the hour?"

I stop mid-sidewalk. "I can make it."

I'm oddly elated by the development.

This happy about a doctor's appointment? God, I'm pathetic.

"Really? Gosh, that would be wonderful. Otherwise, the time slot is lost."

I don't think I've ever heard her this cheerful.

"I just need to get some groceries home. What time?" I resume walking in the direction of my apartment, picking up my pace.

"You've got forty-five minutes," she says with a chuckle. "What luck."

"I'll see you then."

Physical fitness and medical testing are just part of the job for any commercial diver. I can't suit up if I don't pass routine tests or if a medical doctor fails to certify that I meet numerous medical requirements, such as adequate hearing, visual acuity, and full lung function. The medical scrutiny is even more intense if you sustain an injury.

By the time I enter Dr. Andrews' hyperbaric medical practice, I'm ready to be poked and prodded and given my customary work-up.

I settle into a waiting room seat and pull out my phone to put it on do not disturb. A notification bubble displays on the screen, but it's not Mom. This time it's Greta.

Greta: I have no idea if you're terra firma
but I'm calling in the reinforcements.

Well, this certainly is intriguing.

Violet: I'm not supposed to be, but I am.

Greta: ???

Violet: Hurricane warning.

Greta: Oh shit.

Violet: Whatever. What's up?

Greta: Bella. Things went south with the
love interest.

Violet: The boss?

Greta: Oh yeah…about that. Act surprised.

My brow furrows.

I glance over at the receptionist's desk, where the "no cell phones" sign is taped front and centre. Fortunately, she's distracted, so I continue.

Violet: Surprised?

Three dots bounce on the screen.

I mentally urge her to get the message out before I'm caught out by the receptionist or called in to see the doctor.

Greta: I probably shouldn't have mentioned
anything about Kent when we texted a
while back. I think she wanted it on the DL.

I chuckle.

Violet: Well, I never seem to see you guys, I
don't think that's a problem.

A little self-deprecating humour about my loner status.

Greta: Yeah, that's another matter we need
to address.

I shift in my seat.

Greta: But first, Bella.

Violet: KK. What do you need?

Greta: I need to get back to work…I'm on
an epic job at the University right now. I'll
message later but keep your night free.
We're on a rescue mission.

I suspect this involves alcohol…and maybe copious amounts of junk food.

Violet: I'll hit the liquor store. Text me your order.

Greta: I love you.

"Violet," Ruthless Receptionist is standing a few feet in front of me.

Shit. Busted.

I expect to be reminded of the strict "no cell phone" rule, but she smiles at me instead.

Who knew filling an abandoned appointment slot was the way to this woman's heart?

"Let's get you into the examination room." She gestures to the hallway behind her.

"Oh, yes." I stash my phone and follow her.

Paper crinkles as I shift in my seat on the examination table. Dr. Andrews stands to better reach the two sheets of paper that have just spat out of the small printer set up on the counter next to him. The action sends his stainless-steel stool scraping against the linoleum.

"Okay, here are your chest x-ray and bloodwork requisitions. You know the drill." He hands them over to me and I eye them to see that they're exactly what he says they are.

I certainly do know the drill. I've been going through

these standard tests ever since I started diving, about ten of those years with Dr. Andrews. At this point we've developed a shorthand communication style as we autopilot our way through the checklist of questions and mandatory requirements.

"Anything else you want to talk about?" he asks, returning to his seat.

I've always enjoyed the man's informal nature. It's made many awkward conversations so much easier these last several years.

I'm not sure if it was seeing Blond Toddler at the grocery store or maybe the timing of my mother's call right before the appointment, but my mind turns to something that's been running in the background for years. An open browser that I've never closed despite disagreements with Charles or cautions from others who advised against it.

"Well…" I begin.

Dr. Andrews waits patiently.

"I would like to get some information about more permanent birth control." The words are rushed. I need to get them out before I lose my nerve.

"Permanent?" He raises a brow.

"Yes."

"What do you mean?" The same brow furrows.

He's the doctor. It seems odd that I need to explain it to him.

"Well…um…you're the doctor, so you tell me," I joke.

He sits up straighter.

Shit. I hope I haven't offended him.

It's odd that I'd need to talk about this with a doctor who specializes in diving medicine, but reproduction is bizarrely interwoven with my job. Pregnancy is considered a temporary medical restriction. If I get pregnant, I can't dive, so Dr. Andrews has become well acquainted with my reproductive health. Plus, if I go ahead with a procedure, it will be Andrews who follows my recovery and clears me to dive.

"This is unexpected," he replies.

"Well, it's the unexpected that I'd like to prevent." I give a nervous chuckle.

He opens my medical file and takes a look. "You have an IUD."

"Yes, I do."

"The efficacy rate of the IUD is extremely high. Why do you think it's not enough?" He closes the file and turns to face me.

I feel a sudden rush of defensiveness, which seems odd considering it's *my* body we're talking about.

I mirror his posture. It's a coping mechanism I've developed over the years—matching male size whenever I feel vulnerable.

Why do I feel vulnerable right now?

"Um…I…" I can't seem to formulate a sentence.

"And you do know that *permanent* birth control..." His verbal underscore of permanent is laced with unprecedented condescension. "Doesn't protect you from sexually transmitted infections."

Jesus. What does he think I'm doing on my Saturday nights? Spoiler: The only balls I'm fondling are of the yarn variety.

"I realize that, yes," I reply flatly. "Neither will my IUD."

"And once done, there's no going back?" He awaits my confirmation. I find it more than a little annoying.

"The permanent part is what I'm actually going for."

"The IUD will stop periods too, but procedures like tubal ligation will not."

"I still often get periods with my IUD, though," I explain.

"Really?" He looks like he doesn't believe me. I don't dignify it with an answer.

He turns back to his computer and begins to type. I'm not sure if he thinks the conversation is over. Regardless, I refuse to fill the awkward silence.

"Continuous use of the pill is another effective means of eliminating your menstruation." He's speaking with odd formality now, talking to the computer monitor in front of him, not me.

Agitation is starting to build as this unfamiliar side of Dr. Andrew reveals itself, unfurling its dark tendrils.

I'm forty years old; I know about the goddamn pill.

Is he seriously mansplaining birth control right now?

I take a deep breath and reframe things.

"It's not about my periods," I begin. "I don't want to use prescriptions anymore. I'm tired of sticking IUDs in my body. I know I'm not going to have children, so permanent prevention seems like a better choice." I take a deep breath, feeling better having said it.

"What does your partner think?"

Um. What?

Anger expands in me, like an air bubble right before it's about to pop.

He turns, waiting for my answer. Like this is a pertinent factor.

I have news for him: It's not.

"I don't *have* a partner," I spit out, wondering if the heat in my face is visible.

"I thought you'd mentioned one before."

Pop.

My stomach twists with betrayal.

I've trusted this man for years, built a lovely rapport with him, and it feels like the informal conversation and idle chit-chat we've shared in the office is now being used against me.

"We've broken up," I state flatly, despite the fact it's none of his business.

"Is this a recent breakup?" He smirks, like he's solved the puzzle...like I'm a problem to solve.

"I know what you're suggesting."

"I'm sorry?" he says.

"You're suggesting that wanting to do this has something to do with my recent breakup. It doesn't."

"I'm not suggesting anything."

Dr. Andrews and I are approximately the same age and yet right now, it strangely feels like he's a parent and I'm a child.

My face turns hot.

My right shin itches where the lingering effect of razor burn has started to heal.

The reminder only incites more rage.

"Look." I pause for emphasis. "You know better than I do that forty is not an ideal age to have children. I have no expectation that my circumstances will change and believe even less that my desire for children—or really lack thereof—will either. I'd like to proactively explore my options."

Dr. Andrews shakes his head. "I think you should take some time to think about this and not make any hasty decisions. As your doctor, Violet, it's my responsibility to advise you against unnecessary procedures that present risks."

The condescending use of my name mid-sentence does me in.

"I've had plenty of time to think about this, Dr. Andrews," I state loudly.

In fact, now that Charles is out of the way I finally feel the autonomy to do this for myself.

"With time, you might change your mind." He begins collecting items, like the conversation is closed.

"Please respect my decision."

Dr. Andrews stops and faces me once again. "I have nothing but respect for you, Violet."

It's only now that I realize how the power balance has been tipped in his favour from the start—to him I'm just Violet, but he gets to be called Dr. Andrews.

"Do you respect me enough to assume that I know my own mind?"

Dr. Andrews stands. "Let's talk about this again next time."

Next time.

At next year's checkup.

I've been completely brushed off.

I'm not feeling so lucky to have *scored* this appointment now.

I stand, once again mirroring his posture and matching his size.

"I don't think there's going to be a next time."

His face turns red. Now it's his turn to be angry. "Violet, I—"

"No," I cut him off. "Pro tip: Listen to your female patients and don't presume you know better when it comes to *their* bodies."

I get four blocks away purely on rage-fuelled adrenaline. It's at this point that the haze lifts and I realize I've just walked out on one of maybe two hyperbaric specialists in my geographical area and am likely screwed.

Well, shit.

I find a bench on the sidewalk and pull my phone from my pocket with a shaky tattooed hand. My adrenaline is already starting to crash.

Greta: Get wine. Red. Maybe white too.
Good to have options.

I'm going to need a drink or two myself.

Violet: No problem.

Greta: Fair warning, Bella is in full-on man
hate mode.

I can't help but snicker to myself on the bench.
    Good, I'm in the mood for a proper man bash.
    Bring it on.

CHAPTER 22

"He should lose his job over this." I take a generous swig from my wine glass.

This *Kent Armstrong* is yet another disappointing example of men shitting the proverbial bed.

I'm a titch punchy tonight.

Combine the embarrassing effects of what's going on with Cooper and my reproductive wishes being summarily dismissed by my doctor, and I'm perhaps not in the best frame of mind to provide objective support to my friend Bella, who's just found out that her partner has deceived her.

I'm woefully distracted and only half listening when the topic of Bella's amazing collection of feminist T-shirts comes up. Greta and Bella's cousin Sarah name their favourites. I pick her *Smashing the Patriarchy is my Cardio* shirt and when she smiles, I can't help but note how remarkably composed she is, particularly relative to how poorly I seem to be managing my own feelings after dealing with far less.

The oldest and supposedly wisest of the group, I'm

often labelled the surrogate big sister. I need to push my own issues aside, get my shit together, and be what my friends need today.

"I'm not feeling very strong or successful these days." Bella sinks deeper into her overstuffed couch.

So much for that idea.

Her words twig something in me, and the anger and resentment of these last few days finally spills over. "Don't do that, Bells. You're letting shit that you had no control over steal your power."

My inner feminist can't stand how she's letting a man take the wind out of her sails. They're meant to take her bright and beautiful self far and wide—wherever she wishes to go. But if I'm honest, I'm doing it too…and I hate myself for it. I want to get over this, but when Greta suggests that forgiveness is the answer to Bella's problems, I internally scream.

"I'm not going to forgive him," Bella shakes her head, resolute.

Thank god. Not that I want *her* to suffer—I want this Kent dude to suffer.

"That's the spirit." I raise a glass in toast.

"Stop that," Greta pushes my hand away and I pull my glass back just before it spills on Bella's white couch.

Greta rambles on some bullshit about the true power being the choice to forgive, and I feel my eyes involuntarily roll as I grab a handful of gummy worms from the bag on the coffee table.

She must spot my eye roll, because she spitefully snags a worm from my hand and stuffs the entire thing in her mouth.

I'm not exactly sure what's up with Greta. Maybe she's got her own shit going on too…she isn't normally this philosophical.

"Why are you being so bloody rational?" I shake my

head. "I want to be a stubborn asshole. I want *Bella* to be a stubborn asshole." I surprise even myself with my frankness.

"What's going on with you?" Bella's brow furrows.

Shit. I've made this about me, and it's supposed to be about Bella.

"Is this because of your breakup with Charles?" Greta asks.

Three sets of eyes land squarely on me.

I wince. "No, Christ! That's history. Completely irrelevant. This has nothing to do with Charles. Moving on."

I can't move on from Charles fast enough, to be honest.

Cooper, on the other hand? I'm not exactly sure what's stopping me.

Sure, he's handsome and charismatic, but I've been in the presence of beauty before.

I scratch my itchy razor-burned legs as conversation around the coffee table continues.

What I've never quite experienced before is this monsoon of attraction. An intangible thing that draws me in and holds me to him.

I need to relinquish this. I need to get past it.

I know I can get over the embarrassment and awkwardness on the platform—I have no choice in the matter. Surely my regret will dissipate too.

It's these other uncharted feelings that are more difficult: not only how I feel about him, but how he's made me feel about myself.

The problem is, when he said he thought I was incredible, for just a moment I believed him.

The app tells me our Uber is five minutes out. I'm a bit tipsy after tonight's wine, so I lean against one of the planter boxes that flanks the entryway outside of Bella's apartment while we wait.

"I'm a bit worried about you," Greta says.

"You've had just as much to drink as me." A devilish giggle escapes me.

"I'm not talking about the wine." She leans a hip against the planter opposite mine.

It's past midnight. I'm exhausted after an emotional day. I'm not in the mood for deep, meaningful conversation, but I'm also too tired to fight her.

I let the moment hang. Greta fills the void. "If it's not Charles, *who* or *what* is it?"

"It's just…" It's hard to parse what I'm feeling and put it into words, particularly after several ounces.

I glance over at Greta, who's waiting patiently for me to speak.

"I'm just…" I bend down to scratch a shin. "Bad at love," I finally spit out.

Greta's brows raise. *"Bad at love?"* Her tone suggests I've just declared the sky is green or that plumbers can do their own electrical.

"Yes. Epically bad…really." My shoulders drop.

"Okaaay…" Greta drawls, skeptical.

"I'm done with it. I don't understand men. I don't think I ever will." I kick at a rogue pebble on the pavement with my Tretorn. "They piss me off."

"They *are* an enigma." Greta groans. Something tells me she's got her own shit going on, but now that the words are flowing, I don't stop to question her.

"I don't know how to read them, what they want, or what they want from *me*. Maybe I'm just done with them."

"Let's back things up, shall we?" Greta shifts her weight

against the planter and crosses her arms. "What's happened?"

God, where do I start? Charles? Cooper? Dr. Andrews?

I release a long breath. "Ignore me. I'm being dramatic. It's just been a shitty day…week…maybe month?"

"No."

"*No?*" I'm taken aback by her blunt response.

"Why aren't you talking to us? Problems like this don't pop up one day, they accumulate over time. Allow me to use an electrical reference—it's my language."

I laugh. I love how Greta always slips a little of her profession into everything she does. "Permission granted."

"You don't wait 'til your entire panel needs rewiring to call your electrician. You call when one fuse or one outlet doesn't work." She tucks a few of her lustrous, dark locks behind an ear.

I release a long sigh.

Shit. The woman's brilliant.

"Oh no…wait a minute." Greta's brow furrows. "It's worse." She stands and steps forward. "You're DIY-ing it." She winces, like she's bitten into a lemon.

"What are you talking about?" I reply defensively.

"You're trying to fix shit all by yourself, aren't you?"

"I can handle things on my own."

"Oh no you don't. You're part of this tradie family. You don't *get* to handle shit on your own." She's back to crossed arms and sour face.

"Tradie family?"

It elicits a chuckle from both of us.

"You know what I mean," Greta says. "Our women-in-trades family. Why are you waiting 'til your entire panel is on the fritz to come talk to us?"

"My panel is just fine, thanks." I gesture to my breasts, hoping the joke will distract her.

"Your panel is spectacular, but friends help each other.

Just like we rallied around Bella tonight, we should be supporting you if you're hitting a rough patch."

"I'm fine." I wave her off.

"Clearly you aren't." The serious tone Greta uses gives me pause.

Am I fine?

"And even if you *can* handle shit on your own," she continues, "it doesn't mean you have to."

The Uber pulls up to the curb, putting an abrupt end to our conversation. Despite my long history of avoidance when it comes to talking about myself, I'm surprised to find that relief doesn't follow.

CHAPTER 23

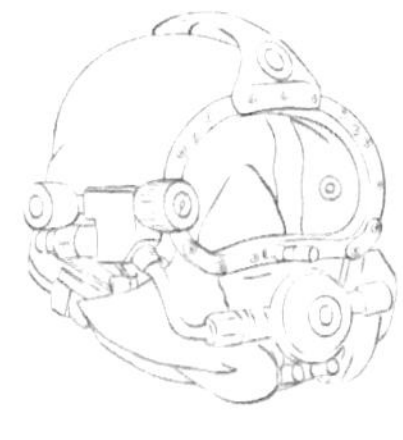

Steve isn't at the heliport when we reconvene several days later.

Like scattered points that converge on a random, pre-selected map location at the start of each two-week work period, we're different people from different places, brought together by our unique skill set and perhaps a twisted thirst for adventure.

I take a long pull from my water bottle and glance over at JT. My sunglasses are having trouble blocking out the midday sun at the helipad.

I'm about to ask JT where the hell Steve is, when the *real* tall drink of water arrives.

Shit.

Cooper has had his golden hair trimmed while on break, and it only serves to accentuate his goddamned symmetrical cheekbones and sharp fucking jawline. As he steps up to join the group, he removes his mirrored sunglasses. I try in vain to avert my gaze, and the bright eyes that emerge make my traitorous chest ache.

This isn't good.

I'm not given even a minute to find my bearings before he approaches.

He comes up alongside me. "Violet, can we talk?"

I steel myself, taking a deep breath, and turn to face him.

The seriousness of his expression is completely incongruous with the ridiculousness of his Twisted Sister T-shirt.

Dee Snider's tarted-up face stares back at me. It's extremely distracting.

"What the hell are you wearing?" I ask.

He looks down the front of himself.

"It's…a…T-shirt?" His brow rises.

"It's ridiculous," I spit out.

His eyes pan up to mine, alight with surprise. I see his entire body soften, his shoulders drop. "Are you dissing Dee?" He clutches his chest in mock horror, and the way his hand lands, it perfectly covers Dee's mouth.

Shit. Don't laugh. Do not laugh.

I want to be mad at him right now. I want to hold a grudge. But the adorable look on his face and that comical band shirt are conspiring against me.

It's not like he ever made me any promises. I'm the one who read everything wrong.

With a single deep breath, I let the resentment go. I surprise myself with how easy it feels to do it; it's certainly something a younger version of Violet never would have done.

My face breaks into a smile. I rub my forehead.

When I look back up at him, a beautiful smile shines back, revealing perfect white teeth that could skim a lovely trail along my neck if they weren't already skimming Lauren's.

Lauren.

As if on cue, she rolls up with her wheelie case.

Great. Guess we have more sonar requirements on this rig.

I watch closely to see what plays out with her and Cooper, but surprisingly I see nothing exchange between them.

His eyes are still fully on me.

"Are we okay?" He takes one step closer. He slips his mirrored sunglasses back into place and when it's clear he doesn't know what to do with his hands next, he stuffs them into his jeans' pockets.

I think about mojo, about precious group chemistry.

I think about what's best for the team.

I let out a resigned sigh.

"Yeah," I say. "We're good."

The relief that crosses Cooper's face is palpable. I'm oddly relieved too.

"Hey, Bruce," I hear JT shout. "Where's Steve?"

I turn and watch as Bruce and another man approach from the terminal.

The look on Bruce's face is hard to read.

"Steve's taking a leave of absence." Bruce gestures to the man on his left. "Bob here is going to step in for him."

We all nod and say our hellos.

"Leave of absence?" JT asks, surveying the crowd. "He okay?"

Bruce nods. "He will be. He just needs to sit this one out."

How do you say he has PTSD without saying he has PTSD?

Bruce steps forward. "You good, Violet?" His chin rises.

I guess he's worried about losing *two* of his crew to the dark demon.

"I'm good, boss," I'm quick to reassure him.

Bruce smiles softly and nods.

One look over at Bob and I already miss Steve. Bob has a

surly look on his face and appears not to give a single fuck about making a good impression, because he's scrolling his phone and standing three steps back from our circle.

Nice to meet you too.

My eyes pan over to JT and he's shooting me a look of concern.

So much for mojo.

"How are the private accommodations *this time*, Princess?" JT stabs a cherry tomato with his fork and bites it off the tines. I hear the sound of his teeth scraping against metal because the dining room is still so quiet and calm.

We've met here way ahead of everyone else and I'm sure JT has set up this little tête-à-tête very much on purpose, so he can grill me.

"Fan-TAS-tic." I flash a smug grin.

My room is actually a glorified closet and has a peculiar smell, but I won't tell him that.

"How is life back in steerage?" I tease.

"As cozy as ever. We're singing campfire songs at Camp Crusty Cabin." He rolls his eyes.

"Quarters a wee bit tight, are they?" I snicker.

"Not any tighter than usual, but morale is decidedly low." JT lets out a tired sigh.

"Bob?" I ask.

"You mean the Man Who Personality Forgot."

I grimace. The man does appear to have all the charm of a piss-filled wetsuit, but I was holding out hope that I'd just misread him.

"Why do you think I was so eager to meet for dinner?" He saws away at his dense cafeteria chicken parmigiana.

"I figured that was just a ruse to get me here for the inquisition."

Shit. Here I was, hoping to avoid the conversation, and instead I waded right in.

I sip from my water, wishing it was wine.

JT stops mid-slice. "*That's* open for discussion?" He studies my face for a reaction.

"There's nothing to discuss." My cheeks grow hot. The contents of my plate suddenly become very interesting.

"What happened?" His voice is soft and kind. I know he isn't just after the latest gossip; he cares and wants to help. *Helping* me right now, however, would be letting me move on and forget.

"A gross misread, that's what happened." I take my first bite of battered fish and it tastes not unlike how I imagine an Amazon delivery box would.

JT's face sours after taking his own first forkful. "Even the food is terrible. Christ, we need Marsha."

It's like the mojo gods have decided to flip us the middle finger.

"Violet, I've been along since the beginning. I've seen it all. You did not misread anything." JT sets his fork aside, clearly giving up on what looks like a tomato-sauce-covered shoe insole.

I'm quick to shut it down. "We really don't need to revisit this, thanks."

I have no interest in retelling—or worse, reliving—the story. It's a tale as old as time: woman falls for man's charms, woman gets burned. The end. I'm eager to turn the page.

"V..." His voice trails off.

Christ, JT's relentless.

"Whatever went down—"

"He wasn't alone, alright?" I snap.

He sits up, then leans back in his seat. "What?"

He's asking *what* but I know he means *who*.

I breathe in deep, then release it slowly.

"Lauren."

"*No.*" He shakes his head. "No way."

"I know what I saw, JT."

Yep, the sight of her casually sipping from her water bottle—as if her presence in that cabin was as natural as easing into a pair of well-worn work boots—is indelibly marked on my brain.

My Amazon box sits like lead in my stomach.

"No. Fucking. Way." He's shaking his head even harder now.

"You can shake your head and say *no* all you want; she was there in his cabin when I showed up."

He tosses his napkin onto the table in an act of capitulation.

"Well, I'll fucking be. Did *not* see that coming."

"So, if it's alright with you, I'd like to move on and forget all about my little transgression."

"There was no *transgression*, V." He lowers his voice, as several rig workers file into the dining room for their dinner.

I bring my own voice down to meet his. "I know all about risks—I calculate and mitigate them every damn day. In a moment of weakness I took an uncalculated one, and my pride took a hit." I shrug. "I won't let it happen again."

"Shit." JT's face looks the way my chest feels: pained. "If you miscalculated, then so did I."

My thoughts turn to that intimate moment in the shower, when I was sure I'd heard him say my name.

Maybe he did, but it's irrelevant now.

"For the sake of the team, we need to move on." I pick up my fork and make another attempt at the food on my plate. Stomaching this terrible excuse for dinner has become a metaphor for my life: One bite at a time and setting my own preferences aside, I *will* get it done.

We settle into a comfortable silence, absorbed by our thoughts and perhaps at a loss for what to say.

"He's a good guy, you know," JT finally says.

"Yeah, yeah."

I'm annoyed by the statement, and even more annoyed by the fact that it's true.

"Seriously." JT leans in, seeking to convince me. Despite what's happened, I don't need any convincing. I let the moment hang to spite him. To spite Cooper too. To coddle my bruised ego.

Cooper and JT certainly have hit it off these past few weeks. Let's face it, we all have. The rapport he has with the team has made Cooper's cover-off of Patrick's paternity leave practically seamless. The team chemistry has been amazing; no one can deny that.

"Uh-huh," I mumble, shovelling a forkful of salad into my mouth. Thank god for salad; you can't really mess that up.

JT leans in further. "He knows about my bisexuality," he says quietly.

I stop mid-chew and look at him.

The first thing I feel is jealously, truth be told. It took JT years to tell me. Not that I'm entitled to know his personal business at all.

The next thing I feel is happiness—that he's found someone to talk to and share his true self with. It kind of warms my heart.

"Wow. That's…amazing."

He nods. "Yeah…I mean, I didn't just come out and tell him at the breakfast table." He chuckles. "Pass the peanut butter, I'm bi." He laughs at his own joke. JT is the funniest guy he's ever met.

"He was talking about someone he knows who had

recently come out as bi and that he wished he could be a better support to her." He pauses to take a drink from his water glass. "I decided to tell him."

A wave of admiration for them both washes over me.

"That's wonderful."

"It felt good to talk about it." The moment the words are out, I see he regrets them. "Not that I can't talk to you," he quickly adds. "I know I can. But this seems different somehow."

"I get it." I really do.

Another few beats of silence follows.

"Maybe don't give up just yet," JT says.

No, no, no.

My ability to suck it up and get on with things is contingent on the very fact that I *do* give up. Give up any thoughts I've had of Cooper and me being more…of my being what he wants…of him being what I need.

"Don't," I reply curtly.

JT rests his elbows on the table. "Maybe there's more to the story, V. Maybe you need to hear him out. I've heard him ask you to talk."

The weak hold I've had on things starts to slip. Annoyance and hurt shift into anger.

"I don't care what kind of bromance the two of you have going on. I'm not interested in *hearing him out*. In my experience, the simplest explanation is usually the right explanation."

I sit back in my chair and drop my fork, the twist of my stomach convincing me my dinner—as well as this conversation—is over.

"We didn't read it wrong," JT insists.

My face grows hot. "Listen, I don't care what you have to say, and I don't care what *he* has to say, I'm not going to hold onto some silly notion that he's into me when clearly he's not."

God, do I really need to say this out loud?

"V—"

"I'm not going to keep talking about this just because you saw fit to tell him you're bi, JT!"

At that moment, the entire cafeteria seems to go still.

JT's face turns red.

My entire body goes cold with the realization that I'd raised my voice to indiscreet levels...at the very moment that Bob, Nick, Bruce and Cooper entered the dining room.

Fuuuck.

JT rubs his face with his hand.

"I'm so sorry." My voice barely registers above a whisper.

"Oh, *now* you decide to speak quietly," JT quips

Christ, even when I'm outing the poor guy he has a sense of humour.

My already dodgy stomach turns sour. I truly feel sick.

I look up at the faces of our colleagues and it's clear they've heard me.

Bruce and Cooper share a wince. Bob has a look of disgust.

Yep, making a great impression there.

My eyes shift back to JT who, despite my horrific mistake, is smiling.

"Fuck, JT. I'm so, *so* sorry."

He flashes a sheepish grin. "Well, that's one way to get it all out in the open."

CHAPTER 24

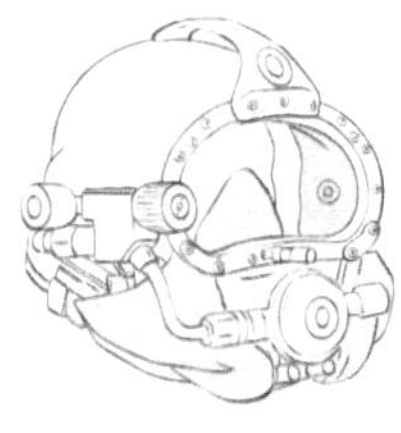

What a colossal fuckup.

The combination of hot morning sun and shame is working to sweat me right through my cotton shirt and PPE. I move equipment and prep for the day's dives happy for the distraction, eager to park my thoughts.

It's only partly working.

I wipe my brow with my hand, pausing to mentally list my recent missteps and internally cringe.

I'm literally and figuratively a hot mess.

I'm so deep in my own self-deprecating thoughts that at first, I don't notice the commotion across the deck.

When voices rise, I start listening.

"I'm not sleeping in there again tonight," Bob snaps.

I stop working and rest my hands on my hips, openly watching the exchange.

Bruce's face is red—too red to be blamed on the summer morning heat.

Cooper and JT mill about, bent over bins of cable and fussing with equipment. They share a look of visible annoyance.

This Bob guy is a charmer.

Looks like someone doesn't think the shared accommodations meet his standard. I've always been a bit envious of the guys, thinking the camaraderie of bunk beds and common quarters to be a team-building and morale-boosting experience. I guess Bob doesn't share this opinion.

I chuckle to myself. Hah…and JT calls *me* Princess.

"I'm not sleeping next to *that* guy." Bob points at JT.

I'm not chuckling anymore.

Cooper stands abruptly, face growing dead serious as he steps forward.

He's clutching his wetsuit with a death grip. I imagine he's fantasizing that it's Bob's neck he's got his massive hand around.

"What did you just say?" Cooper demands.

Bruce is on them in an instant. "Okay, let's dial it back, guys."

JT's eyes shift between them.

I take a step closer.

"I refuse to spend another night next to one of them." Bob flashes a look of disgust at JT.

Cooper's expression turns ice cold. "What the fuck is that supposed to mean?"

"Let it go, Coop." JT's voice is resigned, like he's saying this because it's nothing he hasn't heard before. This incites unprecedented rage in me, but I can't hold a candle to Cooper.

The look on his face is a unique mix of ice and heat.

Cooper's eyes could at once freeze another's soul, and out-burn a welding torch.

"Say it," Cooper spits out. "Say what we both know you're thinking. Have the spine to own it."

Bob simmers in place, a nasty snarl on his face. His wheels are turning.

The entire group hangs on his next move.

Bob's words are laced with hate. "I'm not laying my head next to some pervert."

At first, I can't believe I've heard it—surely, he didn't just say what I think he did—but then Cooper's reaction confirms it.

He's two feet from Bob in the span of a heartbeat.

"Cooper," Bruce warns. "You touch him and you're going home."

Bob flashes a sinister grin. "Freedom of speech, buddy. And I call it like I see it." Pure evil smoulders in his eyes. "And all I see is a fucking fa—"

The entire homophobic slur doesn't make it past Bob's mouth before Cooper's fist meets it with abundant enthusiasm. Bob crumples to the steel deck.

A few shocked seconds pass as everyone processes what's happened.

Cooper opens, closes, then shakes his fisted right hand.

Glancing down at the crumpled pile of asshole in front of him, he points at Bob. "Worth it."

Holy shit.

He strides off towards the accommodation quarters.

My body acts without me, carrying me just steps behind him until I'm at the door to the cabin.

I watch in stunned silence as he pulls out his bag and starts packing. His bright yellow speaker is the first to go.

Everything is happening so quickly. Half of me is still back at the homophobic slur, wanting to pull the bastard back up so I can punch him again myself.

Cooper isn't the one who should be packing. Bob—that sad excuse for a human—should be going home. Or maybe I should, for opening my loud mouth in the first place.

Everything's gone pear-shaped.

My instincts tell me to stop him, but he's already stuffed half his belongings into his duffle bag.

Stop.
No.
The words spill out of me.
"I'm going with you."

CHAPTER 25

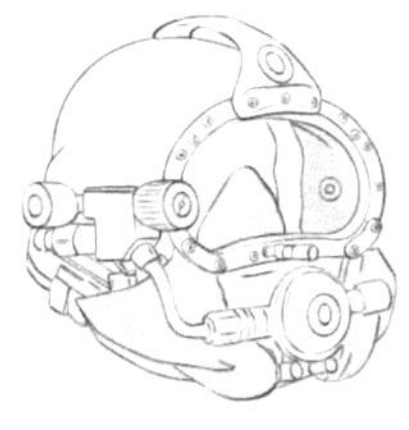

There are three qualities that any man can possess that, when combined, become my kryptonite.

Intelligence.

Wit.

Willingness to stand up to a bully.

Wrap that into a package like Cooper's and it's outright dangerous.

After witnessing his defence of JT, any grudges that I may still have been holding onto at this point are null and void.

Redemption arc officially unlocked.

Even if we're never going to be more, Cooper is my friend. He's proven he's worthy. The real question might be: Are we all worthy of *him*?

"You're not coming with me, V." Cooper collects various toiletries that are scattered around his corner of the cabin and tosses them into a shaving kit. I pan the room and see clothing and belongings everywhere. We've been on this rig for less than twenty-four hours; that this cabin is in this sad state already, kills any romantic notions I've been holding on to about having bunk mates.

What's that awful smell?

"Well, I'm not staying behind with Bigot Bob." I step aside, allowing him to access the counter behind me, where his laptop is charging. "And they're going to make you pay for the airlift. It's my fault Bob knew about JT—I should've kept my mouth shut. The least I can do is split the cost."

Cooper stops to look at me. "I can afford a helicopter ride."

Of course he can. We all can. We get paid extremely well; what we lack is the opportunity to spend it.

Cooper pauses mid-pack and examines his punching hand.

"You need ice," I say.

"I think Bob needs it more." Cooper attempts to hold back a smile.

Surprised by the joke—that he's made it so soon—a chuckle escapes me.

I cover my mouth with a hand. "I shouldn't laugh."

When he looks up at me, we both crack. Hysterical laughter fills the small space.

"This is not what I expected to find," JT says from the open doorway.

We spin around to face him.

"Sorry, man," Cooper says. "I shouldn't have acted on your behalf like that." His face turns sober.

He returns to his duffle bag, rolling garments and cramming them in.

"You're not the one who needs to apologize, Coop." JT enters the room as Cooper zips his bag. "Or the one who should be going home." He sits on a bed.

"I'm going too." I cross my arms. "It's my fault that Bigot Bob found out in the first place."

"Yeah, but it's not your fault he's a dickhead," JT remarks.

"Holy shit. What was *that*?" Lauren steps across the

threshold too, eyes the size of saucers. "Wait…" Her face sours. "What's that smell?" She pinches her nose.

"I believe they call it homophobia," Cooper quips. "And it's coming from that side of the cabin." He gestures to the one bed in the cabin that's properly made.

Figures.

"If V's going, I am too. No one would be dealing with any of this shit if it wasn't for me, and I have zero desire to stick around if you know what I mean." JT grimaces.

"Going where?" Lauren asks.

"Bruce is going to send him home." JT gestures to Cooper.

He'd been warned. If I know anything about Bruce, he's a man of his word. Cooper is definitely going home.

"Don't leave me here with that asshole. If you guys are going, so am I."

We all exchange confused looks.

"We don't even share the same employer, Lauren." Cooper sounds a titch annoyed. I guess whatever was *on* with the two of them is *off* now.

"I don't care," she spits out. "I'm not staying behind with that sociopath."

And just like that, one colleague's disciplinary action turns into an act of solidarity.

All four of us go.

Running away from an offshore oil platform doesn't end up being the passionate and theatrical temper tantrum it's intended to be. Turns out it's hard to make a dramatic exit when leaving requires logistical planning and costly execution.

By the time the helicopter arrives, our group of rebels has grown to six. Two more oil workers who heard about what transpired have joined us in an outright refusal to stay on board with Bigot Bob.

The first problem is finding our ride. The next is deciding on a destination. We end up with a compromise: a pricey chartered helicopter ride split six ways that will take us to the closest resort town with a safe place to land, options for accommodation, and access to an airport.

My pulse has been at a steady trot since Cooper's fist hit Bob's face, and it doesn't seem to want to slow down. It didn't let up through packing, or through waiting and pacing, and certainly not through boarding.

Bailing on Bruce is the boldest thing I've ever done, and it feels like an out-of-body experience when our Uber drops us at the only place with vacancies to accommodate all six of us with zero notice: Preston Villas.

I fall in love the moment I see it.

An old fifties-era village, it's quirky and quaint. Its vintage neon starburst sign still promises cable TV and electric heat. The stifling temperatures that hit us the moment we're off the water ensure that we won't be needing the latter.

Laden with gear, I throw my hair up into a messy bun and fan myself with a tourist brochure before attempting to find my cottage.

The six of us scatter in every direction. The sound of palm fronds in the wind serves as our soundtrack as we drag our pelican cases—*clip, clip clip*—down flagstone paths to individual bungalows, each painted their own tropical colour.

My diamond-shaped hotel keychain tells me I'm booked in at cottage fifteen, and when I find it, I break out in a wide grin. It's bright, bold, and beautiful pink.

I can't wait to send a photo to Bella.

With a push of my hip, I force open the sticky door, bracing myself for what I'm about to find. The reasonable nightly rate we've been given hasn't instilled a lot of confidence in the quality of our accommodations, but we've checked in anyway. We don't plan on staying long—just long enough to book our flights and find our own routes home.

I stop in my tracks the moment I'm inside.

It's like stepping back in time when the door clicks shut behind me.

Furnishings and textiles of every imaginable colour lie before me. Ottomans in avocado, a sofa that's tangerine, lemon-yellow curtains, and armchairs upholstered sky blue. The walls are painted in fresh aquamarine and covered in mismatched frames.

I drop my belongings, eager to get a closer look. I study the artwork. It's an eclectic mix of psychedelic abstracts and retro postcards. It's hard to tell if they're new or old, because while they seem to be from another era, their style is utterly timeless.

As I set my hotel keychain on the teak wood entryway credenza, it's hard not to feel like I've stumbled upon treasure—like we've come across a goldmine on our way to a debit machine.

When I catch myself smiling in a mirror, I notice that my heart is calm and steady for the first time in hours.

A knock startles me.

Adjusting my sweaty, messy bun in the mirror, I take a deep breath, examining my reflection before moving to answer the door.

I expect to find JT, but it's Cooper standing on my flagstone doorstep.

His hair looks damp from a shower, and he's already changed into a vibrant Hawaiian shirt and shorts that show off his summer tan. He slips his hands into his pockets, looking like an advertisement for casual cool.

A drop of sweat tickles me as it travels down my back.

He turns to face me after examining the pink exterior of my cabin. "Isn't this place incredible?" He cracks a wide smile. "My bungalow is yellow."

His eyes are as bright as my cabin's walls, and his face is full of joy. It's the same adorable expression he'd shown remembering his grandmother's kitchen and her clacking knitting needles.

It's typical that Cooper would have precisely the right outfit for the occasion, as if he'd planned it. The world, it seems, is no challenge for Cooper Brooks' unrivalled adaptability.

"How is it possible that you had vacation wear with you?" I gesture to his outfit.

He shrugs, looking down at his playful shirt. "It's what I wore to the airport."

A pang of sadness throbs inside me. I know they arrived at the helipad separately and seem to be *off*, but I still picture Lauren and Cooper frolicking on their shared time off—lounging poolside, youthful bodies in the sun.

I push the feeling aside and stand taller. It's a *good* thing I found Lauren in his room. If the last twenty-four hours have proven anything, it's that when boundaries are tested on the platform, only chaos ensues.

But maybe a little chaos is fun.

The voice in my head surprises me. I ignore it and wipe my sweaty palms against my heavy work pants.

"This is all I've got." I point to my Carhartt T-shirt and steel-toed boots. "Wheelie cases filled with clothing that's meant to cover and protect."

He pulls his sunglasses from his shirt pocket and flashes a pearly grin. "Well then, looks like we're going shopping."

CHAPTER 26

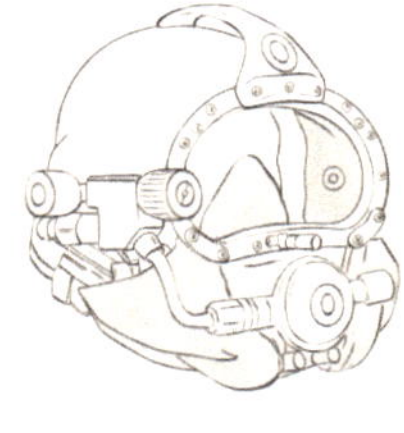

It's weird and wonderful to be alone with him again.

After canvassing the crowd, it's not surprising that no one wants to join us in a hot walk through town. Naps and swims in the resort pool are quickly arranged as makeshift bathing suits are sorted.

I'm equal parts thrilled and terrified at the prospect of playing tourist with Cooper. But then again, this roller-coaster ride of emotions seems to be the status quo since Cooper turned up instead of Patrick on that derelict seventies-era oil platform set for decommission.

The first thing to go are the boots. I track down sandals and gladly wear them out of the store. After peeling off sweaty work socks, my body temperature drops several degrees.

I'm not fussy, clothing wise, and I'm eager to get a few simple pieces and then head back to the comfort of the group.

Cooper, on the other hand, is determined to take his time. He walks—no, *strolls*—slowly along the quaint sidewalks and attempts to engage me in conversation. My lingering embarrassment over Cabindoorgate is holding me back.

"How was your time off?" He nods to another cheesy gift shop on our left. It's the shorthand we've developed to determine which stores either of us might want to see.

I shake my head *no*, but answer, "Fine."

I'm not sure I'd call the past two weeks *fine*, but I'm not in the mood to discuss the hot garbage of my doctor visit or the state of my emotions after finding Lauren in "level three, cabin sex".

I swallow hard and hope the flush of my cheeks can be attributed to the sweltering heat.

Cooper hesitates, studying me briefly before moving on.

"Let's go in there." I point to an upscale women's clothing store that promises locally made jewelry and sustainable fabrics.

The bell of the door chimes as we enter and feel the instant relief of the satisfying air conditioning. Three women, all dressed in cream linen, politely greet us. I chuckle as their eyes catch on Cooper.

"Can we help you?" one woman asks him. They haven't even noticed me yet.

Ever the polite and charming man, he removes his sunglasses and smiles. "Hi there. My friend…" He gestures to me, standing two clothing racks over. "She needs some lighter clothes."

I push my own sunglasses onto my head and shift my boot bag in my hand. I adjust my crossbody purse that feels like it's digging into me.

The saleswoman brightens when she spots me. "We can certainly help."

As she approaches, Cooper sits in a chair in the corner and pulls his phone from his pocket, resting one foot on his opposite knee. Is he always this at home, wherever life takes him? I, on the other hand, spend most of my time feeling like a square peg in a round hole.

"What did you have in mind?" the woman asks me.

Suddenly self-conscious, I wonder if I'm in the right kind of store for me. The tattoos on my arm stand out against the store's calm and serene neutral palette. It's definitely not the colourful second-hand shop where I usually pick up my Doc Martens and vintage tees.

"I'm…not sure," I answer after several seconds.

I pan the store, taking in the racks of clothing.

"Oh, this'll be fun. Can I pick some things out for you?"

I turn to face her and she's wearing a delighted grin, holding her hands in prayer position.

An odd sense of relief finds me. "Please."

Settling into the change room, I rifle through the dozen or so items I'm expected to try. There are a few misses, but I fall in love with a dove grey linen romper and a simple bone coloured linen tank dress.

I'm hesitant to leave the confines of the change room, but when Jenny—the salesperson—urges me to show her, I crack open the door.

"Oh, honey—it's beautiful," she says about the dress.

I search behind her, making sure Cooper isn't in the line of sight. I'm not sure why the act of showing myself fully dressed feels so exposing.

"Thank you." I keep my voice quiet, not wanting to bring attention to myself.

Despite my best effort, Cooper steps up behind her, catching a glimpse of me through the small opening.

A rush of heat floods my cheeks.

I'm surprised when pink colours his too.

"Wow," he says after several beats.

His eyes drag across the ink on my skin.

I look down at myself, at the exposed tattoos along the right side of my body. Vine leaves trail down my arm, disappear under the dress, then reemerge on my leg to cross my bare foot.

He's never seen this much of me before.

After a few quiet seconds, Cooper clears his throat. "Looks…great."

He heads back to the front of the store.

"I think your boyfriend likes it," Jenny says with a smile.

"Oh, no; he's not my boyfriend," I'm quick to correct her.

"Sure, sweetie." She winks and steps away to assist another customer.

I wear the linen dress out of the store.

High on the effects of Cooper's gaze, I impulsively grab an expensive navy linen slip-dress before heading to the register.

Take my money.

We're three blocks down the street before either of us speaks.

I'm relieved to be free of the burdensome clothes that covered me and yet also feel vulnerably naked. I don't really think it has anything to do with the garments I've shed, it's more to do with the feelings that flooded back when Cooper's eyes studied me.

They'd felt like more.

Right when I'd learned to expect less.

"Shit, let me help you with the bags." Cooper reaches for the heavy bag that holds my work clothes. Our hands brush as he takes it, sending a shot of electricity up my arm. We both awkwardly try to step away, but he zigs when I zag and we manage to somehow walk right into each other.

Fuck.

When we've finally righted ourselves on the sidewalk, I see his Adam's apple move up and down with a hard swallow.

In the next moment—like a terrier spotting a squirrel—Cooper catches something over my shoulder. A grin spreads over his handsome face.

"Come this way." He scoots around me, checking both directions before crossing to the other side of the street.

One of my brows raises involuntarily, but I follow him to the end of the block.

He stops in front of a hair salon and looks at me with a smile.

"What?" I finally ask, no idea what's running through his mind.

He steps toward me.

"Remember when you said that you used to have the purple streak—the violet—in your hair?" He takes his sunglasses off, as if to be sure I'm really paying attention.

I shift my crossbody more out of habit than necessity. "Yeah?"

"Do you want to put it back?" His eyes brighten.

"Put it back?" I echo.

"I saw how you looked longingly at that photo of yourself, V. If you want purple in your hair, you should have purple in your hair." He points a thumb at the door of the salon behind him for emphasis.

How are we talking about purple streaks and hair salons? I'm still back at stolen glances of leg tattoos.

When I don't speak, Cooper continues. "I saw the sadness in your eyes when you told me it needed to go."

"That's being a bit dramatic." I roll my eyes.

"To be frank, the only thing that needs to go is Vampire Accountant, who doesn't seem to want you to be yourself… doesn't see that *yourself* is enough."

A laugh escapes me at his use of the old handle.

Vampire Accountant.

Ancient history.

I never told him it was Charles who didn't like the purple in my hair. Somehow Cooper still figured it out. Then I realize Cooper doesn't even know we've broken up.

"He's long gone." I shrug.

Cooper's eyes widen. "Oh." He doesn't even bother to hold back his smile. "Well then, so should any reservations about being who you want to be."

Something wide and expansive opens in me.

Hope. Possibility.

I've been focusing on the sad parts of a life spent alone. But what about all the good parts? Living it on my own terms, having true autonomy. Piercing my nose again if I want to, dying my hair any colour of the blessed rainbow, tattoos left unapologetically uncovered.

"I don't want the purple streak in my hair." I really don't. That's the Violet of the past.

"Oh," he replies again.

I hear a note of disappointment in his voice, but as his face begins to fall, excitement bubbles up in me like air from a cylinder.

"Just the tips." The words spill out.

"Pardon?"

I giggle. "The tips. I've always wanted violet ombré tips."

Cooper laughs. "I have no idea what the hell that is, but let's go get it for you."

"Yeah?" I ask, suddenly unsure. "It's not a little on the nose? You know…*violet* and all?"

Nervous excitement flutters in my belly.

Cooper looks excited too. "Yeah…I mean, no."

His smile is kind—one that reaches his beautiful turquoise eyes.

He wants to do this for me.

I want him to give this to me.

I nod.

He grabs the handle of the salon door. "After you, Violet Thomas."

With the help of his gorgeous smile and trademark charisma, he gets me an appointment within twenty minutes. Of course he does. And I get back a small part of myself that I'd thought was lost forever.

CHAPTER 27

Cooper Brooks has the patience of a saint.

He quietly waits the ninety minutes the stylist needs to create her work of art. Sitting casually in a chair at the front of the salon, he only leaves once to grab a coffee from a nearby shop sometime between the application of colour and the completion of processing.

As he scrolls his phone, I wonder if he's used to waiting. Does he have sisters who taught him to be patient like this? A mother who took him along to tedious appointments? A father who taught him how to queue and wait? Are places like these foreign or familiar? We really don't know much about each other, aside from the few stories we've shared in the galley while I taught him how to cast on and purl.

It's better that way.

"Violet."

My head snaps back to the mirror in front of me and I watch pink hit my cheeks as I realize I've been caught staring.

Bonita—the stylist—grins but doesn't call me out for it.

"What do you think?" She runs her fingers through my lustrous, wavy mane.

I look at my reflection and see a cascade of long, layered silvery locks with the perfect shade of lilac interspersed throughout the bottom third of my hair. The colour is a reverse fade: light and subtle at first, transitioning to bolder hues at the tips.

She calls it balayage, I call it bloody beautiful.

I smile wide, revealing two generous dimples in the mirror.

Cooper approaches and I see his patterned shirt and tanned grin emerge behind me.

"Well?" he prompts, studying me eagerly.

"I love it."

I don't know if it's the feel of his eyes on me or the hair I'm referring to.

Both?

A spark catches fire in my green eyes. Is this what happens every time I look at Cooper?

"I'm glad," he says to my reflection. There's that kind and gentle smile again.

"We'll need to put it up…to spare your beautiful dress," Bonita suggests. "The dye might stain it."

Cooper drifts back to his spot at the entrance. With just four pins, Bonita effortlessly creates a dreamy up-do that I'll never—for the life of me—be able to replicate, all while casually discussing care and maintenance.

When I get to the register and pull out my wallet, Bonita puts up her hand. "It's taken care of."

I spin around to face Cooper, who's pretending to be interested in a senior lifestyle magazine.

"Cooper, no."

"It's a gift," he states. "From Steve."

I roll my eyes.

He shrugs.

"Let the man pay," Bonita whispers behind me.

I turn back to face her and sigh.

She smiles. "You deserve it."

Do I?

I outed my friend with my big mouth and blew apart our entire work team. Then there's Bruce: the supportive boss I've abandoned to *hang* with the Sexiest Man Alive™ and get pretty purple in my hair.

I'm not feeling all that deserving right now.

"Don't." Cooper's stern voice startles me. He steps closer, resting his hands on his hips like a schoolmaster. "I know what you're thinking and…don't."

"I—"

"One little mistake doesn't undo how wonderful you are."

I swallow and turn back to Bonita, who's looking at Cooper with love in her eyes.

My own heart swells.

What is it about this man's praise that's so utterly believable?

He wants to do this for me.

I want him to give this to me.

I release a long, slow breath.

"Thank you," I say to Bonita. My voice is quiet.

"Thank *him*." She nods in Cooper's direction.

"Steve, you mean," he corrects her from behind me. "Thank Steve."

"Right…Steve." She gives Cooper a not-so-subtle wink.

I collect my things and we head for the door.

Cooper pulls the handle for me. "V, I'm staaarving."

I wince. Poor man has been wasting away in a waiting room chair.

"Oh, Cooper, you've been so patient." I adjust the bags in my hands and step out onto the sidewalk.

"Yeah." He pauses at the threshold. "I have."

The double meaning of his words makes me stumble in my new sandals. He reaches out to grab an elbow—to help me get my footing—but I step back just out of reach.

I'd call this his usual shameless flirting, but his face doesn't look like it's a joke.

The humid outside air grows stifling. I might as well be back in boots and PPE.

His eyes remain fixed on me. They're heavy. The weight of them sits squarely on my chest.

A few beats pass.

My mouth turns dry.

"I need a drink," I force out.

Cooper clears his own throat. "Yeah, let's drink."

Cooper's plate practically overflows with enchiladas, seasoned rice, and beans. He dives in like it's day one on a job in the Bahamas and that plate is the Caribbean Sea. A few grains of rice spill over the back edge.

His insatiable appetite never ceases to amaze me. I try not to imagine the activities all those calories could fuel.

Not now.

I can't.

Not now that he's been with Lauren.

That ship has sailed.

I chuckle and dip a tortilla chip into my guacamole. "Have you always eaten like this?"

"I'm sorry?" he asks, still chewing.

"Like a teenage boy," I clarify.

He swallows and washes his food down with a drink from his lime-stuffed beer bottle.

"Could you imagine what my parents' grocery bills must've been like?" He grimaces.

"I'm sure they're glad they're not still feeding you in a post-COVID economy." I chuckle and take a swig from my own.

"Yeah, lucky for them, Erica and Addy always ate like birds. Grace, on the other hand, outdid me at the kitchen table for a few years there."

The moment hangs as the names register.

"Erica and?" I try to recall.

"Addison, Erica, and Grace. My sisters." He explains.

Well, shit.

Those text messages weren't from his conquests. They were from his siblings.

This is…interesting.

He returns his attention to his plate. I watch in rapt fascination as he uses his large, tanned hands to cut into a cheese-filled enchilada and takes a generous bite.

I catch a glimpse of his bruised knuckles and wince.

The unrelenting heat and frequent reminders of how I've let JT down have killed my appetite, but I'm grateful for the cold beer and snack in our shaded spot on the patio. A little time to catch my breath and be still for a few moments after the drama.

We'll have to get back to check in on JT soon.

Cooper wipes his mouth with a napkin and sits back in his chair. "Do you come from a big family?"

"Only child of divorced parents. I *am* my family."

Shit, I didn't mean for that to come out so cynical.

"Pretty much the opposite of me then." He wipes at the condensation dripping down the side of his bottle.

"Yeah." I've been reluctant to ask Cooper about himself: his life at home, the people in it, even where *home* is. Something always stops me from getting too personal. When we're busy on the platform, it's easy; I can shift the conversation to technical stuff. Cooper's always eager to learn and I have ten extra years of diving stories to tell—tips and tricks to share. Here on a restaurant patio with nowhere to go and no work to hide behind, it's more of a challenge.

"Four of us kids meant six around the table at home." He smiles wide. There's a tiny piece of black bean skin on his front tooth.

It's fucking adorable.

"Are you younger? Older?" I ask.

"I'm the baby." He finds the skin there and wipes it away with his tongue.

I knew it. Boys with older sisters always seem to know how to treat women—no, *people*—with respect. One step out of line and girls are going to set their baby brothers straight by any means at their disposal.

I laugh, more to myself than at Cooper.

"That doesn't surprise you, does it?" His smile shifts to that charming one, the one that renders most weak. Thank goodness we're both wearing sunglasses to throttle those powers.

"Nope."

It's no wonder the ninety-plus minutes in the hair salon didn't faze him. He comes fully trained—waiting room broken.

God bless sisters.

"Another drink?" Our server's voice interrupts us.

We both sit back in our chairs.

Were we just staring at each other?

"Um. Yeah. Sure." I stumble over the words. "Another beer, please." I raise my bottle.

"You sure you don't want one of our little umbrella drink specials?" He gestures to a woman at another table, drinking a pink cocktail from a highball glass. "They're quite—"

"Beer," I snap. "Please," I add, softening my tone.

The server retreats, heading straight for the bar, eager to leave the table.

When I look at Cooper, his brow is raised. "Get the lady a beer, STAT."

I take a deep breath and lean my crossed arms on the table. "I don't like it when people think they know what I *really* want."

He fills up his fork with more rice. "This sounds like a story."

Should I tell him?

My gauge for judging what I should or shouldn't tell a man is clearly broken.

I've tried being what I think they want. Fail.

I've tried being what *they* think they want. Epic fail.

Maybe I should just try being what I want.

I ponder my next move as I crunch a tortilla chip, pausing to shamelessly double-dip into the guacamole pot.

Being single means never having to share your guacamole.

"While we were on break, I went for my routine medical," I begin.

"Hey, me too!" Cooper shovels in another mouthful. He chews, waiting patiently for my story to unfold. It's the same calm, measured Cooper from the salon.

Cooper Brooks: Steady as the sea at sunset.

A reassuring breeze cools the back of my neck, as if to say, *"It's okay…keep going."*

"I asked about…something, and it was summarily dismissed as something I couldn't *really* want," I continue.

"Something?"

I breathe in, breathe out.

"Permanent birth control."

His eyebrows shoot up in surprise. "Oh." He washes his bite down with more beer from his bottle, hesitates, then takes another swig.

Yep, this is definitely a two-swig conversation.

The moment hangs as the server returns with our next round.

"Can I also get a water, please?" I ask before he leaves our table. The beer is going down dangerously fast.

"Absolutely." He nods and heads directly back to the bar.

"Dude isn't going to step out of line this time." Cooper chuckles.

I smile sheepishly, feeling a bit guilty about snapping at him now.

Our server returns promptly with two glasses of water and leaves us just as quickly.

I remain silent, letting Cooper decide what direction our conversation goes—giving him the out.

"Well..." Cooper moves some rice around on his plate. "That sounds...permanent."

A defensive element kicks in. "I'm forty years old, Cooper."

"You're not old." The firmness he packs into that statement is endearing, but doesn't change the fact that I'm "geriatric" in the reproductive realm.

"Too old for motherhood, even if I wanted it—which I don't, by the way."

I begin to worry I've waded right in on a far-too-personal topic.

Cooper sets his fork down and leans back in his chair. "Fair enough. And that's your choice to make."

Points, Cooper.

"Thank you." My chin lifts. I take a refreshing drink from my water glass.

"So, what did they say?"

More points for not assuming gender, Cooper.

"*He* suggested that I needed time after my recent breakup."

"Ouch."

Yes. He gets it.

"He seemed to think—"

"That you don't really know what you want."

We both cringe.

Cooper raises his bottle to his lips. "Oops." He takes another drink.

"Right? And on that subject...the only *oops* I want in my life right now are at the scale of leaving my wetsuit outside in the rain, not..." I don't bother to finish my sentence.

"What did you tell him?"

Frankly, I'm surprised Cooper's this interested in the conversation.

"He insisted he *respected* me." I emphasize with air quotes. "I asked him if he respected me enough to know my own mind."

Cooper's face breaks into a wide grin. "Well played, Thomas."

I love his little act of solidarity, but I still worry I've shared too much.

He pushes his plate aside and leans against the table, rubbing his chin. "Well, I certainly know how shitty it is when someone discounts what you bring to the table."

"What do you mean?"

Maybe by sharing a bit of myself, I've given him the green light to open up too.

He hesitates, then continues. "People tend to take one look at me and dismiss me as the labour. Definitely more style than substance."

Shit. I instantly replay past conversations and scenarios, worried I've objectified or discounted him. But I come up empty.

I mean, yes, the man is beautiful. I'd have to be blind not to notice. But he's incredibly smart, and capable...and kind...

"Wait, but what about that *vast vocabulary* of yours?" I grin, remembering those first days on the frankenrig.

"Crosswords and brain puzzles." His face pinkens. "You knit, I do those to pass the time."

I've just spilled my reproductive truths and he seems shy about revealing his simple pastimes: God, this man.

He looks down at his bruised hand and frowns. He clenches it. "Maybe this swollen fist just proves that I'm exactly what people think I am: more brute than brains."

"No." I'm unequivocal in my delivery.

"No?" he asks. There's a hint of vulnerability in the question.

"One little mistake doesn't undo how wonderful you are."

We share a smile as I use the same words he spoke to me just hours ago.

Our eyes catch on each other's and hold. The air between us feels lighter, having shared our stories, but also thick with newfound connection.

My phone reverberates against the table, startling me. I flip it over.

JT: clryton and jmes are froking rickstars
theyree the bst

Oh lord. Incoherent babble text. Reserved for only when JT has found a tequila bottle.

Shit. "We better get back."

CHAPTER 28

Turns out sailors on shore leave can't hold a candle to offshore workers who have abandoned their post.

Rushing back to Preston Villas to assess the situation, Cooper and I enter a rowdy scene. The resort's outdoor bar top is covered with empty shot glasses, another round is being raised and clinked, limes waiting in hands. Unknown patrons are interspersed with Lauren, JT, and the others. Clayton and James—the other rig workers who defected with us—pat JT on the back supportively.

Quite the party.

It would seem that Lauren, Clayton, and James can hold their liquor.

JT? Not so much.

A couple of glasses of water later, after a good game of hide-the-tequila-bottle, I feel like we've avoided JT-over-the-toilet territory.

But who can blame him? In the last twenty-four hours JT has been outed to his colleagues (thanks to my epic fuckup), been on the receiving end of homophobia (thanks

to Bigot Bob), and fled an offshore oil platform by helicopter (thanks to our dramatic exit).

It's a tequila-worthy day.

Leaving Cooper to manage JT, I find an empty table set
away from the crowd. I need a moment to collect my
thoughts and regroup after the race back to the resort.

I sit and enjoy the breeze as it passes through the open
patio, listening to Bob Marley tell us not to worry about a
thing.

I'm not entirely convinced.

From my vantage point, I watch as the party continues
at the bar. Cooper leans against the polished wood top as JT
continues to talk his ear off. I can only imagine what he's
telling him, and cringe slightly at the thought. Whatever
he's saying, it's keeping Cooper entertained. He can't stop
smiling—beautiful flashes of white teeth against tan skin—
and offers up the occasional laugh, hand covering his
mouth when JT gets undoubtedly off-colour with his
remarks.

JT is funny on any given Tuesday on the platform. With
his filter removed, JT could do stand-up comedy.

Despite the stillness, thoughts swarm. There's so much
to process. Contentment over my hair, which feels like a
return to myself, nerves about our unprecedented exodus
from the work site, a hint of regret about the loss of
romantic opportunity where Cooper is concerned, and joy
that we've found a new path as friends.

I watch as the happy scene plays out in front of me.
Laughter, punctuated by pats on backs. Shouldn't we be
feeling bad about what's transpired? Sad that someone
could be filled with so much hate over someone's sexual
preferences? Guilty that we've left Bruce high and dry?
That's not what I see here.

I see five colleagues embroiled in adventure, sucking the
Thoreau-like marrow out of life along with their limes.

Kindred spirits out of their comfort zones, making the most of the situation at hand.

Inspired, I grab my phone and begin to type.

> Violet: I put the purple back in my hair.

A reply arrives almost immediately.

> Greta: YES! I always loved Violet's violet.

My face breaks out in a grin.

> Greta: Wait. Aren't you off on an oil
> platform in the middle of nowhere
> right now?

> Violet: Long story.

> Greta: I've got time.

I check my watch. Greta's hours are all over the place. Lately she's been working nights at the university, doing electrical work while we're all snug in our beds, just to avoid disrupting lectures. A diver's shifts aren't exactly a breeze, but I've always been thankful that our work conforms to the movements of the sun.

I consider my words… then opt to go all in.

> Violet: Cooper punched a homophobe in
> the face and got kicked off the platform. A
> few of us left in solidarity.

> Greta: Wait, what? Who the hell is Cooper?

Who *is* Cooper?
Which version of him do I give?
A respected colleague? JT's hero? A dear friend?

"I thought he was the answer to my sexual prayers."

It's like my subconscious has spoken, but it's someone else's voice I hear.

I look up to find Lauren standing in front of me, sheepish expression on her face, hands in her denim shorts' back pockets.

"Mind if I sit?" She gestures to the chair beside me.

I pull it out for her and gesture to the seat. I don't want to be one of those women: the kind that find themselves at odds over a man. Lauren is a lovely person, smart and kind, and I can't hold my injured pride against her.

She sighs as she sits. "That's why I was there…in his cabin that night."

Despite my eagerness to hear her out, I can't help the pang that strikes as I'm brought back to that cringe-inducing moment at Cooper's door.

"You don't owe me an explanation; it's none of my business." My face grows hot with embarrassment.

"Oh, but it is."

I go to speak, but she raises her hand.

"I had to shoot my shot. I mean, look at the dude: the man is sex on legs." Lauren gestures in his direction. We both turn to look at him.

We watch as he slips his hand up under his shirt and scratches his flat stomach.

If I had access to those abs, I wouldn't stop pawing them either.

We both emit slightly dreamy sighs.

"But he wasn't having any of it." Lauren's words bring me back to the table. "And once you came to the door, he couldn't get me out of there fast enough."

Wait…what?

"By the time you turned up," she continues, "he'd already turned me down. He said he was involved with someone."

Shit. Is he in a relationship back home?

Wherever *home* is.

My stomach twists. My brow furrows.

I look back over at him and he's already looking at me. An elbow rests on the bar top, and JT still natters beside him. Cooper flashes me a handsome smile and rolls his eyes when JT isn't looking. He discreetly mimics chatter with his free hand.

My face relaxes.

I love this shorthand we share. Signals meant only for me.

Are they really just for me, though?

My eyes don't leave him.

"He's never mentioned a partner." My words drift into the cool breeze.

Lauren ignores my comment.

"As soon as you knocked on his cabin door, I knew who he was quote-unquote *involved with.*"

My head snaps to Lauren. "Who?"

Lauren laughs. "Do you really not know?" Her eyes are wide with surprise.

I pan back over to Cooper, who's waiting with another gentle smile. We look at each other in stillness as the room carries on boisterously around us.

Lauren's words break through the din.

"It's *you*, silly."

CHAPTER 29

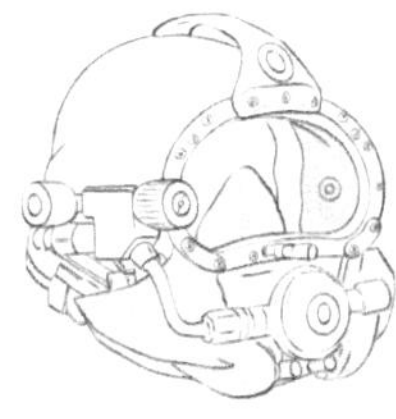

The silver fox across the bar boldly winks at me and raises his glass in my direction. A fresh bottle of beer sits before me on the high-top table, compliments of my new…friend.

At least he didn't send me an obnoxious umbrella drink.

This is exactly the type of man I should be focusing my attention on. He's closer to my age, extremely handsome, clearly interested, and not a work colleague. Green flags all around.

And I'm not the least bit interested.

My eyes seek out Cooper, but he's not at the bar.

Lauren's words still ring in my ears.

"It's you, silly."

Words I never expected to hear, words that change everything.

After a few suspended seconds, I realize I've left Greta hanging. Slightly numb, I raise my phone to type.

Violet: I'm going to have to talk to you later.

Greta: THAT LONG PAUSE IS VERY
INTERESTING, VIOLET.

She's pulled out the all caps.

Bubbles dance on my phone screen.

Greta: Like I said before, don't DIY shit.
What's going on?

Oh god. So much is happening at once.

"Looks like you've caught someone's attention." JT's words startle me. The dude is ridiculously stealthy.

Lauren leans toward me. "The plot thickens."

Things are moving too fast. I need more information.

"You mean you and Cooper…" I trail off.

"Nope, nada. Nothing." She sits back in her seat, taking a generous swig of her drink before continuing. "And it's been awkward as fuck. I haven't been able to make eye contact with either of you since."

The last piece slots into place. She's been avoiding me because of *her* embarrassment, not mine.

I still can't find Cooper.

I need to reply to Greta.

"You should go talk to him." JT nudges me, gesturing to the grey-haired man at the bar.

My head spins. I need space.

I stand and head straight for the bathroom.

I cling to the counter with one hand, my iPhone with the other, trying to catch my breath.

Pocketing my cell, I run the cold water and rinse the beads of sweat off my upper lip.

The face that looks back at me in the mirror is almost unrecognizable.

I don't recall ever feeling quite this before: a bizarre mix of opportunity and fear.

Before I can second-guess it, I lift my phone and dial.

"V?" Greta's concerned voice answers.

"There's a guy."

She chuckles. "Of course there is."

A silent moment passes. God, where do I start?

"Where is he from?" Greta asks.

"I don't know."

"What?" I can hear traffic on her end of the line.

"I've probably caught you at a bad time. I can let you g—"

"Not so fast, girl." A car door closes. "I want to hear this."

Shit.

I guess I'm doing this.

With one long breath out, I finally let the words flow. "I don't *want* to know where he's from, Greta. First thing he's telling me where he lives, next I'm touring his hometown on Google Earth trying to see where he gets his groceries. Then comes the restraining order."

I check to make sure the bathroom wall is clean before leaning against it. Dammit, I wish I'd chosen a more hygienic place for my personal crisis.

"Whoa. This guy's *restraining-order* worthy?" If it's possible to hear someone smile, I can in Greta's voice right now. Of course she's having fun with this.

"Not the point, G. The point is we see each other every

other two weeks; we're not turning our lives upside down for each other."

"Wait, wait…you've thought about it, though." She chortles.

When I don't answer, she continues. "This is Cooper?"

Cooper. Just the sound of his name on my friend's lips makes my chest ache.

"Yes, this is Cooper."

"Why are you five steps ahead? Maybe he has a tiny penis or something."

"Greta!" A shocked laugh spills out of me.

"Wait…have you *seen* his penis?"

At that I start to laugh—really laugh. "No, I have not."

"Well, get on it!" Greta orders. "I mean that quite literally by the way…"

I look at myself in the mirror; this time it's my familiar face that smiles back. Just two minutes with Greta and I've found myself: shoulders dropped, brow smooth, colour returned. I continue to watch as I finally say it out loud for the first time. "I want to."

I let the words sink in—more for my own benefit than hers.

"I know you're cautious. Your even keel is just part of why we love you. We can always rely on Violet Thomas. You're solid as one of Bella's rocks."

"Stone."

"What?"

"She works with stone, not rock. She's a stone mason not a rock mason," I clarify.

"Whatever…work with me please?"

"Sorry, continue." It's my turn to chuckle.

"You're holding on so tight to something, V. I'm not sure what. Maybe it's time to just let go."

"Let go?"

It's never occurred to me before, how this tense feeling I

always seem to have isn't much different from the exhausting grip of hanging onto a platform in the midst of the current. Terrifying and tiring, it's an endless fight against an intangible thing.

Letting go. God, what a relief it could be. I release a long, slow breath just at the thought.

The question is, if I do let go, will I sink or swim?

"I'm so sorry, V. I have to go." I hear Greta's car start up.

"KK, sorry."

"Don't you dare apologize. Do you see what you just did here?"

My brow furrows, not sure what she's talking about.

"You didn't DIY it—you came to me for help."

A couple of seconds pass as it registers.

Wow. I did.

"I'm proud of you," she says softly.

My throat tightens.

Maybe there's hope for this only child of divorced parents who's always just managed on her own.

Little bubbles burst in my chest. I'm proud of me too.

We say our goodbyes and I stand tall, adjusting a few stray strands of my platinum hair.

Hold on, or let go?

Sink or swim?

Only one way to find out.

CHAPTER 30

Within five determined steps of the washroom, I'm cornered by the silver fox.

"Whoa." He reaches to steady me when we nearly collide.

I step back defensively, eager to restore my personal space.

"Hi there." He offers a sly grin. "Thanks for the drink."

It takes me a moment to register what he's said, but when I do, I correct him. "I didn't buy you a drink."

"Sure, sweetheart."

Sweetheart? Eww.

"No, I'm serious." I take one more step back for good measure. "*You* bought *me* a drink…remember?"

"Sure, let's go with that." He winks. "Why don't I buy you another?"

I didn't buy this guy a drink. He claims he didn't buy one for me.

WTF?

I look back over at our group of renegade divers who—with the exception of Cooper—have congregated around my old table.

I find JT in the small crowd, and the instant we make eye contact, he looks down at his feet.

Guilty.

Oh, JT…what have you done?

"I heard you guys are a bunch of scuba divers."

I reluctantly turn back to face him.

We're not. We use surface supply. But I'm not going to waste my time explaining the difference.

The man is like an impressionist painting—best viewed from a distance.

Up close, his symmetrical features look sharp, almost severe. The sly grin he keeps giving me and the cologne he's marinating in, aren't turning me on. In fact, they're turning my stomach.

"Um…yeah," I finally force out.

"A professional *diver*, huh…" His mouth curves into a smirk.

Oh god, please don't make a sexual joke.

I mentally prepare myself for what's coming—spoiler alert, it's not me.

"I'm a pretty skilled *'diver'* too…Betcha I could show you a few tricks about going down."

Damn you, JT.

"Is everything okay here?" Cooper's voice hits like a deep inhale of one hundred percent pure medical oxygen.

I spin around to find him behind me and flash him the Save Me™ eyes.

He doesn't miss a beat.

"Wanna get out of here?" he asks.

"Oh god, yes."

"I'm going to choke JT when I see him next."

"You think he's behind this?" Cooper moves to take one of my shopping bags out of my hand. "Let me help."

The juxtaposition isn't lost on me. Cheesy pickup lines from Silver Fox one minute, chivalrous bag-carrying from Cooper the next.

Cooper is probably fifteen years younger than my patio predator, yet carries himself with exponentially more maturity, and certainly more class.

I let him take each bag until I'm left holding just my cross-body and perhaps the largest infatuation I've ever had for a man.

Who says chivalry is dead?

We resume our leisurely walk along the resort's network of flagstone paths that lead to our cabins.

"Oh, there's no question he's behind this," I reply.

Startled by a noise beside us, we pause, but resume our amble when a critter scurries off into the brush.

"'*Betcha I could show you a few tricks about going down.*'" I groan.

I almost lose one of my sandals when it catches on the edge of the footpath, but recover it and work to slot my toes back into the flimsy shoe. "Christ, Cooper. He even called us '*scuba divers*,'" I mutter as I struggle against the plastic.

"Oh, fuck." I can see Cooper's eyes roll in the lamplight as he watches me.

When the footwear fights me, he grips my arm to provide support while I adjust my shoe.

The movements we make are fluid, completely natural. So second nature, in fact, that it takes us a few seconds to realize what we've done: while I'd recoiled defensively from another man's touch just minutes ago, my body had intuitively leaned into Cooper's.

In the next moment, the same instinct that brought us together forces us to step apart.

Cooper clears his throat. I straighten my skirt.

We continue walking.

"The pickup line is tacky, but in all honesty, I probably used something similar on some poor woman ten years ago." Cooper adjusts my bags in his hand.

"The difference is that *you* grew up."

"Oh god, I hope so. I'd never try that now." He chuckles.

"Just goes to show you that sometimes people *never* grow up. Sometimes age is irrelevant."

A silence lingers, loaded with words unspoken: *Maybe it's irrelevant for us.*

Trepidation builds in me as the pink hue of my adorable cottage comes into view.

Our moment is coming too fast, too soon.

When we land on the raised step of my cottage door, a cold panic sets in.

I need to stall.

I'll tell him a story to buy time.

I turn sharply to face him, surprising Cooper. "My first month as tender," I jump right in. "I accidentally caused a bar fight when I misunderstood what a teammate meant when he asked if he could see my Kirby Morgan."

"What?" Cooper's voice is filled with an alluring mix of curiosity and delight. His wide, white smile telling me to *go on.*

"In my defence, I was a rookie on my first shore leave who'd still not learned to hold my drink, and with the noise of the crowd I'd thought I'd heard *curvy* instead."

Cooper lets out a full belly laugh that makes my pulse race with approval.

He covers his mouth, like he always does. Like he needs to stifle his joy in case it's too much.

My tattooed hand reaches up on its own accord and pulls his down.

"Stop, don't cover it," I say between my own giggles.

He grabs my hand back, pulls it. "Don't cover what?"

The strength and authority in the movement sends a rush of heat through me.

"Your smile."

He pulls my hand once more, just a quick tug that brings me scant inches from his mouth.

The lamp lights are dim, but there's enough brightness to show me the sparkle in his eyes.

Jesus, where's my bail-out bottle when I need it?

Butterflies work in my stomach.

Will I ever overcome what's inside me and find the strength to close the gap?

Neither of us moves.

Neither of us breaks the silence.

Does he feel this connection? The charge between us?

"Violet." Cooper finally fills the void. "I'm so glad…"

"Glad?"

I'm searching for clues, for hints in every syllable.

One more long, loaded silence.

"So glad that we're friends."

Friends?

Friends.

That word should fill me up inside—his friendship is a gift to me from the universe.

With one word it feels like he's handed me a winning lottery ticket and at the same time broken my heart.

A raw ache builds in my chest as he slowly releases my hand.

I watch as it drops.

Hold on. Let go.

This isn't the letting go I'd imagined.

He takes a step back, setting my bags at my feet. "Goodnight, V."

I slot my key in the lock and reach for the door's handle. "Goodnight, Cooper."

The silence of the moment is punctuated by the loud click of my cabin door latching shut.

Once inside, I lean my head against the closed door, allowing it to rest on the hard, cold surface. My heart is lodged in my throat, but my pang of sadness shifts to resignation as I step away, dropping my bags with a thump before heading toward the bathroom.

I'm halfway down the hall when I hear a knock that stops me in my tracks.

A little burst of joy explodes in my chest.

Hang on.

Turning on my heels, I rush back to the door, pulling it in haste.

Cooper is standing there when it opens, chest rising and falling—like he's run a city block in the two minutes it's taken him to go absolutely nowhere.

"Did you forget something?" I give a friendly smile, afraid of false hope.

Hang on.

He runs a hand through his sandy locks and furrows his brow.

The moment hangs.

"I left..." he starts.

An excruciating pause. One step forward.

"I left without this."

In a heartbeat, his two large palms envelop my face, spanning me from ear to jaw, and then his lips find mine: hot and hurried, not a second to waste.

CHAPTER 31

The power of his kiss forces me backward two full steps.

We let the door fall shut behind us and in an instant I'm spun and pinned against it; there's a thud as my ass hits the frame.

There's no apology after, just a low groan from Cooper to accompany my own gasp of surprise.

He angles his face to take the kiss deeper, I open my mouth to let his tongue slide against mine. My heart beats wildly in my chest, but despite my nerves there's an unmistakable sense of relief having his lips on mine at last. I lean into him and let out a contented sigh.

The radiating heat and spicy smell of him cage me, but I don't feel trapped. No, I'm finally granted freedom—to touch and grab muscle and skin as he, in turn, does mine.

Cooper kisses like he welds: hot, competent, attentive, skilled.

He pauses, pulling at my bottom lip with his teeth. I open my eyes to find him watching me. He nips harder, then grins against my mouth.

Thump, thump, thump.

I can hear my blood pump in my ears.

I draw in a breath.

Afraid he might stop—might step away—I grab at his shirt, fisting fabric with my hands, pulling him back in.

His next rhythmic, confident tongue-strokes make me picture him naked and fucking me, makes me hot between my legs.

When I arch into him, his hands drop to my hips.

His strong arms first guide me to the right, but we trip over my shopping bags, causing us to chuckle.

Then he takes us left. I'm not really sure where we're headed, but Cooper's searching for a place to land. We're a clumsy mess of movements as we blindly kiss our way to nowhere, bumping our teeth, and knocking into a lamp.

Kiss, step, kiss, step, kiss, step, kiss.

Eager hands caress and cup. Mine find his stubbled jaw, his find my ass.

There's no laugher left in us when he hikes me up on the top of the entryway credenza. Both my dress and my breath hitch as my skin hits the cold, hard surface.

A sandal falls from one foot.

Cooper's hot palms blaze a trail down my bare legs and instinct has me wrapping my thighs around his hips.

The other shoe follows the first.

Our frantic pace finally slows to a sensual, exploratory meter: a kiss for each hot breath. Cooper pulls back from me slowly, tugging at my swollen upper lip as he goes. When he steps back to study me, my stomach flops and flips.

Is this really happening? I'm still back at the knocking door.

This close I can see that his eyes aren't just turquoise, they're a half dozen different shades of blue. I reach and trace a brow, let my finger follow his beautiful cheekbone, let it line his soft, full lips.

He closes his eyes, takes a breath.

I should probably say something; we've still not said a single word.

It's like we're both too…overcome. We need to register the moment.

His warm palm rests on the back of my neck, fingers reaching towards my nape. Examining the outline of my face, he considers me. "Can you take this down for me?" He touches my now surely tousled updo.

"Down?" I barely get out.

He studies me intently. "I want to run my fingers through it."

Heat rushes to my cheeks.

We've crammed our tongues down each other's throats but somehow *this* makes me blush?

Lifting my hands from his broad shoulders. I go in search of the four little hair pins carefully inserted by Bonita just hours before. Feeling my way, I find each one and coax them from my tangled hair. With each removed pin, more purple tips spill across my shoulders and chest, until they're a cascade of untamed curls.

Cooper watches where my platinum locks fall, where the newly violet tips skim the neckline of my dress.

When I expect him to reach for my hair, he runs both hands up the outside of my thighs, up under the hem of my dress.

He searches my eyes and I give a slight nod.

Peeling the bone-coloured linen away from me, he lifts it over my head, discarding it on the floor.

When he's done, his eyes have changed, blown-out pupils blocking the blue.

His hot hands skate up the sides of me until they meet the strands at the back of my neck. Slowly, he weaves his fingers through. He's tentative at first, in that way that boys are: unsure of how it's done, afraid to catch or knot it.

"So soft." His hands pull slightly when they finally confidently comb.

My nipples harden under my modest white bra.

He bends to run his nose along my neck, his tongue trailing along behind. Still his fingers work in my hair. "Just as soft as I imagined you'd be."

It's hard to breathe.

He's so careful. So meticulous. Just like when he's cutting pipe.

His eyes pan over me, examining the ink that trails along my skin—taking in his fill.

He studies me like a work of art. Maybe I am. I'm torn between wanting to study him like a painting too—like the masterpiece he is—and wanting to rip his goddamn clothes off.

I grab at the buttons of his shirt and begin to slip each one through its corresponding hole, but once the top few are undone, he reaches behind himself and impatiently pulls it over his head.

I've seen his chest many times before, during quick shirt changes on deck, or when his wetsuit's been pulled down to his waist, but the sight of it still makes me pause in reverence…out of bloody respect.

I'm literally jarred from my trance when Cooper grips my hips and pulls me to the edge. He grinds against me, his hard length showing me he's feeling the same.

Oh god, this man is so beautiful—so decidedly out of my league—but propped up before him, with unshaved legs and a shabby bra, I feel like a fucking goddess.

I reach between us and stroke the impressive bulge in his shorts.

"Fuck, V." He drags a breath in through his teeth.

His words hit me. The same ones spoken that day in the shower. Same guttural moan at the end.

That's when I know that I heard exactly what I thought I

did…that he touched himself with *my* name on his lips and no one else's.

Emboldened, I grab his belt and unfasten the buckle, making quick work of the pin. The weight of his pockets makes his shorts drop. My hands cup his navy blue boxer-briefed ass and I revel in the shape and feel of him.

Jesus. Sweet. Christ.

Pulling him closer, I line us up: heat against heat.

"Fuck, yes." He's short of breath. "We're doing this."

It's a statement, not a question.

Like I need any convincing?

"Right here." He grinds against me.

"Here," I echo, voice breathy.

Blood rushes to where he's touching me.

Oh god, that's the spot.

"Right now." He bites down on my shoulder.

"*Now*," I plead.

With that single word, I seem to flip a switch in him. Both his hands roughly pull back the cups of my bra, exposing my breasts. He takes one hardened nipple in his mouth, sucking and flicking it with his tongue. Instantly I'm wet, slick from the languorous movements of his mouth, first on one breast, then on the other.

"That feels so good." My head falls back against the wall.

"I'm only getting started," he whispers against my chest.

There's a pang in my belly, an excited fear that makes me worry I'm in over my head—this feels a bit like drowning.

Cooper runs a palm up my inner thigh. The tips of his fingers stop short of exactly where I want him to touch me. Where I *need* him to touch me.

He does it again.

I tilt my hips to try to connect and bridge that gap. It elicits a chuckle.

"You want my fingers, Violet?"

His voice is like velvet in my ears. Sensuous syllables that tempt and tease.

Shifting my hips, I tug at the white cotton of my panties. I can't get them off fast enough.

As Cooper helps pull them down my legs, his devilish grin turns truly wicked.

There's that pang again.

I swallow hard.

Torturous seconds pass before he finally drags a long finger down the centre of me. I release a relieved sigh.

I arch my back, offering up my breasts to him again. He cups one and nips at the other, all while that single finger drags deliciously back and forth.

Skilled, indeed.

I grip the edge of the credenza, hips bucking off the hard surface. I don't mean to do it, but I need to help, need to get him there.

"There?" he asks, lingering in exactly the right spot, making sweet circles.

"God, yes."

"Or there?" He boldly plunges one finger in.

My gasp makes him do it again, harder. I hold on tighter, digging my heels into the front of the cabinet.

He moves back and forth, harder work with his fingers, softer swirls with his thumb, and all I can do is rock my head against the wall behind me and bite my lower lip.

I open my eyes and see this beautiful man in front me: sun-kissed skin and golden locks, muscled forearms working to coax me over the edge. It feels like a dream.

The first clenches of release squeeze and Cooper's eyes flash up to me.

One side of his mouth turns up, satisfied. "You're close, aren't you?"

He slides a second finger in, and the tight friction steals my breath.

I feel myself slipping and I so desperately want to let go.

"Cooper…" I whimper.

But I'm wound too tight.

After several seconds, I'm still firmly on the edge. I reach for his waistband, worried I'm taking too long.

One hand stops me, grabbing my wrist. "No."

Startled by the command, my eyes seek his in concern.

His lids are heavy, but his smile is light.

He threads his fingers through mine, then holds my hand behind me. As his teeth skim up the side of my neck his fingers work inside me.

"Don't give. Just take." Hot breath and lips brush my ear.

My hips shift in time with his movements, sweat beading on my skin, until one last curl of his fingers leaves me teetering on the edge. With one more hot moan of my name from his lips, I have no choice but to let go.

CHAPTER 32

Fail to plan, plan to fail.

Clever words often said to me by my militant diving instructor. Drilled into me from day one and meant to keep me safe when stakes are high, and sound when certainty is low. Little does he know that they inspired me to never leave home without a multi-pack of condoms.

"Grab my purse." I gesture impatiently to the spot on the floor where my crossbody sits next to my shopping bags. A bit self-conscious, I adjust my bra back to its proper position as Cooper flips his wallet shut and tosses it next to his discarded shorts.

He scratches at his defined abdomen. "I can't fucking believe I don't have one."

I'm actually glad he doesn't have one. It means that—while he'd certainly been thinking about it—he's not been gunning for my pants.

Still propped precariously on the credenza, I watch as he grabs my bag from the pile and hands it over to me. Moving back to his rightful place between my legs (amen) he rests his hands on my thighs, as I hastily zip open the pouch. Three foil-wrapped packages peek back at us from the inside pocket. I pull one out and toss my purse over with his wallet.

When I look back up at him, he's watching me with a raised brow. "You don't leave much to anyone else, do you?" His thumbs find the tops of my hips, reminding me of my nakedness from the waist down.

I shrug. "It's not the man's responsibility to provide the protection."

The moment hangs just long enough for me to start feeling silly sitting on this piece of furniture.

"Should we move?" I sit up straighter, hands crossing to cover my parts.

Cooper steps back and slowly peels down his boxer briefs until he's wearing nothing but a self-satisfied smile.

I don't even attempt to conceal the thorough examination I give him, eyes bouncing from one beautiful sight to another. I survey the smooth, tanned planes of his chest, ropey muscles of his arms, the strong, thick mass of his thighs. He has hollows at the sides of his ass that you could drink from, and they're definitely making me thirsty.

"Do *you* want to move?" The look he gives me is brash and cocky—full of his signature Big Diver Energy. A pulse returns to my crotch. My nipples ache.

I couldn't move right now if I tried.

He steps closer. I can smell the earthy spice of him, feel his heat, see exactly where the vee of his abdominal muscles lead.

My hands grip wood tightly—palms damp with nervous sweat—but my legs open in reply.

"Didn't think so." He bites back his smile, teeth resting on his lower lip, and watches himself run one finger up the centre of me. I tilt my hips forward, chasing his moving hand.

His height and the dimensions of this blessed piece of

furniture are facilitating near perfect alignment of every zone.

My legs fall further apart.

"That's it, Violet," Cooper praises. "Nice and wide, so I can see."

My face grows hot, newly shy. Like I've not already moaned his name six ways from Sunday. In my forty years I've never heard words like these before—ones reserved for smutty romance novels, not found in real life.

I run a hand down the taut muscle of his stomach—the one I've wanted to paw for weeks—and see his hard length twitch.

Holy shit.

Cooper grabs the condom, carefully opening it before rolling it on.

I swallow the choked noise that escapes my throat.

We're really doing this.

His next movements are restrained, measured. He takes his time as he leans in closer, carefully studying me as he cradles my jaw until his hot lips land on mine. This kiss is slow, sinful, thorough, a suggestion of languorous motions to come.

The skill of his kiss leaves me weak and pliable in his hands, and he knows it. He nips at my bottom lip and reaches to grab my ankles, folding my legs up like some sort of posable toy, setting my feet at either side of my hips.

I've never been this open—so completely exposed to another. But any shyness I perhaps should have slips away with the first long, drawn-out slide.

Each delicious inch of him is better than the last as he eases himself in.

The position is like fucking magic—somehow, he knew it would be. His body holds my legs back, freeing his hands to pull my bra away again in time with the second thrust.

This one forces out a gasp. It's a mix of pain and pleasure as he stretches me to fit him just right.

He throws one hand up against the wall behind me for leverage with his next push. The other stays behind to work my hard nipple.

Each stroke of his thumb is electric, each swing of his hips, alchemical. Combined: He casts a spell.

"You feel incredible." The wizard speaks.

"Coop—" is all I get out, lost to another wave of bliss.

"You *look* incredible." He pulls back enough to watch where our bodies are joined.

I follow his eyes, see him pull almost all the way out before slipping decisively back in.

Watching us like this—watching *him* watch us like this—makes me feral.

"Fuck…" I groan. My short nails scrape his biceps, up his shoulders and along his neck. When I get there, I grab his head roughly, pulling him in for a brutal kiss.

He answers with a twist of my nipple, sending a new charge between my legs, a rush of heat to my lower belly. The sounds our bodies make as they come together, sweat-covered skin against sweat-covered skin, creates another layer of seduction.

My hips try in vain to meet his as a familiar tension starts to build, but in this position, I can't shift and it's torture. The need to move—to match each of his strokes—is almost unbearable.

"Fuck me harder." The words tumble out of me. I don't even recognize them.

His large hands fall to my ankles, holding me as I squirm. "Hold onto the table," he demands.

My fingers run a trail along Cooper's damp skin and then find the wooden edge again. I grip it for dear life just as he throws his hips once, then twice, as far as he can go.

I draw in a sharp breath.

"Fuck, V...fuck..." His voice is strained and gruff, hovering at an edge. They're the same sweet words I heard in that bathroom, the same sinful sound I've replayed every night since.

With one more deep stroke, my body makes the connection; Cooper delivers exactly what it needs.

It hits me like a cold plunge, the shock making my body shudder, my legs shake. As I ride out the tremors, Cooper finds it too. With one deep, guttural moan he follows. Taking strained breaths he holds me in place, rolling his wicked hips in ways I swear could throw me right back into the deep.

As our chests rise and fall, there's a pause as we work our way toward stillness. I let my legs fall down the front of the cabinet. Maybe it's mild disbelief, maybe it's repose, but we stay like this for long seconds.

I run a hand through my tousled mane, wiping damp strands away from my forehead. Cooper helps me, hands carefully collecting my hair and gently setting it behind my shoulders. When our eyes finally meet, his brow is furrowed with a pensive expression.

"You're quiet," I say softly, a little afraid to speak.

Let's face it, I was unsure of where we stood *before*, I'm at a complete loss now that it's *after*.

A wide smile crosses Cooper's face and I swear it's the most beautiful and reassuring thing I've ever seen. He plants a hard kiss on my stunned mouth, knocking twice on the wooden top of the credenza. "I'm trying to figure out how we can take this with us."

CHAPTER 33

"What's your favourite number?"

I wake the next morning to sunshine and smiles.

Confused in my drowsy state, I peek over at the digital clock on the bedside table.

5:15.

Looks like someone's an early bird.

"Um…that seems kinda random." I pull the covers up to hide my chest.

"Humour me." He runs a warm hand along my exposed hip, and that's when I notice the sheets have slipped off to reveal the entire tattooed side of my body.

I move to cover that too, but Cooper grabs my hand, threading his fingers between mine. The thrill of this small gesture scares me more than the darkest depths.

I focus on the conversation at hand.

"I don't know…twenty-six?" I shrug.

"Twenty-six?"

"Some of my favourite people have birthdays on the twenty-sixth," I explain.

Cooper pulls himself in closer, kisses the fingers on my

grasped hand. "Mine's on the second—August second—not the twenty-sixth." His eyes sparkle with amusement; he teases me with a grin. A brow raises as if to ask, *Can I still be your favourite?*

My eyes pan down his brazenly naked golden skin.

Yep. Early riser indeed.

My mind drifts back to the night before, to tongues and teeth, hands and heat, and I decide—resolutely—that he's indeed my favourite.

"Why? What's your favourite number?" I adjust the pillow sitting under my head.

"It's 432." He's unequivocal.

My stomach flips with surprise because I know that number—I know 432.

He adjusts his pillow beside me. "That's how many leaves you've got from your fingers"—a gentle squeeze to my hand—"to your foot." He nudges mine with his.

That's 432 leaves for 432 dives.

Each season early on in my career, I tallied all my dives. Every single tasking, all individual missions. At the end of every season, I had that year's dives marked indelibly into my skin—a leaf for each one—until I ran out of room. When I was young and inexperienced and started the ritual, I'd never imagined it possible…that I'd dive so many times that I'd lose track of them in the end. One hundred dives a year is what I've averaged. That's approximately fifteen hundred dives, fifteen hundred slow resurfaces, fifteen hundred gambles, fifteen hundred wins.

"You counted each leaf?" My face grows hot at the thought that he's done this while I was sleeping.

"I did." His voice drops. "You don't think I've wondered these last few weeks exactly where that vine goes?"

He uses a single hot finger to trace a path down my side.

It should probably tickle; instead it's a tease—a small sample of what I now know those skilled hands can do.

"And that's how many kisses I'm about to deliver."

I gasp in surprise as he shifts down and grabs my ankle.

With the same meticulous care and painstaking detail he uses to run a line of weld, Cooper sets out to kiss each greyscale leaf as they trail up the side of my body. By the time he gets to my hip, I'm aching with need. When he takes his time to trace the needle-drawn lines beside my breast with his tongue, I have to press my thighs together for relief.

As his endless kisses finally stop at the last one at my hand, I impatiently grab at his stubbled jaw, eager to close the gap.

The weight of his body as it shifts to cover mine is delicious. Between strokes of my tongue, I open my legs to let him settle there. He's full and hard and I can't decide which I like more: how he feels against me or how his tight backside—which had been so cruelly out of reach to me last night—feels against my palms. I grab at his butt and grind shamelessly against him. Why choose?

The second I feel like I'm in control, Cooper has things turned—literally. In one swift movement he puts me on my stomach. I grip my pillow as he licks a trail down my spine and then cups both of my butt cheeks with his massive hands.

I can't help but arch my back and push up into them.

He groans approvingly.

There's a muttered curse and a throaty moan behind me.

"Cooper Brooks," I speak around my pillow. "Are you an ass man?"

He fondles me, pawing and kneading my muscle. "I'm a YOUR ass man."

I swear I hear him growl, feel the nip of teeth on one cheek.

"And I'm torn..." He slides back up to rub his hard length against my behind.

Heaviness builds at the apex of my thighs.

"...between taking you just like this." He pulls me up by the hips so I'm on my knees, rocking against me when I get there.

My heart races.

His lips brush the skin on my ear as he leans in to speak softly. "...or begging you to climb on top so I can watch you come."

Holy. Fuck.

A pulse begins in every erogenous zone.

Instinct has me turning to face him. I need to see him. Right. Now.

The gaze that finds me makes me feel like a bloody sex goddess.

He studies me with hooded eyes. "Christ, you're so fucking sexy."

From him, the words sound preposterous.

Like Karsh saying I take a good picture, or Monet saying I'm good with a brush.

But with those five words, I become the centrefold pinup he's just scotch-taped to his wall.

"I want to be on top."

Who even am I?

"Holy. Fuck."

It takes me a few seconds to realize that *he's* the one who's said it.

On impulse, I somehow flip us around and straddle him, aging body be damned. I'll put myself on full display if it means I get more of this—more of him.

His tanned hands caress my freckled skin, gripping and

squeezing, like he's testing how they fit. One grabs a hip, the other a thigh. With each firm grasp my heart thumps in time with the pulse between my legs.

I roll my hips to rub against him and his hands shift to cradle my breasts.

"I've got 432 leaves for 432 dives." I lift off for a moment and then settle back down.

Cooper's eyes fall closed, his head settles deeper into the pillow. "Leaves…dives…" He's having trouble finding his words and I relish the moment.

Another lift. Another roll.

He releases a low groan.

"That's what the leaves are for." I start to fondle his defined pecs, lose a few seconds to his washboard stomach. "I used to add a new one for each of my dives."

I watch his Adam's apple rise and fall.

"You don't anymore?" He manages.

"I ran out of room."

His eyes snap open, catching fire. I feel him grow harder underneath me.

"How many?"

I love that he *needs* to know.

"Into the thou…sands." I emphasize the *thou* and practically purr on the *sands*.

His thumbs find my peaked nipples. I know it's a devious trick—an attempt to literally take back the upper hand—and with his first pass I submit, willingly leaning into them.

With a pinch and a pull, I'm reduced to head throws and throaty moans.

My next hip roll is hot and slick.

"God, you're so fucking…competent." When he says it, it's pure dirty talk, entirely unlike the last time I heard it… during my annual performance review.

"You show great promise yourself, junior," I tease.

The moment the word's left my lips I worry I've crossed a line—that, with the age reference, I've taken things too far. Instead, he reaches a long, muscular arm over to where the remaining two condoms sit on the bedside table.

One foil package is placed on his abdomen before he lifts me like a doll to shift me back onto his thighs. I watch in awe as he tears the wrapper and works it slowly down his length. I realize I'm openly staring when his hands fall uselessly to his sides.

My back straightens, caught in the act.

Our eyes meet. His normally cool blue pools have an unprecedented heat.

He thrusts his hips once in a flagrant display of erection. "Better show *Junior* how it's done."

"I—" I attempt to speak but can't direct my tongue.

I'm supposed to be the one in charge here; I'm the one on top. But let's face it, I haven't been in control since fate landed us on the same ramshackle rig weeks ago.

Butterflies work in my stomach as I take him in my hand and shift back into position. He does nothing to help me, just flashes his cocky grin as I attempt to take command.

The smug look on his face falls the moment I sink to take him in.

His white teeth bite down on his lower lip when I pause before taking it further, until he's fully seated inside.

The delicious stretch constricts my breath. There's a beautiful mix of pleasure and pain as my body adjusts, and I sigh. Cooper sighs too—a similar combination of rapture and relief.

My hands fall to his strong chest, searching for leverage as I start to move my hips.

Working like that for several seconds, I enjoy my front-row seat to Cooper's undoing. I watch keenly as Cooper's brow creases, then calms. I revel in his attempts to speak that lead only to stutters. I smile when he moves to touch me but clutches the bedsheets instead.

"You *can* touch me." I chuckle.

"I won't…" He pauses to catch a breath. "Unless I'm told."

He's certainly committed to his instruction.

I lean to take his jaw in my hand, kissing him hard, nipping at his bottom lip, dragging my knuckles along his coarse stubble. When he tries to bite back, I pull away.

"Put your hands on me." I order.

I'm expecting enthusiastic grabs or hard squeezes, but instead he teases me with one finger, skimming the space between my breasts. He charts a path down to my belly and then cruelly stops.

Lower. Lower, my body begs.

Chasing something I can't quite find, I move my hips harder, faster. It feels so good, but it's not enough.

My mind fixates on that finger. On where it is. On where it needs to be.

"You're so…" He circles my belly button. "Incredible."

There's that word again.

One I never really noticed before, one I now always want to hear.

He runs his thumb across my bottom lip, and I playfully bite, attempting to lighten the moment. I expect him to pull it away, but instead, he pushes it further. I swear I feel him twitch inside me as my tongue latches onto the pad of his thumb and I take one long, hard draw against it.

His thumb pulls out with a slight pop, and he grins devilishly as he moves it down to where we're joined. Like some sort of sexual unicorn, he effortlessly finds exactly the right spot to circle and swirl and send me swimming.

Waves of pleasure lap against me, each successive one more powerful until I think I might go under.

I reach back to grab his muscular thighs and lean into him.

"Please?"

I don't know what I'm asking for. Maybe for him never to stop.

When my head falls back, he grips my hip, meeting each of my thrusts with his own. And still, that thumb works, slow and steady, like the cadence of the sea.

Heat and pressure build.

So close, I'm so incredibly close.

My eyes pan down strong arms and shoulders, across Cooper's muscular chest, seeing his expression coloured with ecstasy. Knowing I'm the one with him in this moment—putting that look on his face—feels like a fever dream. It's a far-fetched tale that future me won't believe.

My gaze falls to where his hand squeezes my hip and I spot them: faint stretch marks on pale skin. From there, my eyes catch on the slight curve of my belly.

My body tightens.

It was one thing getting lost in the moment in the dimly lit entryway last night, it's another here in the brightness of day.

Release slips further from reach.

"Please don't stop." His voice is strained and urgent.

I hadn't even realized I had.

I study his face. His eyes implore me; there's a concerned furrow to his brow.

It's oddly intense.

Of their own accord my hips roll, letting us slip back into rhythm.

His brow remains fixed, but his soft smile returns. "God, you…you feel…" He sucks in a breath. He trails his hand up my side. "You feel like a reward for every good deed I've done in my life."

Something new sets off like fireworks inside of me.

I let my hands fall to the hard planes of his chest. Purple curls cascade over my breasts, and with his calloused fingers gripping the stretch marks of my skin, we move together, crashing like two frantic souls caught at sea.

CHAPTER 34

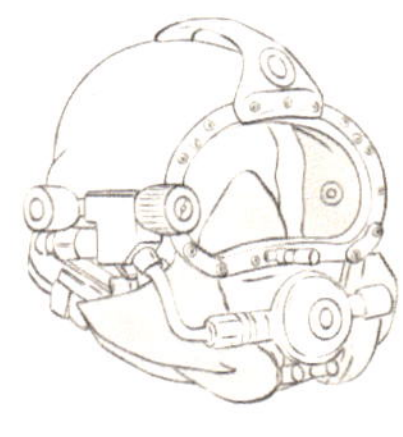 I really hope I don't get a UTI.

Sucking back another generous slurp of my cranberry juice, I let the ice clink as I set my glass on the condensation-soaked coaster.

I know full well that this sugary drink has little-to-no medicinal properties, but it's the best I've got for prevention. It's been a while since some of my parts have had this much of a… workout.

Summoned back to the hotel bar patio for a late lunch by JT, Cooper and I opted to arrive separately. We're not exactly sure what to do about our situation. When the group text arrived saying there was news from Bruce, we agreed to go the less controversial route: Cooper went back to his yellow cabin, and I showered and left from mine.

The loop-de-loop my stomach made when a freshly shaven and showered Cooper Brooks sauntered to our table nearly had me falling from my barstool.

"So, Bruce says Bigot Bob is gone," JT announces to the group.

Murmurs of "good riddance" and "thank god" escape the small crowd.

Fortunately, Cooper has chosen a seat at the far side of the table. Unfortunately, I have a perfect sight line to his hands each time he raises his pint glass to his lush lips.

I watch his movements closely, completely preoccupied, knowing exactly what those hands and lips can do.

I'm not sure how I'll manage when we're back on the rig and expected to work together, but that's a future Violet problem.

"So, what does this mean?" I ask.

JT takes a drink of his Bloody Mary. "We're going back." He drops it on the table with dramatic thunk.

"You're okay with this?" James ask.

Clayton and James are good people. Their moral compass brought them along with us. The same moral compass has made them fast friends.

"Yeah, yeah," JT replies. "He's assured me that Prince Charming won't be there when we get back tomorrow."

Tomorrow. One last night in paradise.

My eyes find Cooper's across the table. He gives me a wink. My face heats.

When he stands to walk to the washroom, I do my damnedest not to check out his ass as he walks away. I fail epically.

JT breaks me from my reverie. "So, Violet…"

These men should wear bells, because he's somehow slid into Clayton's chair next to me, which I hadn't even noticed he'd vacated.

"You look a little…depleted," JT teases.

I roll my eyes. "You're the one with the hangover, JT. How are *you* feeling today?"

"Nope. You're not changing the subject." He shakes his head adamantly.

Speaking of subjects, there's one that still needs addressing. I turn to face him for emphasis. "You sent that grey-haired guy a drink last night and said it was from me."

JT flashes a brash grin, zero regret on his face. "I also sent one to you and said—out loud *to everyone*—it was from him." Pride beams from his smug little smile.

"Why?"

"Sometimes people need a gentle nudge," he replies coyly.

"I wasn't the least bit interested, JT."

"It's not *you* or the silver fox I'm talking about." He raises a brow and gestures to the empty chair on the other side of the table.

Cooper? He thought Cooper needed the nudge.

JT, you romantic mastermind

"After that failed visit to his cabin, neither one of you was going to make the move. Once you had a reason to leave and he had a little perceived competition, I knew things would come together nicely." He tents his fingers like an action film villain.

JT hides behind a persona of benevolent innocence. Turns out he's got a mind for MI5.

"You little shit."

JT chuckles. "Am I wrong?"

Heat hits my cheeks. "No,"

"Fantastic!" he crows.

My eyes pan our table. "Keep it down."

"Oh, come on—there's nothing to hide here. It's fucking amazing." He nudges my arm with his elbow.

"*We work together,*" I loud-whisper, checking to make sure no one's paying attention to our side of the table.

"Whoa, clutch your pearls. You mean two consenting adults have ended up in a workplace relationship? That's, like, *never* happened before." His feigned shock almost cracks me up.

Forget deception, it's sarcasm that this guy is master of.

"Okay, okay, point made." My face still holds onto its heat.

"No one gives a shit, V. Fill in your disclosure form with HR and try to keep your hands off each other during work hours. End of story."

Eager for the conversation to be over, I murmur in agreement.

I watch as something registers, lighting up JT's face. "Oh…" He practically titters. "You're totally not going to be able to keep your hands off each other during work hours, are you?" He squeals in delight.

My stomach flips, the heat of embarrassment now encroaching my chest. I watch it colour my pale skin.

"JT. Don't," I say under my breath, glancing around conspicuously.

He snickers. "I'm going to love seeing cool and collected Violet Thomas get all worked up and frazzled on the platform."

"Hey, I can keep things professional."

Thankfully, Clayton returns to his seat, forcing our discussion to move on.

One thing JT isn't wrong about is feeling depleted. Aside from a protein bar Cooper and I shared mid-morning, I haven't eaten in hours. Once everyone is back around the table, a server takes our orders. Between ironing out details about travel plans and collegial storytelling, we all dive into our meals when waitstaff arrive with food and refreshments.

I'm taking a heaping forkful of huevos rancheros and Clayton is telling me about the perils of working on the monkey board during windstorms when my phone lights up on the table in front of me.

Cooper: Work up an appetite?

Sitting up straighter, I glance across the table. He's watching me with his phone in his hand.

A smile forms as I type out a reply.

Violet: Eat your lunch.

Cooper: Keeping me fed. I see where this is going.

I hide my phone on my lap, keeping my eyes on my plate to maintain a straight face.

My phone vibrates.

Cooper: I want you to look at me the way you look at guacamole.

I giggle—yes, *giggle*—as I notice the generous double order of guacamole on my plate.

I type out my reply.

Violet: I really like guacamole.

I bite my bottom lip as I hit send.

Cooper: I think you're going to like me
more.

My eyes snap over to him.

He flashes me a broad smile that's all levity and life. My heart feels too big for my chest.

I force out a ragged breath.

I think he might be right.

Chairs have been pushed out from the table and napkins tossed on empty plates as the low hum of our group's chatter competes with the bar's sound system. Full bellies are lending themselves to quiet contentment while we people-watch, sitting back and enjoying the warm breeze. I'm thankful for my new linen romper as it keeps me cool against the summer heat.

Cooper must be thankful for it too, based on the long looks he gives me when I get up from my seat. The thrill I feel each time I catch his eyes on me only compounds when I spot my newly violet tips, left loose to toss and tease.

Simply put, I feel beautiful, and more myself today than I have in months. Zero regrets.

I'm mid-conversation with Lauren when, over her shoulder, I catch a sparkle of mischief flare in Cooper's eyes. Watching him lift his phone from the table, I know the buzz is coming seconds before it hits my pocket.

Cooper: How much longer do we need to
sit here?

Violet: Is there somewhere else you'd
rather sit, Brooks?

He doesn't answer right away. I'm taking a drink from my
pint glass when his next message comes in.

Cooper: I'd rather you were sitting on my
face.

I choke on my beer.

It takes me several minutes, and Lauren's vigorous back
smacks, for me to pull myself together. Another text is
waiting for me when I finally do.

Cooper: I'm sorry, did that offend your
feminist sensibilities?

Violet: I'm just not used to men being so…
direct.

Cooper: For the record, the sexist version
of that text would've had me expecting to
sit on yours.

Violet: Are we really having this
conversation right now?

Cooper: True equality isn't that I shouldn't
talk dirty to you, it's that we're free to talk
dirty to each other.

Cooper: Liberty and pleasure for all.

Violet: I don't think that's how the line goes.

JT: You two are sexting right now,
aren't you?

Looking over at JT, I see him pan between Cooper and me.

With our flushed faces and wide grins, the two of us couldn't look more guilty than we do right now.

JT's thumbs begin to move on his phone screen.

JT: Shameless.

Violet: Go away.

Cooper: Harsh. Was it too much?

Violet: Shit, no! Sorry, that was meant
for JT.

Cooper: Phew. I wondered.

Violet: It's all incredibly hot, Cooper. I just
wasn't expecting you to be quite this…
forthcoming.

Cooper: Well, if we do things right, we'll
both be forthcoming at least three times
tonight.

Oh my god.

Laughter bubbles up in me at the audacity of his words.

I look up self-consciously when I realize I've released a shocked cackle.

I can tell by the expression on his face that he's particularly proud of that text. The playful look I get from Cooper across the table lights me up inside. It makes me want to light him up too—to be just as playful back.

I consider my words carefully.

> Violet: As you're so faithfully committed to feminist principles, there really is only one truly equitable arrangement that ensures both parties are on a level playing field.

> Cooper: Oh yeah?

I see him raise a contemplative brow.

Silly boy has no idea what's coming.

I type out a simple two-digit number, take a deep breath, and hit send.

Cooper nonchalantly checks his message just as the server arrives to check on drinks.

Red cheeks give him away. His Adam's apple moves up and down with a swallow.

He spins around in his chair. "Um hi…" He gestures urgently to get the server's attention. "We're going to need our cheques, please."

CHAPTER 35

When I wake, a reassuring breeze is blowing the sheer curtains at the open sliding glass door. Something has stirred me, but I'm not sure what it was. The room is quiet. Just the sound of birds chirping at the first signs of daylight break the silence.

I check the time on the clock.

4:47.

The red glow of the clock's light glances off the torn condom wrapper on the bedside table—the third and last condom wrapper—left discarded in the night.

I settle back under the covers and attempt to fall back to sleep.

Cooper's large form faces away from me, a massive reassuring mound under the covers beside me. He's a sound and silent sleeper. Spicy warmth comes off him in waves. Everything about the man is a comfort. It occurs to me that I sleep better with him here.

Don't get used to it, the little voice inside me warns.

I let out a quiet, resigned sigh.

Just as I'm drifting back to sleep, I hear it. It takes me a moment to register what *it* is, but once I do, it's unmistakable: Cooper's soft moans. Not satisfied moans, but uncomfortable moans. Moans that signal warning, verging on distress.

I sit up and watch his stillness, unsure of what to do.

His leg jerks, twitching in response to whatever's he's found in his dream.

"I can't get out…"

Cooper's words are low and slightly slurred, but they're unmistakable and laced with panic.

This is no dream, it's a nightmare.

"Ah…" A cry muffled by his pillow.

I want to wake him, put him out of his misery, but with one full body flinch, he wakes himself. "Fuck."

I silently watch as he rolls over onto his back and blinks his eyes open. After a few long seconds, he spots me.

"Shit, did I wake you?" His voice is groggy.

"Are you okay?" I don't even bother to answer him.

He releases a long breath. "Yeah."

He pulls the covers down so they gather at his waist. Light dances over the contours of his chest, highlighting every dip and curve. I smooth a hand across his skin, wanting to calm him.

He clears his throat. "Sorry."

"Don't apologize," I'm quick to reply. "You had a bad dream."

Well duh, Captain Obvious.

I feel like I'm fucking this up. I pull my hand away.

"Don't." He grabs me, pulling it back to where it was. He sets his own on top. "It helps."

A long, silent moment passes. I let him take the lead.

"I was in the Gulf, on a rig construction project…" he begins.

I curl up beside him, setting my head into the crook of his shoulder. The need to comfort him swells in me.

"I had to go into a confined space to tack-weld two lengths of thirty-inch pipe together."

Fuck, confined spaces. My gut wrenches. Even after fifteen years, I still dread them.

I form small circles on his stomach while he speaks, hoping it makes an ounce of difference.

He responds with strokes along my arm.

"I was so worried about—oh, you know—not *electrocuting* myself...that I didn't catch things had shifted in the current."

I imagine the scene and shudder.

"When I tried to backtrack my way out, the exit was blocked. The crew was right on it; I could communicate no problem with topside—I was fine the entire time. It only lasted seconds. But that single moment, that sudden panic...I guess it's never quite left me."

I'm speechless.

Working with him every day, you'd never guess it. Mr. Happy-go-lucky, Mr. Yellow Speaker, Mr. Dee Snider T-shirt has inner demons.

I sit up and study him in the early morning light. "Shit, Cooper."

"Lie back down." He pats the spot next to him

I don't move. "Are you seeing someone about it?"

He runs a hand across his face and sighs.

He'd better be seeing someone.

"Cooper, this is serious."

"Violet, I'm fine. It's just a few bad dreams."

"There's nothing *just* about post-traumatic stress, Cooper."

He doesn't reply.

"I really hope this isn't a *tough guy*, toxic masculinity thing." I feel a little bad about giving him the gears right after his nightmare, but not bad enough to back down.

"Fuck, Violet." He chuckles. "You're such a goddamn

ball buster." He pulls my arm until I fall back down beside him. "Yes, I'm seeing someone. A really great therapist, actually."

Relief washes over me. "Good." I nestle back into him.

I want to ask him a million questions. Is he doing CBT? Is he being properly supported at work? Did Steve's incident trigger anything? But I let things lie.

The instinct that kicks in—to study, to protect, to mend—is unlike anything I've experienced before: some sort of autopilot engaging in me as strongly as it would on the platform.

"No one knows about my dreams." He speaks softly and plants a kiss on the top of my head.

My chest tightens, heart swelling with the privileged access he's just granted.

Tilting my head back affords me an unprecedented view of his features. Upon close examination, I see fine lines that frame his eyes, ghosts of yesterday's smiles in the shadows of his face. A man who seemed so vibrant—the personification of youth—suddenly showing the mark of age, patina revealed by the morning's raking light. Evidence of lessons lived and learned. A measure of unexpected wisdom. It only makes him more handsome to me.

I raise a finger and trace the laugh lines next to his lips in an intimate moment loaded with unexpected intensity.

Cooper must feel it too because—with typical charm—he quickly breaks the tension, sending us into a gentle roll. He works me onto my back and wedges himself between my legs, caging me with his forearms. "You need to tell me a secret now too, since you know mine."

His lips sit torturously scant millimeters from mine. The look he gives me makes me wish I had some dirty little secret to tell him. A naughty kink that adds some sort of sexual street cred to my Friday Night Knitting Club.

But I have no secrets to share. I'm the most boring person I know.

Except…

I let the words leave me with my next breath. "I saw you."

Cooper's brow furrows. "Saw me?"

No turning back now.

"Once…in the shower." I squeeze my eyes shut, and in an instant I'm back in that sterile tile-and-steel washroom, frozen with fear and fascination.

When I reopen my eyes, Cooper is smiling back at me with great interest.

"Well, this is an interesting and unexpected development." He wiggles his hips and settles deeper between my legs. I definitely feel things…stir.

Street cred, established.

"Go on." He nudges my crotch with his.

Easy fella, we're fresh outta condoms.

I take another breath and continue. "It was the platform with the broken bathroom lock."

Oh god, am I really doing this?

My chest presses up against his when I try to take in more air. His own hot breath hits my cheek.

"I didn't mean to, but…" I pause.

He drags his nose along my neck. I swear he takes a sniff of me.

"That's very distracting," I tell him.

"It's working just fine for me." He nips at my ear, and I can tell by what's happening below the waist that things are indeed working for him.

"I didn't mean to walk in, but the door wasn't locked," I rush to explain. "You were in the shower but facing away from me."

"I didn't even notice. Did you just walk back out?" he asks, still nestled into my neck.

"I did…after." I swallow hard.

He pulls back far enough to study my face. "What do you mean *after*?" He raises a brow.

"After I saw that…you were…busy?" It comes out like a question.

Surprise dawns on his face.

Shit, maybe this isn't giving *hot*. Maybe it's just giving *creepy*.

"Wait, was I…?" he asks.

"You were."

He rolls over onto the bed, howls with laughter, and remains like that for several minutes.

I think he wipes away legitimate tears before he turns to face me. He props his head on one hand and rests the other on my naked stomach. "This is like a romcom."

"Where are you watching your romcoms? Because the ones I've come across on the Hallmark channel don't feature masturbation."

"That's a shame."

"Indeed."

He circles my belly button with one finger, a delightful new habit he's seemed to form, and it does transcendent things to me.

"I remember that day."

His voice is as smooth as the zipper he pulled down that afternoon on the platform. It gives me the same rush it did then. My body temperature increases several degrees. I pull one foot out from under the covers.

"That was the day I helped you with your gear."

I pull the second one out too. "Uh huh…" I murmur.

His finger travels up between my breasts. A shiver passes over me, goosebumping my skin.

"It made me wonder what it would be like to take *all* your clothes off."

Heat rushes to every erogenous zone.

His finger circles a nipple. "I wish you'd joined me."

Sweet Jesus. Aren't I the one who's supposed to be sharing secrets?

He thumbs the hard peak. "I had to touch myself just to keep from touching you."

God, the words just keep coming. Smutty sonnets inked in sin, marking me like the tattoos on my skin.

"What did you see?" His lips find my shoulder, kiss a trail along my collarbone, linger at the base of my throat.

"One hand, up against the tile."

He licks the hollow of my throat.

I close my eyes and suck back a breath. "Legs spread."

"And?" He takes my other nipple in his mouth.

I struggle to answer. "You touched yourself…and said my name."

"Show me." The cool breeze from the window hits my skin when he draws back the covers and pulls me to stand.

Just like that day on the platform, he grips my hips and directs me, controlling where I go. He walks us to the edge of the room, then turns me, taking small steps until I'm just inches from the wall. Once we've stopped, he carefully shifts my hair away from my neck, tucking it over my shoulder.

"One hand up," he tells me.

He threads his left fingers with mine and sets our joined hands against the wall.

Our proximity makes it impossible for me not to feel his hard length against my ass. I lean into it, but he pulls away.

"Legs spread." He slips a knee between mine, working them apart until I'm in a wide stance—just like he was that day in the shower.

"Is this how it was?" His lips brush the back of my ear. "Like this?" His question hits me like the pressure of a hundred-foot dive.

"Yes." My voice is breathy, barely above a whisper.

I wait in anticipation, wondering where his other hand will go. He sets it lightly on my hip.

"Touch yourself."

His command makes me ache.

Burning lips brand the back of my neck.

For some reason I don't even question it, don't hesitate for a second before moving my right hand between my legs.

I'm already hot and slick, and I sigh with relief on the first pass.

With no inhibition, I move in circles, shifting my hips to work in rhythm. When I do, I close my eyes, remembering what I saw. The water as it flowed over his skin, drops hitting the tile between his legs. I remember how his shoulder moved decadently, up and down. Up and down.

I match his tempo now.

Cooper stays silent behind me, squeezing my left hand tight, urging me on. He's determined to keep me solo, and each time I try to arch back into him, he inches me gently forward. But knowing he's there, that he's watching, is enough. He might as well be working my hand, moving my hips.

With each swirl of my fingers, sensations build, but my position is limiting; I need my second hand.

I let out a frustrated groan.

"What do you need?" Cooper asks.

"I need, I need…"

I don't know what I need.

Cooper reaches around to cup a breast. His soothing caress is followed by a sudden decisive pinch that sends a shock of electricity between my legs.

"Oh god," I whimper.

"Is that what you need?" Cooper repeats the movement, pulling harder.

It feels so good it makes my glutes clench.

"Again." I throw my head back, arching into him.

He delivers a sustained squeeze to the other ripple, so intense I suck in a breath. I draw out each sensation, slowing my pace and dragging my middle finger until every millimeter of movement seems to take seconds, revelling in each sweet circle.

Release hits like a long, sustained ride. I crest its wave and stay there, surfing the tide.

"Say my name." Cooper bites my shoulder.

And with one final shudder, I do.

CHAPTER 36

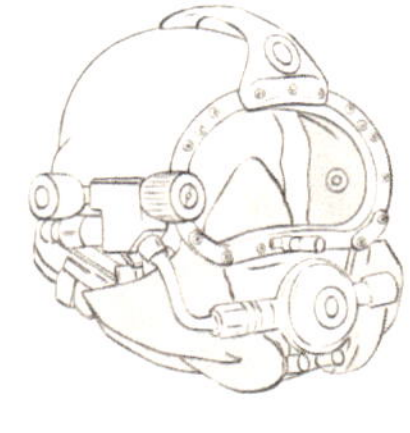

Cable lines smack against metal framework, causing a metallic clang. The flare boom groans against the wind. High-vis-clad workers brace themselves on the monkey board. One figure pats the straps of their fall-arrest harness like a sign of the cross, praying it'll hold.

"This is bonkers!"

I have to strain to hear JT's shout over the ambient noise on the platform.

Grabbing more gear, I work quickly to get everything back to its rightful place. The workday's been cut short by high winds, but there's still plenty to do before we can seek refuge inside.

When the safety manager sends us packing, we never put up a fight. Not only because there's zero tolerance for cowboy bullshit out here, but we'll be damned if we're going to survive running electricity through water just to die getting blown off the platform.

Yes, die.

Certain death.

Because while we might be surrounded by water, a cannonball done from these heights might as well be diving onto concrete. I try not to think about it, but there's a boat permanently moored below, just waiting to retrieve our broken bodies in case it ever happens.

I start moving faster.

Catching sight of Cooper working diligently across the platform, my already adrenaline-addled heart takes off in a sprint.

Shit.

A summer fling with the paternity leave back fill.

I'm in way over my head.

If only there were five-point harnesses for romances.

Dropping my PPE and work gear on the floor of my cabin with a loud sigh, I let the metal door fall shut behind me. It's a relief to no longer fight the wind, to peel back the heavy, cumbersome layers of protective equipment and settle on the bar stool at the small high-top table in the corner of my room. The sound insulation works well to block out the noises from the platform, but I still hear people shouting jovially as they pass outside my door on their way to their own cabins.

Removing my hard hat, I pull out the elastic that holds my ponytail, grateful to tousle my hair and massage my scalp. I catch movement in my periphery and almost startle, until I remember that one entire interior wall is covered in mirror glass. It's a clever strategy to make the place seem larger—less like a glorified closet—but they clearly didn't solicit the opinions of forty-year-old women in the design phase. I cringe every time I need to dress. I can't even change my mind in here without bearing witness to it. I shudder.

A faint hum sounds from my work bag. It takes several seconds to recognize that it's my phone's vibration, and several more to track it down amidst spare clothes, snacks, and other sundries.

Cooper: Feel like doing some knitting?

My face breaks into a grin.

Violet: Is this a euphemism?

Cooper: I knew you were just using me for
my body.

I bite my lower lip as I type.

Violet: Are you just using me for my knitting
needles?

Cooper: It's the socks. I'd do inexcusable
things for those beauties.

Standing to retrieve my project bag from my suitcase, I reach to the very bottom and grab the skein of yarn that I'd stashed there weeks ago. It's a cheerful, variegated yellow that's squishy, soft, and smells of pure lanolin Cooper would love it.

Do I dare?

I can't.

Two pairs would be coming on *way* too strong.

Wouldn't it?

> Cooper: Really this is just a ploy to get you
> to the galley. The gang is here, why did you
> go to your cabin?

Well, shit. I'd assumed *everyone* was going to their cabins.

> Violet: I dunno.

When the phone drones again, I prepare for a witty retort but instead…

> Charles: I've come across a purple
> cardigan I believe is yours. I'd like to make
> arrangements to get it back to you.

I instantly grow cold.

I'm shocked to hear from him. Less shocked by his tone.

As per typical Charles, he's all business.

Ah yes. The purple cardigan.

THE cardigan.

One I hand-knitted, with lovely yoke lace details, that fits like a glove. I'd searched high and low for the right shade of lilac, deliberated over fingering weight or DK, spent months on the hunt for the perfect mother-of-pearl buttons for it. Meant to be just a pretty little summer sweater to keep away the evening breeze. I loved that cardigan. Until it became THE cardigan. The one I used to hide my sleeve of tattoos that seemed to make Charles so uncomfortable in the company of his friends and family. The one I used to cover up the inconvenient parts of me.

That cardigan is a metaphor for our relationship.

Hours spent in crafting it.

Care taken to make it fit.

In the end, not at all what it was intended to be.

Christ, what a terrible relationship. How could I steer so wrong?

And yet, here I am. Knitting bag in hand once again.

Cooper: Are you coming?

My chest grows tight.

I contemplate the stitches. Projects made and projects planned.

Eager to push it all away, I stuff my knitting bag back into my suitcase.

Violet: I think I'll pass.

Three bubbles dance across my phone screen.

Cooper: Everything okay?

Violet: Just tired.

Tired of second-guessing. Tired of missteps.

Cooper: Okay.

I leave them both on read.

CHAPTER 37

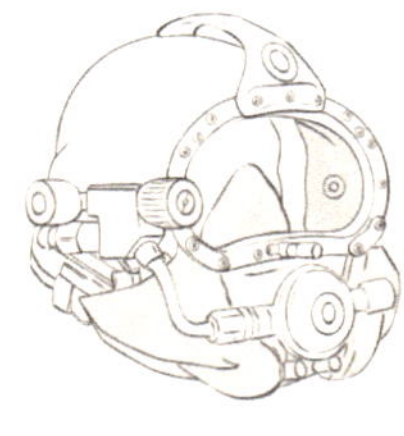

I'm fine. Totally fine. Everything is fine.

It's been several days, and so far, Cooper and I have managed to maintain a professional distance. We work as any two colleagues would, politely interacting on the platform. Every favour followed with a *thank you*, every request enhanced with a pleasant *please*.

Aside from the odd knowing look or lingering glance, we're fine. Completely fine.

Taking time and making space is smart. Not only because we need to keep things professional here, but dialing things back is also a wise course of action. A "burn hot, burn fast" fling is fun, but I need to keep a level head and remember I'm on the rebound and that geography—and reality—are conspiring to ensure this won't last.

It's not like I've really thought about a future with Cooper. With my romantic history, I know better than to do that. But even if I had considered one, he's not in the same stage of life as I am. He's in the *all-my-friends-are-getting-married-and-having-babies* stage. I'm in the *all-my-friends-*

have-realized-he-was-actually-a-narcissistic-asshole-and-getting-divorced stage.

I won't burst his thirties bubble.

Another busy day of diving is wrapping up. Cooper's yellow speaker cranks out its customary classic rock while we clean. As we work diligently to finish out the day, wetsuits are partially peeled back like banana skins as we tidy and put away.

We work to the sound of the one album every single one of us can agree on (Led Zeppelin's legendary album *IV*) eager for hot showers and generous suppers.

When my last piece of equipment is stashed, I finally remove the neoprene encasement that's been making me itch.

Hanging it on the hook of my equipment locker, I enjoy the first rush of air on my skin.

I've been doubling up on my dives: wearing athletic shorts over swim bottoms under my wetsuit. Partly for modesty, mostly to prevent chafing. Spotting sweatpants in my bag, the thought occurs to me that it'd feel a whole lot better wearing *them* than wet shorts on my walk back to my room. A quick pan of the deck and I confirm that no one is in line of sight. Even if they were, it's not like I'm naked underneath.

I turn to face my locker and decide to make quick work of it. I peel off the clingy Lycra shorts and they drop in a wet heap. In my haste to bend and retrieve them, I feel my bathing suit bottoms ride up. Cool air kisses both butt cheeks. I quickly thumb the fabric, pulling it back over my ass and restoring modesty with a gentle tug of both hands.

Grabbing my oversized pants, I work fast to slip the generous fabric over my thighs, resorting to rolling down the waistband several times when the fabric swims on me.

Turning, on autopilot as I gather my things, I stop short and freeze when I find Cooper standing a few meters away.

He's watching me, face clad with an uncharacteristically serious expression. He takes a swallow, panning the length of me with hooded eyes, as Robert Plant sings about levees breaking and Bonham bangs on drums.

We stand for a few seconds in silence, my pulse thrums in time with the bass.

Crap. Did he just see…?

My heart gives a legitimate schoolgirl flutter when I remember his earlier words to me.

"I'm a YOUR ass man."

My entire body grows hot.

He adjusts the front of his wetsuit.

Oops.

"I'm just gonna…" I point a thumb in the general direction of elsewhere.

"Uhm." A muscle flexes in his jaw. His face turns an unprecedented shade of pink.

Cooper is definitely *not* fine.

I'm only in my cabin for a few seconds before I hear knocking.

I'm no fool; I know exactly who it is before I open the door, and it's a full-on moral dilemma as two sides of me battle it out at the doorway. My sensible side tells me letting him into my cabin is not advisable—certainly not in keeping with the *let's keep things professional here* policy I've adopted thus far. My other is asking, *Um, woman, have you seen him?*

Turns out, I don't get to decide.

The moment I open it, the door is pushed aside and Cooper waltzes in.

I quickly check left, then right, to make sure no one's witnessed it before I let the door fall closed behind us.

"Sure, by all means, come right in." I'm a little taken aback by his assertiveness. I mean, the man is always bold, but this crosses into brazen territory.

He spins on his heels to face me. "You knew exactly what you were doing back there!"

Wait, is he mad?

He certainly seems heated.

My brow furrows. "What are you talking about?"

"I'm trying to stay professional here, and you're exposing your hot little ass!" His eyes light up like a beacon as he emphasizes *hot* and his tone gets slightly guttural when he says *ass*.

I cross my arms, slightly indignant. "Well, isn't this typical male behaviour? I was wearing a bathing suit, for fuck's sake. Skin exposed for mere seconds. I put on pants. Get a hold of yourself."

Wait. Did he say hot?

Little?

Hot little?

"Oh yes...parading around in your hot little grey sweatpants. All low-hanging and shit..." He grimaces as he glances down where my rolled waistband rests on my hips.

He's said *hot little* twice.

He looks physically pained.

His face and his words are not matching up If not for these helpful adjectives, I'd be thinking he was horrified, maybe even disgusted.

"What?" I gesture down the front of myself. "They're *sweatpants!*"

I know about the Legend of the Grey Sweatpants™—the alleged godlike transformation of the average male when the garment is worn—but I've never subscribed to that theory. I've certainly never heard about this in reverse. Are grey sweatpants on women a *thing*?

He waves at me emphatically with one hand. "You're all abs, ink, and bikini top. And those goddamned grey sweatpants that look like they'd only need a wee tug from my hands to come right down."

Oh, my.

Yep, apparently a thing.

With one sentence, my need to check his clichéd male behaviour over what I'm wearing transforms into a new need to…well…feel his hands tugging my sweatpants down.

"Wait, I have abs?" My hand skims my torso, in search of them. Perhaps also in search of one good reason why Cooper's hands aren't on them.

Cooper takes a step forward. "Yes." His breath catches on the way in, making him gently shudder.

I always compare myself to Young Violet, who was built like a brick shithouse. To my eyes, any abs I may have once had were hidden long ago by extra pounds and lost to lack of discipline. Present Violet has softer curves. I certainly have a strong core from daily, hard physical work, but now there's only a hint of shadow where muscles form. In my opinion, one would have to look carefully to find them.

The expression on Cooper's face tells me he's been looking quite carefully.

"And I imagined running my tongue along them about a dozen times while you wiggled your sweet fucking hips to 'Misty Mountain Hop.'"

Oh.

Fuck.

The cabin seems to shrink suddenly, air becoming thick and difficult to breathe.

"You really shouldn't be in here, Cooper."

My legs step toward him of their own accord.

"Doesn't the *shouldn't* part make it better?" The sinful smile he gives me threatens to incinerate my bathing suit bottoms and set fire to my pants.

I release a nervously excited laugh. "Christ, you're bold."

We can't do this.

I give myself a mental pep talk.

But my mind immediately imagines doing *this.*

In fact, I find myself searching the tiny room for the perfect spot to do *this* but quickly snap out of it.

"Are you asking me to hold my tongue, Violet? I thought it was your favourite part."

My cheeks grow hot, my heart thumps in time with a new pulse between my legs. Several parts of me awaken, throbbing and tingling entirely without my permission, like they've heard him say it too.

Cooper flashes a cocky grin. He knows.

"You shouldn't have come to my cabin."

"Would you rather come in my cabin instead?" He gestures coyly to the door.

"What? No. That's not—"

He bites his bottom lip, holding back a grin.

He's already turned me on; now he's attempting to fluster me out of my clothes.

"Don't turn my words around." I try—and fail—to keep a straight face.

"Oh, you're gonna love it when I turn things around." He raises a brow.

Dear god.

I remember the feel of his hot hands on my ass, positions proposed in that pretty pink cabin of ours.

I consider them all over again now.

Cooper steps toward me. Just a small step. It feels like a test of the waters. One foot in to check the temperature, assessing the response.

"V." It's all he says. Not a statement, not a question. Just a cue for me to decide.

He takes one more step. The move feels daring in these small quarters. We're only inches away from each other, but somehow, I know this is his last. If we're to close this gap, it's up to me to take those steps.

I've never done anything like this at work. Even in my younger years, with opportunities abound, I've always kept a distinct separation between business and pleasure. I've carefully conducted myself with exemplary performance and behaviour, the epitome of professionalism. That level of conduct is just part of my character, an inextricable part of who Violet Thomas is. But if I'm being honest, it's also because—as a woman among men—my bar is set higher.

Part of me fears the fallout: What if we get caught?

But a bigger part of me is curious. It hears the voice in my head that's telling me to be bold. To be more like Cooper. To *live*.

Sure, play it safe outside of this cabin, where it's paramount—when lives are at stake. But in here? Life is short, death is just one failed dive or one unfortunate fall away, there's no time to waste.

It took courage for me to walk to his cabin those weeks ago. To risk—and yes, relinquish—my pride on a glorified booty call.

"Fuck it," I mutter, drawing from that same reservoir of courage now as I uncross my arms and close the gap.

CHAPTER 38

 In two determined strides I'm on him, taking his jaw in my hands and kissing him hard enough to knock teeth.

Cooper sighs when he touches me, and it makes my entire body hum with delight.

He hesitates only seconds, waiting until we've found our rhythm—tongues stroking and mouths biting—before reaching to pull down my pants.

We laugh against each other's lips.

"Fucking pants," he manages to mutter mid-kiss.

He was right. Just a tug from his hands sends them falling to my feet. It feels like my centre of gravity goes with them, knocking me off balance until I brace myself against the closest wall.

The reflection of my movements and the feel of my palms hitting cool glass shock me. I'd forgotten about the wall of mirror.

"Shit, are you alright?" Cooper asks from behind me.

"Yes." I laugh at myself.

I look up at the reflection of him behind me in the mirror and watch as our smiles transform to something else. Eyeing one another in the glass, I see a shift from playful amusement to darkness and decadence. Something electric arcs between us.

I move to step away.

"Don't." His voice is deep and demanding.

My chest tightens in response.

Bending down behind me, he helps me step out of the loose pool of jersey fabric that's entrapped me. He stands, tossing them aside.

When his eyes find mine again in the mirror, I relax against his warm chest.

"Take your hair down," he asks. "Please."

I pull at the elastic of my messy bun and let my violet-tipped mane fall.

Channeling the dexterity and efficiency of, well…a welder…he removes my damp racer-back bathing suit top. It's nothing like the borderline shoulder-dislocating effort it usually is.

I rearrange my messy hair, letting it sit modestly across my chest.

Cooper watches his own hands in our reflection as he pulls my hair behind my shoulders, then carefully studies me—mostly naked—in the mirror. Only my black bathing suit bottoms remain.

I squirm a little under his gaze, focusing my eyes on him so I don't need to see myself.

He steps back, peeling off his graphic tee with the classic, male, one-hand-over-the-back pull. Then I get to watch as the universe's gift to the denim industry removes his well-worn jeans.

He doesn't stop there.

I study him like he's a masterpiece, a work of art in

ropey forearms, muscle, and tan, as his thumbs slot under the waistband of his grey boxer-briefs and pull them down.

He calls *me* incredible. It's absurd.

Cooper confidently steps up behind me. His sparkling turquoise eyes laser-focus on my reflection, and the power of them forces me to swallow.

It's clear he's not the least bit uncomfortable on display and thank god (and his exemplary genes) for it. But I think he notices I am.

"I love your body."

I should love it too.

This body has been faithful to me through hundreds of dives, carrying me through so many professional and personal struggles, but I still cringe a little when he says it.

Turns out, I'm a fraud.

I send inspirational memes daily to Greta, reminding her to embrace her curves. I celebrate each personal best Bella achieves at the gym. And while I know everybody, *every body*, is beautiful…when I say it about myself, I struggle sometimes to believe it.

"I love these tattoos." He runs the knuckles of one hand along the vines on my ribcage and it makes me shiver.

"And your bellybutton." He watches himself circle it with a single finger. I've always thought it looked strange—part "innie" and part "outie."

"And this spot right here." He runs the finger back up between my teardrop breasts. "It was made for my mouth."

My nipples grow hard under his examination.

His fingers fall to the edge of my bathing suit bottoms. They tease, pulling at the stretchy fabric, but going no further.

"They're damp," I choke out nervously, breaking my conspicuous silence.

What am I even saying right now?

"Are they?" Mischief flares in his eyes. "I've not even started."

Nerves, like bubbles, flitter in my stomach.

There's not been a single day since I met Cooper that he hasn't levelled me with surprise, maybe even intimidated me with his unrivalled charisma. Up to now, he's managed to snare me in his net without even trying, without more than a joke and a smile. It occurs to me in this moment what powers he may have been holding in reserve. Charms and seductions that—if applied with an ounce of real effort —could be downright insurmountable.

The thought terrifies and thrills me in equal measure.

"Let's see about that." He winks.

Buckle up.

From his place behind me, Cooper reaches to skim a finger across the fabric gusset of my swimsuit. It makes my crotch ache and my knees weak. I let my eyes close, and my head fall back against his shoulder, submitting to his support.

He goes for a second pass, and the contact sends a pang to my lower belly. My body trembles.

On the third, he plunges his hand right down the front of my suit, finally—thankfully—skin against skin.

The skim of his lips against my ear mimics the agonizing, delicate trace of his finger as it brushes against me.

"Yep." His whisper sends goosebumps across my skin. "Nice and wet."

Already a heady mix of sensations, his words nearly incapacitate me with lust.

I need more of him. More touch, more taste, more everything.

I grab at the Lycra and pull. I can't get my bathing suit bottoms off fast enough.

When I bend over to pry them off my feet, Cooper paws

at me, capitalizing on my position to grope and fondle my ass.

"Fuck." He growls, grinding against me.

Standing back up, I catch his face in the mirror. I can only describe what I witness as a building smolder, and I notice it perfectly matches mine.

Reaching around to hold his head, I twist to kiss him. In this position it's almost impossible, a clumsy dance of tongues and teeth.

Cooper's large, calloused hands coast over my hips and stomach. Rough and hot, they scratch an itch I didn't know I had. Drifting up, they cradle my breasts, fingers finding my nipples and coaxing me to moan. I pull away from his biting kiss to look in the mirror.

We both watch as he works his hands.

"Look at you. God, you're so gorgeous."

With a rush of shyness, I look away, but he takes my face in his hand and gently turns it back toward our reflection.

"Watch us," he says softly. "See how good we look together."

I've heard words like these before and never really taken them in. Empty words meant to placate me and turn me on. They never do. But there's something about Cooper's tone, his inherent honesty, that makes me look at myself differently this time—makes me try to see with his eyes.

We're a tangled knot of lust and skin. His dark tan is a beautiful contrast to my paler complexion. He's a blank canvas, I'm a work of ink. Fresh-kissed lips grace flushed and fevered faces. My easy curves rest against the hard planes of his built physique.

We're beautiful.

I slide a hand over one of his, weaving our fingers and delivering a gentle squeeze. Then I pull it down with mine, smoothing slowly over my stomach until we land together between my thighs. I leave it there, a silent instruction, telling him what I need.

I watch us, rapt. Two stars in our own X-rated movie. One hand works at my breast, the other builds an intolerable heat. Just as I'm about to submit, he gives a stern "*no.*"

He stops abruptly.

"You're not coming 'til I'm inside you."

Inside me.

"Shit." I freeze. "We don't have any condoms."

"Shit," he echoes. "Okay. That's okay." He moves us into position, back to our silver screen, about to resume play.

"I have an IUD." The words tumble out. I twist to face him. "And I just had my bloodwork done. Everything was fine."

We linger on pause.

He raises a brow. "I had mine done last break."

"And?" I ask.

"All came back okay."

I hesitate for just a moment.

He interprets it as doubt. "Listen, we don't have—"

"I want you."

A smug smile crosses his face. "I know you do."

"No, you *don't* know." My tone is part playful, part pissed. I want to do something unexpected, to knock *him* off kilter for a change. "Let me finish my sentence."

Surprise lights up his eyes.

"I want you…to bend me over that stool in the corner and make me scream your name."

I shock him speechless.

Within the span of a heartbeat, the stool is hauled in front of us.

I'm ordered to fold, arms down, ass up. My fingers cling to the wooden seat.

In just seconds he's buried inside me, watching us, pulling my hair back so I watch too.

He delivers slow, hard thrusts that match each of my breaths.

The fullness of him as he takes me from behind is almost too much.

It will never be enough.

We come together in a sweaty, steep ascent, but in the end it's *him* who screams *my* name.

CHAPTER 39

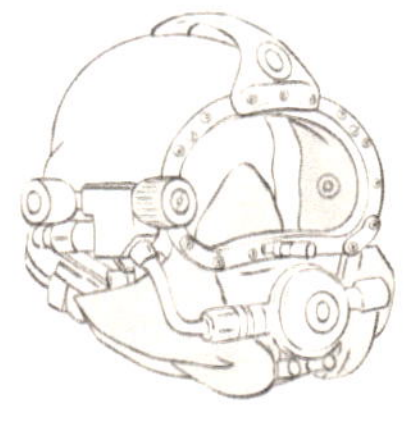

Bruce's scarred, leathery hand grabs the shaker in front of me, then applies salt to his eggs. He's been dining with us more often since Steve left us, even more post-Bob.

Bigot Bob has been replaced by Pierre, a French-Canadian diver with a fabulous accent and a penchant for bringing his own jar of maple syrup with him everywhere he goes.

Pierre is highly skilled and capital-T-for-Team-Player. We love almost everything about him. Everything except that he told Cooper about an old pop star from Quebec named Mitsou, and her song "Bye Bye Mon Cowboy" has now made it into the yellow speaker's rotation.

That damn yellow speaker is going to end up in the drink.

"Don't worry, Cooper." Bruce shovels a forkful into his mouth. "Violet can tell you exactly what to do."

My temperature elevates.

Flow monitoring, Violet. He's talking about flow monitoring.

He takes a swig of his coffee. "And she'll give the what, where, and when, with the injections."

A piece of egg slips down my windpipe, and I cough.

"Mon Dieu." Pierre smacks my back with his hand. "You're okay, non?"

I drink from my water glass. "Yeah. Good. Fine." My voice is hoarse.

Pierre settles back into his chair beside me, gluttonously pours more maple syrup over his pancakes.

Intuitively, my eyes find Cooper's across the table. He's biting back a grin. He gives me a quick, secret wink and it makes the nape of my neck tingle, evoking memories of the delicious pressure created there as he tugged my hair… head held back…telling me to watch.

"Are you okay, V? You're sweating."

I turn to the end of the table, where JT—the observant little bugger—is sitting with a devious, knowing expression. The guy misses nothing. Thankfully everyone else's eyes are on their breakfast plates.

The injections that Bruce is referring to are chemicals that stimulate flow. In the oil and gas industry, more companies are employing chemical injection processes as a means to improve production capacities, increase viscosity, and prevent corrosion along the flow stream. It's one of the lesser-known activities that we perform on the rig.

"When you're getting started, there's always a risk of over-injecting. Just keep that in mind." I note, eager to get back to business.

"Got that, Coop?" JT quips across the table. "Don't get over-excited."

The entire table waits, watching Bruce for a reaction.

When he starts to snicker, the group erupts in laughter.

It's abundantly clear that it will not be possible for these goons to talk about any aspect of this activity without ridiculous inuendo.

"JT." Bruce stands, lifting his tray of empty dishes. "Thanks for volunteering for clean-up detail."

Once he's out of earshot, JT mutters. "Yeah, yeah... what's your line, Coop? *'Worth it'*?"

Cooper flashes a bright, white smile directly at me. "Yep. Worth it."

The warmth of it wraps around me like a blanket. I smile back, knowing the sparkle in his eyes is meant just for me.

"They know, Violet."

"All of them know?"

"Yes, they know."

We're wedged into the single bottom level of the bunk beds in my cabin, but neither of us is complaining. Not when our position of choice these days seems to be on top of each other.

I sigh in resignation.

I'd been lulled into a false sense of discretion, given that we all have private rooms on this platform. I'd figured since no one was aware of Cooper's comings and goings, they were none the wiser. It's not a big deal, I suppose. Like JT said, it's not the first time in the history of the world something like this has happened. What's more important is that we've been careful in front of the others—ensuring it's not impacting our work performance or group dynamic—and we informed Bruce about things as soon as we got back to the rig.

What wasn't part of the discussion with Bruce was any "fraternizing" on company time. Every time we do this, we're taking a chance. We've promised ourselves it won't happen again, over and over. The little pact we make each time he sneaks out of my cabin just ends up being a powerful aphrodisiac.

"Who cares?" Cooper's arm tightens around me.

"Spoken like a man," I retort.

"Hey, those guys have nothing but respect for you. And JT is thrilled."

I bury my face in Cooper's chest. "Oh, god, did he say something to you?" My voice is muffled by warm skin.

Cringe.

"Something about making sure I put your needs first."

"Oh, god." I cuddle closer. If I could be *inside* of his chest right now, it would be ideal.

Cooper laughs. "He didn't mean it as it sounds. He was serious. I think this had something to do with Vampire Accountant."

I need to pull my face away, due to lack of oxygen. "JT wasn't his biggest fan."

"I get the feeling you weren't either?" he asks, brows narrowed in confusion. "Which is odd, considering…"

"It was complicated."

He brushes a strand of hair away from my face. "Try me."

Where do I even start?

Charles was an exercise in futility. But if I've learned anything these past few weeks, it's that the real person to blame isn't Charles, it's me.

"While it's tempting to point a finger in Vamp—*Charles's*—direction, I have only myself to blame for sticking it out with someone for three years when I wasn't even being seen."

Wow. Admitting that out loud feels big.

A sense of lightness follows.

"Well, shit." Cooper strokes my hair. My eyes close from the comforting weight of his hand.

"But here's the thing." When I reopen my eyes, Cooper

is watching me, hanging on my every word. That's what's wonderful about Cooper: his unrivalled ability to make everyone feel like the centre of his world.

He nudges my naked knee with his under the sheets.

I let out a long breath. "I never asked."

"Never asked?"

"Never asked for what I wanted, never told him what I needed." I run a hand along his smooth chest. "Early on in our relationship I told him I liked light roast coffee. He wasn't a coffee drinker…"

"Wait. Vampire Accountant also didn't like *coffee*? Who the hell even is this guy?"

"One doesn't *have* to like coffee. It's a personal preference."

"We're going to have to agree to disagree about this. Anyway, go on."

"He wasn't a coffee drinker," I repeat. "So, he probably thought *coffee is coffee.* The first time he bought one for me, he picked up a dark roast. I hate dark roast, but he'd gone out of his way to get it for me, which was so kind, I couldn't tell him I didn't like it. But then the next week he did it again, and then again. He kept doing it. Each time I sucked back a strong tasting, bitter coffee that I *didn't* like rather than tell him what I *did.*"

"Well, if that's not a metaphor for a bad relationship, I don't know what is." Cooper sighs.

"Right?"

We sit in a comfortable silence for a few seconds. Cooper strokes his rough hand along my arm. Back and forth, like the rhythmic ebb and flow of the sea.

I'm forty years old and I have zero experience with pillow talk. I've either had empty sexual relationships, or Charles. The unprecedented honesty that's happening between us is throwing me a little, mostly because I really like it.

He rises to one elbow and looks at me intently.

"So, then, practice with me," he says softly.

"Practice?"

"Yes."

"With you?"

"That's right." He turns more toward me, letting one leg twine with mine. "Tell me what you like."

We've been lying here unclothed together all evening, but the stark new nakedness I feel at this moment is telling. No one's ever really taken the time to get to know me, to learn what I like—frankly, to even *ask*.

My belly flutters. Heat suddenly fills our close quarters, as if someone's just turned off the AC.

I kick a foot out from the sheets.

Cooper peels back the covers instead.

The instant rush of cool is a relief.

He kisses me once, gently, with his ridiculously soft lips.

I study him, running a finger along his brow. When I do, he smiles tenderly.

"No assumptions, no looking for signals, no reading between the lines." His voice is as soft as his kiss. "Teach me in here, just like you do out there."

I let the moment hang, enjoying our connection, in no rush to speak.

Cooper waits patiently, like we've got all the time in the world; there's nowhere else he'd rather be.

"I like light roast coffee," I begin.

"Yeah, you do," he says with a smile.

I smile back. "And honey in my tea."

"Keep going, honey."

"And full-body kisses." I point to the hollow of my throat. "That start right here..."

He moves my hand aside and plants a single chaste kiss, following with his unchaste tongue.

My breath hitches.

I run my finger between my breasts. "And trail along here..."

Like an apt pupil, his lips follow, showing that he's listening, giving me exactly what I want.

I'm quiet for a few seconds, revelling in the long line of kisses he drops down my stomach. Pressing my own lips together nervously, I worry I might be getting greedy—that I'm about to go too far—then I direct my right hand between my legs. "And end right here."

He studies me with an unreadable expression.

My face grows hot. Have I been too bold?

But in the next moment, he slips off the end of the tiny bed, taking to his knees. My belly flutters as he pulls me by the hips, sets one leg over a shoulder, then takes the other firmly in hand. With one long swipe of his tongue, my head's sent spinning. My body twitches as he works to taste and tease. He lingers at one magnificent spot, eliciting a gasp. Pausing, he plants one incongruously sweet kiss to my inner thigh.

"You know," he says, looking up at me. "There's nothing I won't give you, if you'd only ask."

I draw in a shaky breath, reaching to cup his handsome cheek.

Sure, I'll show him around the platform, all the *whats, wheres, and whens* of the job. I'll tell him exactly how to touch me, what it takes to steal my breath. But in this moment, maybe *he's* the instructor, teaching me how to love.

CHAPTER 40

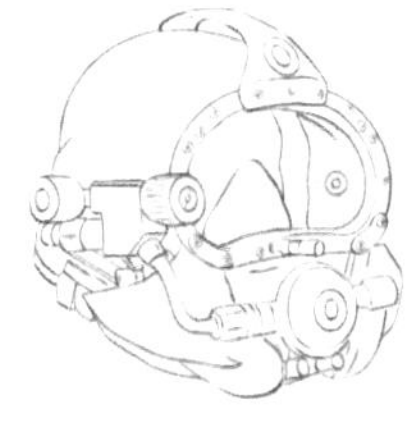

"You still don't know where he's from?"

I cradle my cell phone against my shoulder, grabbing a banana and adding it to my tray. "No, and he doesn't know where I'm from either." I narrowly avoid another platform worker as I turn toward the tables. "Oops. Sorry, dude."

"Sorry for what?" Greta asks.

"Not you, that was…Bobby…I think that's his name."

"So weird. Are those things like little cities?" I hear a drill or similar power tool on her end of the line. Greta's already hard at work, solving the world's electrical problems.

"Sometimes. Always new faces. Sometimes hundreds of people. It can be hard to keep names straight."

Platform life isn't for everyone. People are attracted to the pay rate, but when the reality of the job sets in and they've spent real time away from home, it can take a toll.

"So, what…you're not even a little bit interested in knowing where he's from?"

"Of *course* I'm interested." I settle into a seat, choosing the farthest table so I can eat my breakfast in peace. "One time Cooper left his wallet on the lunch table," I speak softly, so no one else will hear. "Just a snap of my wrist and I could've had my answer. But I resisted."

"This is very weird, V."

"No, it's not."

And—in the grand scheme of things—it actually isn't. We're a transient bunch. It's not unusual for a group of people who are forced together by the nature of their work to not readily share. I worked with JT for two years before I knew his last name. (*Smith*, of all things!) It's funny, in some ways we know each other better than our partners, but under other circumstances, we'd probably pass each other on the street.

"You know where Pierre's from."

I take a spoonful of hot porridge, then blow on it before taking the bite. "None of us had a choice—he wears it on his sleeve."

"Maybe Cooper is Canadian." Greta yells at someone in the background, then returns to me. "Sorry, V."

"Wait, free health care *and* Cooper Brooks? How lucky can one country be?"

We share a snicker.

"So, you're telling me that it's never even come up?"

"Sort of. He tried to tell me the other day."

"And?"

"I suggested he stop talking and do something else with his mouth."

"Daaamn. That'll do it." Greta giggles.

I giggle too, remembering how I had cut each sentence off with a kiss:

"I live on the east side of—"

Stopped by a long, hard peck.

"Just south of—"

Another salacious strike…this time with an ass-grab and a suck of his bottom lip.

"My building's been reno—"

I grab his face with my hands, and slide my tongue past his lips.

By the time I'd pulled away, he didn't remember what day of the week it was, let alone the topic at hand.

"I love seeing this side of you, V."

"My cougar side, is that what you're saying?"

"Cougar? What? No." She sounds confused.

"The age difference…" I remind her.

"I actually forgot about that. More just this version of you, full of life and sass."

Is this true?

These last few weeks it's felt like I've resurfaced too fast, ignored all my depth charts and dive tables and taken ridiculous chances.

When I don't reply, Greta fills the silence. "Aren't you interested in getting to know him? In seeing where things might go?"

A cold panic hits with the mere suggestion.

Arm's length is a comfortable place. A safe distance after the sting of three years of drawn-out rejection. I know there's no comparison between them—Charles and Cooper couldn't be more different. But there is one common denominator. Me. Violet Thomas and her crappy judgement. I've demonstrated it can't be trusted. Flirty texts and fondling are one thing, knowing where he's built a life is another. It's wading into dangerous waters, an easy descent to imagining myself there with him.

"I'm not interested in spending another three years slowly losing myself."

Greta gives an interested hum. "Seems to me that since Cooper came along, you've been more yourself than ever."

"Are you kidding me?" I drop my spoon into my bowl. "I'm taking insane chances at work, I shouted a dear friend's sexual orientation because I couldn't keep my mouth shut, and I've been just shy of screaming *fuck the patriarchy* in the company of you girls. I'm rather unhinged these days, G."

"Hey, just because it's a little messy doesn't mean it's not who you really are."

Well, shit.

I don't even know what to say to this.

Cooper enters the galley, a dizzying display of David Bowie T-shirt and distressed denim. He scratches his belly pensively, contemplating his next meal.

I imagine *him* as mine.

Just weeks ago, those abs were like Bora Bora: exotic, unknown territory that I could only hope to visit one day. Since then, I've planted my flag in those abs, marked them with nails and teeth. Surrendering them—him—at the end of Patrick's paternity leave will be harder than I'd like to admit.

I'm growing too attached.

"Greta, I've gotta go."

Who am I kidding?

By the time that happens, this little fling will have already run out of road. I'll go back to my life and Cooper will move on with his.

CHAPTER 41

I toy with the dog-eared pages of yet another washed-up National Geographic. This one may have literally washed up. It must be standard offshore platform chic: another day, another windowed rig office, another exhausted magazine. Here's hoping this team meeting isn't as unpleasant as the last.

Summoned by Bruce, we all stand awkwardly, exchanging nervous glances.

Is this a long overdue lecture?

Bruce's moment to chastise us for our group snit?

But that doesn't seem like him. Bruce is very much "what you see is what you get."

Pierre checks the forecast on his cell phone but confirms that no troubling weather is on our track. No hazardous conditions are about to send us home.

I glance over at Cooper, who raises a questioning brow. With no intel to offer, I give him a resigned shrug.

Surely this isn't about *us*?

Nah, Bruce would never bring everyone in if it was.

Would he?

Lauren expels an annoyed huff. "He calls us all together and then leaves us here for thirty minutes to stew?"

Ah, see…now that's *totally* Bruce. Always the dramatic entrance after an extended pause.

As if on cue, he enters, bringing the loud sounds of the platform in when the door opens.

"Sorry for the wait, guys." He drops a black hard-cased tablet on the counter. Silence returns when the door closes with a thud behind him.

"Just some updates and announcements to make. Thought it'd be best done here."

Everyone exchanges curious looks. Thankfully, Bruce cuts straight to the chase.

"First, Steve." Bruce crosses his arms and takes a wide stance. "He's doing well and will be returning to the team at the start of the next two-week cycle."

We all sigh with relief, but then turn instinctively to Pierre.

"Le top," Pierre replies, defaulting to his native French. He nods and gives a soft smile.

Poor Pierre.

Bruce—former military man who's all business and practicality—wouldn't think to pull him aside and share this news with him privately first. It's hard not to feel bad for him. His time with us has been brief, but it's been a seamless integration with our team. He will be missed.

I'm so preoccupied with Pierre, I don't register Bruce's next words immediately.

"Next, Patrick."

Patrick.

Wait, what?

"Patrick and his partner have decided it's best for their family if his partner resumes leave. Unfortunately, they're not in a position where both can be off work, so Patrick is returning early to the team."

The entire room shrinks down to Bruce's face, my balance hinging on what he says next.

"Fortunately, another great crew is looking for *two* replacements, so Cooper and Pierre will have the opportunity to join them together."

Fortunately.

Great.

Opportunity.

All words that seem completely out of place with this moment.

My chest tightens. I have trouble swallowing. I lean back against the counter for support.

What the fuck?

I look over at Cooper.

His face falls for a moment before he delivers a Hollywood smile. "You hear that, Pierre? Looks like me, you, and Mitsou are taking a ride."

Oh god. The yellow speaker. Worn-out concert tees. Classic rock and Cooper's unrivalled light. All things that have become inextricably linked with the joy of the platform.

I narrow my focus to the floor, gripping the laminate work top.

It wasn't supposed to happen so soon.

We had weeks—no, *months*—left to go.

I lift my eyes to Bruce. "When?" It's the only word I can manage.

Bruce stands taller, all business, but I see the regret in his eyes. Everyone loves Cooper; even the boss isn't immune to his charms. "Next cycle," he says softly.

His words hit like a winter dive.

The team's leaving the rig for break tomorrow.

We only have one night.

"What suit is trump?" JT asks, adjusting the cards in his hands.

"Hearts," Cooper answers. I catch it when his eyes flash over to me.

An impromptu card tournament has been put together to mark Cooper and Pierre's last night with the team. Sadly, there's no alcohol to numb the sting, but what we don't have in booze, we more than make up for in sugar and shenanigans. There's even a cake.

Euchre isn't the only game being played tonight. Cooper is doing a fine job of pretending nothing's different, and I'm acting like everything's going exactly according to plan.

It's not.

But if the last three years have proven anything, it's that I'm a master at this game.

JT and Pierre are partnered up against Nick and Cooper. The best part of the night is hearing Pierre's Quebecois swear words every time he loses a round. Nick and Cooper are making sure that this happens often.

Lauren and I watch and wait our turn to play the winners.

At the next table, a few other platform workers, including Clayton and James, are enjoying their own boisterous match. Their game is put on hold while someone mops up a spilled beverage. Boisterous indeed.

I try fruitlessly to ignore Cooper, and when my gaze inevitably finds him across the table, he gives me a smile that doesn't quite reach his eyes.

When the cake runs out and euchre winds down, we scatter like papers in the platform wind.

I stand to collect my things. "Off to bed—early day tomorrow," I mutter to absolutely no one.

I don't even know what I'm saying, because every goddamn day is an early one for us.

I only manage to grab my phone before Cooper is standing beside me.

"We should talk."

My phone and stomach both drop to the floor.

"Shit." As I reach to grab it, Cooper does too.

The spicy smell that I now know is his deodorant fills my nose, sending me straight back to a dozen heated moments spent alone with him.

Maybe I can track down his brand and huff it on lonely winter nights.

Pathetic.

Yep. New low.

In my anti-perspirant haze, Cooper beats me to my phone. We stand in unison, and when he hands it to me, he doesn't let go.

Sure, it's a playful tactic, but I'm not the least bit in the mood.

"Give me the phone, Cooper."

He surrenders it, folding his arms. It only accentuates his biceps.

My hands itch to touch them.

I avert my gaze.

Turning back toward the table, I collect my cup and plate.

"Are you…angry with me?"

Oh god, just the sound of his voice makes my chest ache —all the disappointment in it.

When smell, sight, and sound are off the table, what the hell is left?

Bolstering my courage with a deep breath, I turn to face him. "I'm not mad, I'm just…tired."

And I am. It's been only twelve hours since we heard the news, and I'm already tired of wishing things were different. Tired of wishing it didn't have to end. Tired of wondering why we were foolish enough to start in the first place.

Cooper checks over his shoulder, making sure the coast is clear. "Can I come over?"

"I don't think it's a good idea."

Maybe this was *never* a good idea.

"But we might not get the chance—"

"Goodnight, Cooper," I cut him off mid-sentence.

I head back to my room and kick into autopilot, packing my bags and preparing to leave a platform and a man behind. It's as familiar to me as knitting, as innate as knit and purl.

As I wash my face at the mirror, I tell myself I don't want him to visit my cabin. And really, it's true. I don't. It's easier this way. After cutting him off the way I did, I don't deserve his attention anyway.

But it still disappoints me when a knock never sounds on the door.

CHAPTER 42

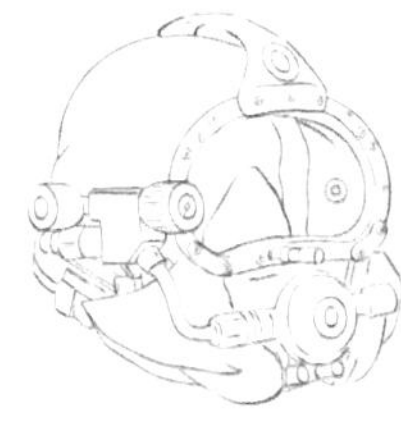

The *thwack, thwack, thwack* of rotor blades is the soundtrack to our snark. The entire group is grumpy as we're transported to the mainland. JT gesticulates over his seatbelt. Lauren laments lost sunglasses. Pierre punctuates his sentences with "esti," which—just based on his tone and emphasis—must mean worse than it sounds.

Cooper and I remain silent, staring out opposite windows, submitting to the lift of the helicopter as it whisks us away.

When we land, it's a bit of a skirmish as gear is located and claimed, and the next team loads up as we're cleared.

I say my goodbyes to the crew, patting Pierre on the back as I pass him.

Taking advantage of Cooper's distraction, I sneak past while he's talking to the guys. I can send him a polite good-bye-text later. Maybe we'll even have some friendly back-and-forth for a few days, until regular life takes over and ten messages a day scale back to two.

It's a tale as old as time: the best of intentions to stay in touch, but zero stamina to see it through. In my version of this story, a cute barista catches his eye at the local café and enchants him with her effervescence and extra cookies. Eventually, I'll be forgotten, so why not just skip to the end?

It's one steel-toed boot in front of the other to get far away, fast.

Clack, clack, clack. My wheelie case hits every crack in the pavement.

It becomes my single focus.

This was only a fling.

No promises made.

Nothing ever expected.

I get to the far edge of the helipad—almost home free—before a large, warm hand grabs my forearm. Startled, I spin round.

"You weren't just going to leave, were you?" A look of panic is on Cooper's face.

I ignore every instinct to make things better, to kiss it all away.

"You were busy. I was going to text you."

"*Text* me?"

It's hard to decide whose lips made it sound more ridiculous.

"We have shit to talk about, V." He removes his mirrored sunglasses. Fatigue colours every corner of his face—dark circles under his eyes, wrinkles to his brow, a strange pallor to his cheeks.

Shit. I've been so caught up in my own crisis, I stopped being a friend.

I know Bruce will make sure he lands on his feet, but Cooper's been thrown for a loop work wise, and I'm too busy building emotional walls to check in on him and see.

I step toward him. "Are you okay? The job…"

He laughs, taking a step backward. "I don't care about the job, Violet. This is about you and me."

I can't read his face. Is it sadness or regret? Or worse…is it guilt I see?

"It's fine. *We're* fine." I shrug. "We knew what we were getting into."

I want to melt into the tarmac.

His face drops. "And what exactly is that?" He slips his sunglasses back on, defensive.

I glance around awkwardly, feeling oddly like the younger one between us, being called out like this.

"No strings or obligations." My face grows unbearably hot under his examination and the mid-day sun.

He drops his duffle on the ground beside himself, rests his fists on his hips. I was expecting a lightening of his countenance, not frowns and pursed lips.

"Is that really what you think I want?" He seems to grow in height; I shrink two feet.

At a loss for anything else to say, I opt for brutal honesty. "I think you could have any*thing* or a*nyone* you want, and in real life I doubt very much that's me."

"Real life." He echoes contemplatively, nodding.

"Uhm," I mutter, waffling under the scrutiny and heat. A bead of sweat trails down my neck. "Do we really need to do this *here*?" I grimace.

I'm low-key panicking. I need to change the setting, change the scene, change the script.

Cooper grabs his bag and straightens. All ten feet of him standing proud. "We're changing our flights. Neither one of us is going anywhere until you've had a taste of Cooper in *real life*."

He boldly walks past, headed for the terminal door.

Well, shit.

That door's my only way out of here.

I have no choice but to follow.

"We're also going to need a reservation at the hotel restaurant," Cooper tells the front desk clerk at the airport hotel.

Apparently, I—like most women—have zero willpower when it comes to Cooper Brooks. Because here I stand, a willing participant in a new game he's labelled "the real life," awaiting our room key.

With a smile, he has us checking in early. A wink gets us upgraded to a suite. One sexy lean across the reception desk and our clerk offers to send up a bottle of their finest.

I'd roll my eyes if he wasn't so damn sweet.

A porter loads our gear onto a cart while Cooper and I scroll flight options on our phones. By the time our elevator lets us off on the top floor, I've spent two hundred dollars in change fees to switch my flight home.

When Cooper opens the suite door, I consider it money well spent.

We're both stunned by the five-star amenities stretched out before us after being confined to our tiny cabins at sea.

I raise a brow sceptically. "Real life, hey?"

Cooper just giggles, and then splays himself like Macaulay Culkin across the king-sized bed.

Trudging over to a chair, I flop down in it and work to get my cumbersome boots off my feet. "*Real life* isn't five-star hotels."

He wiggles his hips deeper into the bed's plush duvet. "Maybe it is with me."

With an air of mystery, he rolls off the bed and heads straight for the door. "Have yourself a nap," he says over his shoulder. "I've got a few things to do."

"Wait, what?" My words meet the back of a peephole, they're answered by a loud thud.

I nap for four hours.

When I wake, it takes me a few seconds to remember where I am. When I do, my belly flops and I cover my face with my hands.

What am I doing?

There are a million reasons why I shouldn't be here. Why it won't work with Cooper and me. Setting aside for a moment that I'm on the rebound, there's the massive age difference between us. But it's the distance that's really the key. Wherever he's from—whether it's two hours or two days' drive away—we can't be on the road working for two weeks, then back on the road again to see each other. Turning our lives inside out, leaving family and friends and homes behind to be together, it's setting things up for failure right from the start.

And that's *if*, when the novelty wears off, he even wants more than what I suspect this is: a summertime fling.

Then there's the rest.

I'm a forty-year-old, tattooed woman who's already decided a family isn't for me. Taking that choice away from Cooper just wouldn't be right. Spending his time—no *wasting* his time—with someone who doesn't want the same things he does, when he could be finding someone else who does, is wrong.

Plus, there's that voice inside my head saying, *You're way out of your league—step aside woman, it's time to leave.*

I roll over in the expansive bed, letting the coolness of the sheets soothe me. My cheek hits a piece of paper.

Pulling it out from under myself, I see a note handwritten in a loopy scroll on hotel stationery.

> V,
> Take your time and shower.
> (I already did while you slept.)
> Be ready for dinner at 6.
> C.

V and C.

They even rhyme.

I only now notice how well they go together.

It elicits a joyful smile, but a wave of melancholy hits me in its wake.

He's not in our room when the clock reads six.

A bit confused and slightly concerned, I check my phone for texts.

Nothing.

I don't send him a message; instead, I choose to be patient. Settling into the lounge area sofa, I sip from my glass of water and get goosebumps from the room's AC.

I wait.

At 6:15 there's a knock at the door.

When I check the peephole, it's Cooper standing on the other side, holding…

I eagerly pull open the door.

"Guacamole?" My eyes grow wide.

His white-toothed grin positively brims with pride.

Shit, this guy is *good.*

We're talking pro-level charm.

"I've been paying attention." He hands me a clear cellophane-wrapped container. It's a common brand found at the grocery store. I shake my head in disbelief, biting back a smile.

I'm duly impressed. It's a million times better than flowers.

Paying attention indeed.

"Sorry I'm late. I ran into traffic."

"Traffic?" I raise a brow.

"Shhhh," he whispers. "This is supposed to be *real.*"

Is this act he's putting on borderline ridiculous? Yes. Does it still make me swoon? Of course.

He steps inside, letting the door fall behind him as I head for the fridge in the kitchenette. I stash the guac with a promise to bring it tortilla chips later.

He clears his throat. "You should know I'm notoriously late."

"You've never been late on the platform." I step forward, setting a hand on my hip in challenge.

"Well, that's because I'm basically captive," he says as he approaches. "And as you suggest, it's not '*real.*'" This time he uses air quotes.

We meet in the middle, and that's when I finally take him in. I pan slowly down the front of him. He's wearing a new white button-down dress shirt, slate-grey pants and—oh my—freshly polished work boots.

"Oh, Cooper." Pointing at his steel toes, I give a *tsk tsk.* "It's gonna take weeks to get it back, all the scuffs and marks and street cred."

"Worth it," he says with a wink.

Right now, that crisp white shirt is begging to be unbuttoned…and to accompany my underwear to the floor.

He takes one more step toward me, just beyond what's considered friend zone, but still tantalizingly out of reach.

The pheromones are coming off him in waves.

I see a tiny cut from shaving on his left cheek.

"You look handsome."

The handsomest man I've ever seen.

"You're beautiful."

Only when you're the one looking at me.

We break out in wide smiles.

I've chosen the navy linen slip dress I bought days ago at the shop with Cooper. It was a last-minute addition to my order that now feels oddly meant to be. It's the perfect date-night dress. With delicate straps, it shows off every ink leaf on my shoulder and fits me like a dream.

When I move to get past him on the way to my sandals, he reaches for my hand. Callus against callus, he threads each of his fingers with mine. When he's done, I shift my gaze up, visiting where the top two buttons of his shirt are deliciously left undone. I take a tour along his freshly shaven chin. Lastly, I arrive at my destination: those stunning eyes that do their best to take my breath.

For a moment, I think they catch a glimpse of my very soul.

He squeezes my hand, just once, before turning toward the door. "One date, a *real* date. And then you can decide."

I expect the restaurant to be stuffy, a hoity-toity affair. Instead, it's relaxed and informal. It's completely unexpected and entirely fun.

There's an open and animated kitchen, with an exuberant chef who makes the rounds. When he comes by our table, we tell him that we're divers, so he sends us a dessert that's made entirely of flavoured bubbles.

We eat, we laugh, we tell stories. It's obvious neither of us wants it to end.

As we linger over our drinks, the conversation finally wanes.

Tension develops quickly, taking up so much space, it might as well pull up a chair. For me, it's a building dread. The looming inevitability, rearing its ugly head.

Cooper plays with his scotch glass, making the ice rattle against the side. Reaching across the table with his other hand, he grabs mine. When our palms meet, my eyes close and I sigh. He's studying me when they open.

"I could look at you all night."

My face heats.

Tonight's look was sponsored by Chapstick; I'm the epitome of low-maintenance chic.

"You don't take compliments easily, do you?" He chuckles.

Ironically, the candle on the table is showing *him* in impeccable light.

"An aging woman's quandary." I pull my hand away to sip from my glass, more from nerves than thirst.

"Ah, there it is."

I raise a curious brow.

"The little reminder of our age difference. You add them every so often, just to remind us both it's there." He settles back in his seat.

Do I really do that?

If so, it's strange. Because—if I'm being honest—setting reproduction issues aside, the more time we spend together, the less relevant this ten-year age gap becomes.

I ignore him and return to the compliment. "Striking, I'll give you. Unique, sure. Beautiful may be a stretch."

"I'll be the judge of that," he replies.

"With purple hair and tattoos, I'm hardly the type to take home to Mom."

His brow furrows, face looking like his dive helmet went foul. "What are you talking about?"

"I'm sure she's hoping more for Taylor Swift, less Megan Fox going full-on Machine Gun Kelly."

He looks at me like I have three heads.

"For the record, your tattoos are a work of art that tell your story. Anyone would appreciate that. And in high school I had a Megan Fox poster in my bedroom, so it tracks."

He empties his scotch glass.

"And Tay Tay may be an entire fucking empire, but she doesn't save lives at a hundred-plus feet."

A heady mix of pride and empowerment comes over me. I attempt to speak.

Cooper raises a hand to stop me, eyes never leaving my face. "Can we get out of here?"

Our server approaches, and this time it's me who says it.

"Cheque, please."

CHAPTER 43

We spill into our room, a horny mess of grabbing hands and biting teeth. The second the door closes, I'm untucking his dress shirt and reaching for buttons. In urgent steps he's got me against a wall, one hand in my hair, the other up my dress.

When I steal a peek at him, he's already watching me. We smile against each other's mouths. I shamelessly bite his bottom lip when he starts to pull away.

"Bed, couch, table. I feel like a kid in a candy store." He abandons my hair, reaching up my skirt and taking my ass in both hands. His eyes widen when he discovers my thong underwear, and he lets out a low groan.

"I know." I slip my hands inside his shirt, run them along his hard chest. "We've been getting it on in a glorified closet; we don't know what to do with all this space."

"Speak for yourself. I know *exactly* what to do." He hikes my five-foot nine-inch frame up like it's nothing and I wrap my legs around his waist.

When we get to the bed, he practically tosses me onto the mattress. I think I actually bounce.

The sound I make is like a squeaky toy, which makes us both laugh.

When he mounts the bed on top of me, one knee between my legs, all laughter ceases.

With a hand either side my head, he slowly, languidly, leans down to kiss the hollow of my throat. My hands work through his hair while he lingers at my neck, feeling the short strands at his nape.

Cooper kisses a trail down to my cleavage, exactly the way I like.

He remembered.

A long lick from his tongue turns my body molten.

"Vibrant." He kisses my chest.

"Vivacious." He licks my throat.

My stomach flutters.

"Voluptuous." Teeth skim my jaw.

Pausing, he looks up at me. "Valuable."

Any initial urge I might have had to giggle at the resurrection of the various V-names vanishes when I see the look on his face. So genuine, so true, so decidedly…*real.*

"All the names I want to give you." His voice is low and tender, like a direct wire communication system straight to my goddamn heart.

I want to barricade us inside this moment. All alone, just C and V. No realities, no limitations, no list of what we can't be.

But…

"This isn't real." The words fall from my mouth. It's barely above a whisper, but Cooper's flinch makes it look like I screamed.

"What?"

I prop myself up on my elbows. "In this little hotel bubble, we might as well be miles from shore again, with all the *real world* we see."

Cooper rolls away, settling in on the bed next to me.

"*Real world.*" He shakes his head. "I had to do something—*say* something—to stop you." He gestures to me. "You were racing off that helipad right in front of me and saying shit like *no strings.*"

"I thought that was what you wanted."

"No." His volume takes me aback. "With you? I want all the strings." He places a hand on my thigh. "I want to get tangled up in knots and wound up with all your wool." He inches closer. "I'm the fucking macrame of men when it comes to you."

His words should make me buoyant, but instead they make me sink. Because as much as I love hearing them, they don't change a single goddamn thing.

"Cooper, we need to be honest, not just with each other, but with ourselves."

"I don't know what we're arguing about."

"Our age difference, to start."

"In all these weeks, how many times has our age difference *really* come into play?"

I think back on every conversation we've had and come up empty. Never.

Cooper's quick to notice my non-answer. "And...that's how relevant it is."

He sits back against the headboard, a delicious combination of messed hair and wrinkled shirt. "You know as well as I do that the numbers are irrelevant. We have more in common than any couple I know who are the same age." He scratches his belly like he always does when he's thinking.

Couple.

Forget about Cooper's confession, it's *me* who's tied up in knots. I need to get untangled. I stand and start to pace.

"You're thirty years old, Cooper. Having a fling with a forty-year-old is one thing, but investing time in a relationship? You don't have time to waste on a woman who won't give you what you need."

"Waste?" His face turns sour. "Nothing about this is a waste."

I cut to the chase. "What if you want a family?"

"I don't."

"You can't say that." I rest my hands on my hips.

"Violet, I *don't*. You know that this profession…this life-style…isn't conducive to pets, let alone kids. I ruled them out a long time ago."

"You're young. How you feel about that might change if you find the right partner."

"What is it you said to the doctor? *Do you not respect me enough to believe that I know my own mind?*" He stands from the bed and approaches me.

Points to Cooper.

I stand taller. "Look, I know how this works, Cooper. I've seen people commit years to relationships, only to fold because of this."

He runs both hands through his golden locks, making them stand on end. "Oh yes, older and wiser." He groans and turns away.

"No. Listen." I step closer, grabbing his arm. "It starts as a tiny, dangling, loose thread that you tuck up inside and ignore until it gets caught on everything. It gets snagged and pulled until the entire seam comes apart."

He turns back to face me. "I know what this is really about." He rests his fists on his hips. "You want to keep playing this game, fine. Whatever." He raises a hand in capitulation. "You pretend that by not knowing where I live, you've managed to protect yourself. That you're spared from really getting to know me or from letting me know you. But it's crap, Violet, and you know it."

He steps closer, until I see the furrows of his eyes and feel the warmth from his breath. "Sure, you don't know where I lay my head at night, but you know I have night-mares when I sleep. You think if you don't know where I get my groceries, you're holding me at arm's length. But you know that behind my smiles are a million insecurities about what people really think of me, that maybe they think I'm not enough. You believe not knowing the geography of our lives protects us, but you have the map to my heart and know every place in it."

"Cooper…" I should back away, but I grab hold of his arms instead.

He takes my face in his hands and runs his thumbs across my cheeks. "And you know it so well because right in the fucking middle is *you*."

It's everything I could have wished for him to say, and I believe every word of it's true. But I'm old enough to know that sometimes what we feel isn't enough.

"We can't—"

"Don't say it." He rests his forehead against mine.

I draw in a ragged breath.

"We need a clean break, Cooper." It's the unvarnished truth, and my chest tightens unbearably when I say it.

He closes his eyes with a breath. Hesitates. Then steps away.

He sits on the edge of the bed, elbows resting on his knees. It feels like a markedly submissive move.

Since we met, it's felt like pushing a stubborn shopping cart that wants to steer left. With one defeated look from him, the metaphorical wheel straightens, and his compli-ance—even though I wanted it—oddly breaks my heart.

"Come here." He reaches a hand to me.

When I take it, he pulls me until I stand in front of him.

He rests his head against my stomach, smoothing his hands along my hips. I run my fingers through his hair.

"Clean?" he says into my chest. "No. I want jagged little edges that cut to the fucking bone. I want a horrible fight. I want us to say terrible things to each other that we never forget and can't overcome. A lasting reminder, like a sliver that gets caught underfoot and stings with every step we take."

I don't deserve to, but I kiss him anyway. A slow and sacred kiss that aims to say everything I can't. That I wish things were simpler, different in so many ways, that I wish we could forget life and just run away.

I slip my tongue past his lips. Like being drawn to the rapture of the deep, I know it's unwise, but it feels too good to resist.

He pauses to slip off his pants, then settles back down on the bed.

His gentle, competent hands slip off my panties, then urge me to take his lap, raising my skirt as I straddle him.

This time when our bodies come together it's a long, slow goodbye.

Reverence replaces euphoria.

There's devotion instead of bliss.

The room's noisy air conditioner is the only sound as I quietly gather my things. I stack my case and bags neatly by the doorway, arrange them as I have for over a decade. I form a messy topknot with my platinum locks, glancing at Cooper's form in bed.

I hesitate at the door.

Hold on.

Spying his cell phone on the bedside table, I tread lightly toward it across the carpet.

Taking the iPhone in hand, I enter his pass code as I have dozens of times before when changing music on his yellow Bluetooth speaker. I push away the feelings of dark deception, the bitter taste of guilt that sours my tongue. This is for the better. Nasty medicine that will heal.

Searching his list of contacts, I find my name. I hit *edit* and then scroll. My thumb hovers at the bottom, but then taps *delete contact.* The phone asks me if I'm sure, and I'm not. I almost hit *cancel,* but take a deep breath and whisper, "*Yes.*"

I delete our text history before placing the phone back exactly how I found it, then turn and make my way to the door. It's like working from muscle memory as I slip silently into the night.

It's not until my plane is taxiing down the runway that I finally let go.

CHAPTER 44

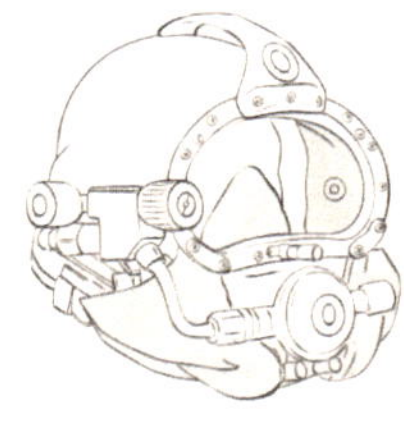They say that people come into your life for a reason, and I believe it.

Whether it's to meet some type of need that you have at a particular time in your life, or to teach you a valuable lesson, people come and go with a purpose. I'm convinced of that.

As I sit on my bed with my phone in my hands, considering my long-overdue reply to Charles, I know with absolute certainty why Cooper came into mine.

Cooper Brooks was a gift from the universe, sent to help me see my worth.

From this moment on, there will be no more covering up. No more changing fundamental parts of myself to make sure I fit in.

I release a shaky breath and type out my rehearsed text.

Violet: Sorry for the slow reply, just back on terra firma. You can pass that cardigan on to someone else. I won't be needing it anymore.

Once the message shows it's "delivered," I delete him as a contact. Each familiar step makes me wince from the memory.

"I'm an expert at that now," I say to no one.

Dropping my phone on the bed, I rise with no new lightness. Closing the door on the dysfunctional past doesn't bring the relief I expected.

Maybe it's because of the Cooper-sized hole left in my heart.

I step into the shower and turn on the water, trying to wash away my lingering doubts.

Well, I know my reason for meeting Cooper. With a new wave of sadness and guilt, I can't help but wonder…what could he possibly have won from meeting me?

CHAPTER 45

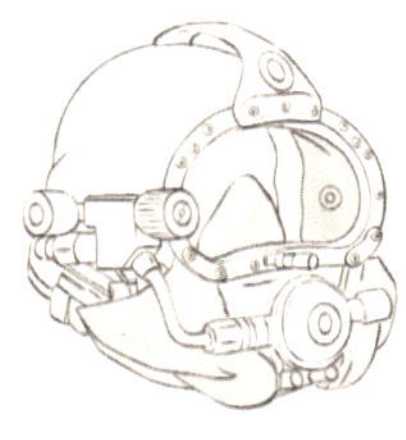

The playback on the television monitor halts and the screen displays a message:

Are you still watching?

I feel the heaviness of judgement as Netflix dares to suggest that I may have perished while watching endless hours of mindless programming.

"Fuck you, Netflix," I say to the screen.

Too drained to reach for the remote, I let it power off.

My cell phone buzzes with an incoming message. I flinch—slightly scared—while checking who it's from.

Greta: What's shaking?

Oh, not much…just the foundation on which I've built my emotional walls…

I sigh with resignation, then fire off a benign message.

Violet: Not much.

I'll leave it at that.

Greta: You sure? I've heard from JT.

My stomach twists.

Shit.

I forgot that they followed each other on social media. They met at my fortieth birthday party. And of course he's been talking to Cooper. It's the one complication I didn't think of when I hit "delete."

Bubbles start to dance on my screen.

Greta: You okay?

Tears threaten to fall. I've done a shitty thing to Cooper, and everyone still worries about the state of *my* heart. I don't deserve them.

Violet: It was for the best.

Greta: That remains to be seen.

Violet: I don't need a lecture.

> Greta: No, what you need is an
> intervention. Get ready. Bella and I will be
> there to pick you up in 30.

I release a long, slow sigh.

I'm in no mood for this.

> Violet: Really, G. I appreciate it, but I'd
> rather just stay home.

I settle in deeper on the couch, looking around at my stark, minimalist surroundings. My gear still sits untouched by the door.

Home.

What a bizarre concept.

Four walls and a yarn stash is really all it is.

Lately, I've been feeling more at *home* on the road.

> Greta: See you soon.

Greta is stubborn AF. But it's hard to be mad when that's part of what I love about her.

"Where are we going?" I say loudly over the car's sound system. Bella has a Beck playlist on in her white Toyota

Prius. I've been told this is typical ever since she connected with Kent, more so since they reunited at a stone masonry conference last week. I'm happy for her, but admit I felt a pang of jealousy when I learned they're back on track.

Greta leans between the front seats from where she's riding shotgun. "To the one place I know will make everything right."

Just a few minutes later, the bright sign of Yarns Ewe Need comes into view. Greta's not wrong. My local yarn store is a burst of sunshine on an otherwise crappy day. The business name—a delightful play on sheep—is a rainbow of colours, flanked by two quirky lambs with knitting needles between their teeth. Marketing genius. It's what brought me in on that first day. The warm smiles and stitching sisterhood are what keep me coming back.

We file into the shop, Greta taking the lead. "Go sniff some skeens."

"Skeins."

"Whatever, you know what I mean." She pulls Bella toward a display of fun project bags; I head straight for the sock yarn.

It's relatively quiet in the shop, with just a few patrons along the aisles. Geraldine is busy ringing in customers; another salesperson is restocking shelves.

As I round a sweater display, I spot Robyn helping a male shopper.

"Can I help you find something?" she asks him.

It stops me in my tracks.

I can tell it's him even as he stands facing away from me.

If that beautiful ass didn't give him away, the dreamy look on Robyn's face would. She involuntarily touches her face, cheeks pink from his attention. A laugh bubbles up in my throat, but I swallow it back. The shock of worlds colliding is set aside as I listen attentively to their conversation.

"I need that stuff for socks—it's thinner. What's it called?" he asks.

The colour on Robyn's face deepens. "Um, ah…"

Oh god, he's going to make her say it.

I watch her shift nervously on her feet.

Seconds pass. I want to end poor, shy Robyn's suffering.

There's another painful beat.

"You want *fingering*," I interject, putting her out of her misery.

He turns.

It's excruciatingly slow. I wait to enjoy the angled lines of his face.

Then it's mine that heats.

I see the flicker of recognition when it registers. "Violet?"

At the sight of him, my stomach does an amusement park twist.

I adjust my crossbody. My brain offers a million questions: *Why? What? When?*

"What are you doing in my local yarn store?" I finally speak.

That he's standing here so casually completely baffles me.

I try to get my bearings, taking stock of the situation.

"*Your* local yarn store? This is *my* local yarn store. I live in the warehouse conversion a few blocks down the road." He gestures over his shoulder. A smile starts to form on his lips.

"That's Kent's building," Bella says, coming up behind me.

No fucking way.

I'm rendered speechless, which gives Greta and Bella a chance to catch up.

"Whoa, this is Cooper?" Greta asks no one in particular, ignoring the fact that we're right in front of her.

"Holy shit, look at him," Bella mutters. "No wonder she's a mess."

What the hell is happening?

I've heard of these moments: serendipitous run-ins of movie-ending proportions.

This can't be what's happening here, can it?

Robyn's head bounces between us, eagerly watching the exchange.

I think I'm having heart palpitations. I'm certainly in a cold sweat.

I glance over at the girls, but despite their running commentary, it's clear that they're not surprised.

"Wait…is this why JT suggested something called *fibre therapy*?" Cooper raises a brow, looking just as dumbfounded as me.

Greta and Bella chuckle.

"JT put it all together." Greta shrugs. "I guess he got tired of waiting for you two to figure things out and decided to intervene."

Cooper scratches the front of his Dee Snider T-shirt. When his eyes find mine, I almost buckle at the knees.

"Can I have a word with you?" He doesn't wait for my reply, instead walks right past me, heading for the door.

He leads us out onto the sidewalk, slides on his mirrored sunglasses, and protectively crosses his arms.

"Cooper…"

He walks in a complete circle, then stops abruptly in front of me.

"I woke up and thought, *Surely she's just gone for coffee,* so I pulled out my phone. I figured I'd send a message, but your entire contact was gone."

My stomach roils with shame. "I'm so sorry." I cross my arms too.

"What the fuck, Violet?"

"I thought I was doing us both a favour. Letting you find someone your own age, to ride off with into the proverbial sunset on your electric motorcycle." I laugh, but it falls flat. "I was making things easy."

"Easy?" His volume and tone make me take a step back. I haven't seen him this angry since he had a fist in Bigot Bob's face. "Would you stop doing that!"

"Doing what, exactly? Being honest? Being *real*?" I ask, stepping toward him.

"Stop thinking that just because you're ten years older, you know what I want or need."

Frustrated, I turn around to leave, to put a safe distance between us.

"And stop thinking that it's not you."

I hang, mid-stride.

Then turn back.

The sight of him makes my heart pound, makes me question every decision I've made.

I've spent years waiting for men, looking for men, misinterpreting men, being controlled by men. I want it to end. As much as I blame the age difference, or the complications of distance, I know I've walked away from Cooper to protect myself. To take back control and make my own future, even if it's one where I'm alone.

The lingering complication? How Cooper makes me feel.

He respects me. Empowers me. Seeks to understand me, even when I'm at my worst. Even when I'm outing friends with my big mouth, or when I'm a shell of myself after years of romantic neglect. I've been determined not to compare them, but where Charles sought to cover and stifle, Cooper celebrates every part of me, shining a light on all the places I've been taught to conceal.

Cooper.

I can't believe he's here. I'm equal parts astonished and scared to death.

After weeks of convincing myself it was impossible, surrendering him to the world, the universe has given him right back to me.

I look down at my grey sweatpants and almost chuckle. The reflection of myself in his sunglasses brings me right back to the day when this larger-than-life man stepped out of the shadows and showed me his beautiful ways. I've never met anyone like him: strong but gentle, bold but at-ease, wise beyond his years. A treasure I don't deserve.

"Walking away is one thing, shutting me out is another." Cooper steps toward me. "Why would you do that?" His eyes search mine.

Wanted.

Beautiful.

Never too much.

"Because how you make me feel terrifies me, okay?" I snap. "We were never supposed to be." I gesture between us. "I was a mess on the rebound, and you were supposed to be a player, just looking for a summer fling. Men were disappointments, relationships were futile. And you came along and changed everything."

My chest aches with each admission. My face burns with honesty.

"Violet." He steps toward me, but I step back. I need the space to say this.

"I expected nothing. Asked for nothing. Just like I always have before. But then you showed me how to ask, taught me that was okay. You raised my expectations, and I dared to want more." I draw in a long, deep breath.

Love unfurls like a blossom in my chest.

"The way I feel for you scares the shit out of me."

"V—" Cooper approaches, wrapping his hands around my biceps.

I set mine against his chest. "Let me say this."

I don't dare look at him. I focus in on his ridiculous T-shirt and gather up my nerve.

"Because if I can be deflated by three years spent on someone who never even made my heart sing, what will it do to me when this thing ends?"

When I finally have the courage to look at him, I find a gentle smile. The trademark Cooper smile. The kind that makes you feel safe, like the centre of his entire world.

"You're..." I swallow. "You're like some kind of hot work, welding back together all the parts of me that I thought were broken."

He brushes aside a lock of hair that's tumbled across my face. I lean into his hand. When he cups my cheek, my eyes fall shut and I sigh.

"We need to make the most of this," he tells me.

"Of our second chance?"

It's hard not to feel like we've been given one.

"Yeah." He grips my hip and winks. It does wondrous things to me. "And our two weeks off."

How is it possible that we live in the same city, only blocks apart?

We were two souls walking on opposite sidewalks, until fate—and now JT—brought us alongside.

His lips inch toward mine. "You know, I live just three blocks down."

"I've heard that line before!" Bella shouts from the store's doorway, where she and Greta stand watching.

Have they been there the whole time?

Cooper completely ignores her, taking my face in his hands. "You're finally doing it."

"Doing what?" I ask, voice cracking.

"Looking at me like you do guacamole."

By the time our lips meet, I know there's no turning back.

CHAPTER 46

Twelve Days Later

Cooper sits on my overstuffed blue couch, wearing my grey trackpants and a frown. He's taken to wearing them when he's at my place. They hit him mid-calf, but they're so large on me that they do fit, and the world is all the better for it. Turns out the romance books were right: they look *that* good. Unbelievably sexy.

I steal another glance. Lord, save me now.

Cooper swears under his breath. He's attempting his first bind-off on a knitted washcloth, and it's not going very well. His massive hands with small needles are a bit of a challenge, but his teacher uses…um…positive reinforcement to keep morale up and spirits high.

"Argh." Another complaint makes it over to me where I'm prepping dinner in the kitchen.

It's our last night at home before we're off to separate platforms, so we're staying in.

Home. It finally feels like one.

I channel my inner schoolmarm and bark at him on the couch. "Oh, quit your whining. Bind off your stitches like a good boy and then we can have dinner." I toss tomatoes into a bowl.

"What did you just say?" He looks up from his knitting with wide eyes.

"Dinner. It's almost ready."

"Not that part."

"Bind off your stitches like a good—"

Even from my distance, I see his eyes darken.

"Oh dear," I murmur.

The project in his hands is tossed, and he stands and marches over, approaching me from behind where I'm prepping our salad.

"Say it again," he says to the back of my neck, voice low and velvety. His hot breath moves the fine hairs at my nape. I giggle.

I drop my knife and turn to face him. "I didn't think that would *do it* for you."

"Neither did I." He sounds genuinely surprised. And genuinely turned on. "You should say it once more, just to be certain."

I wait for a few seconds. Make him pine for it. Then I lay it on thick.

"Come now, Cooper, darling. Bind off your stitches like a good boy."

"Fuuuuck."

He devours my neck like *I'm* dinner.

I groan, covering my face with my hands. "Oh god, we're such a cliché."

"What if your clichéd *good boy* crawled naked to his Queen—would that make it better?"

Heat floods every inch of my body.

"Yep, that'll do it."

The End.

ACKNOWLEDGMENTS

I'm learning that books are like snowflakes; no two are ever the same. *Under Construction* was written so easily, the words flowing through me and onto the page in four short months. Drafting *Hot Work*, on the other hand, I've equated with squeezing out the remnants of an old toothpaste tube. But the words came, slow and sure, and for that I'm incredibly grateful.

This book simply would not exist if not for my diving source. He took the time to meet with me before a single word had been written, and our initial conversation fuelled so much creativity, this story wouldn't exist as it stands today without him. Thank you, Christian. Thank you for your patience through all the questions, for reviewing my offshore platform art while actually on an offshore platform (mind still blown!) and for helping me make this story the best it could possibly be. I take the technical accuracy in my books as seriously as the spice, and for your help to make this one spot on (welding pun!), I will forever be grateful. Any errors or inaccuracies are purely the fault of my own and for the sake of drama.

No one knows the struggle of an author like another author. To my emotional support authors, Heather McPeake, Stefanie Steck, Jenni Bayliss, Alyssa Milani, and Anne Longbridge for seeing me through my struggles. I hope I'm even just a fraction of the support to you that you are to me.

Thank you to Josie Juniper for once again serving as

editor for this project. I think I limited the "lumps in throat" this time, but I'm sure you lost count of the dozen other crutch words I clung to this time. Thanks for your patience.

I want to thank my early readers. I was raw and vulnerable this time, and you held my hand through the editing phase. Forehead kisses to Stef, Heather, Heather, Anne, Laura, Sam, Monja, and Emily.

To the bookstagrammers who showed up to events with bracelets, hugs, and love for *Under Construction* while I was drafting *Hot Work*, thank you. You probably don't realize it, but your words of support spurred me on in those difficult times, when I doubted myself and wondered if I'd ever type "the end" again. Thank you.

Thank you to Mandee, Natalie, and Jess from The Byndery Box for believing in me and my stories. That you chose *Under Construction* as one of your titles will always mean so much to me. I can't wait to see what other adventures await us.

To Patty, thank you for being your wonderful self. That's all I need to say here.

Thank you to Allie Martina and Zipless Podcast for inspiring me to keep going and tell my stories the way only I can—sometimes with only 550 words.

Special thanks to Steffanie S for providing your valuable hair knowledge. I have short hair and haven't coloured it since last millennium…if not for your professional help with Violet's hair colour scene, I would've been lost.

Thank you to Jen's oak tree. If you find it odd I'm thanking an oak tree, then you might not know me—or the oak tree—as well as you should. Jen's oak tree has magical properties. I wrote a lot of words under it's shadow and know it bestowed some magic on these pages. (Thank you so much, Jen!)

I held a wee giveaway to name one character from *Hot Work*. Thanks to Elise for naming James; Clayton's sidekick, who fled the rig with him in solidarity of Cooper's act against Bigot Bob. Thanks for the great name suggestion. Thank you also to Ronny and Mimi for nominating Geraldine and Robyn as knitting shop staff names. I hope they love finding themselves on *Hot Work's* pages.

Paige Moreland, you did it again. What a beautiful cover. I love working with you and what we create together. Can't wait to see what comes next for this series.

Erika Plum, thank you for the amazing offshore platform art that graces an opening page of this book. You absolutely nailed it, and I'm sure readers will greatly appreciate the valuable context that it provides.

Monja De Luca, I want to thank you for your endless support and assistance. You do so many things for me, but the biggest of them all is gifting me with your unconditional friendship. I am so grateful for you.

To my family—blood and otherwise—for encouraging me when I doubt myself and urging me to carry on when I begin to question, well…everything. You steady me when I stumble, and offer support when I don't even realize I need it. Pam, Heather, Emily, Jen, and Mary…thank you. Words will never be enough.

Mom, I miss you. I hope you like the little piece of you I added to this story.

To Dad and my boys. Nothing makes me more proud than making YOU proud.

Mr. Kate Cole. You are my partner in every sense of the word. Thank you for letting me take you out for beers just to then rattle on about storylines and characters that live in my head. Thank you for never once telling me I "shouldn't" do something, but instead, wholeheartedly encouraging me to pursue every irrational dream or outlandish goal I've ever had. You, my dear, are the ultimate book boyfriend come to life. Xo.

Lastly, I want to thank the amazing Women on Site and

their co-founder, Tessa Ferzli. You all provide endless inspiration to me and my stories. What an incredible group of women and human beings you are. I feel honoured to sit among you at each monthly meet-up. If you're a woman in the trades, or a male-dominated profession, look for a Women on Site chapter near you. It will change your life.

ABOUT THE AUTHOR

Since meeting Mr. Darcy in English 101, **Kate Cole** hasn't managed to shake her obsession with all things happily ever after. A sucker for romance, this Canadian bibliophile is a woman in construction in the street, spicy romcom writer in her desk seat. When she isn't reading or writing, she's also a wife and mom in suburbia who can't get enough of Duran Duran or pedicures that match her current reads.

Hot Work is the second novel in Kate's Women in Trades Romance® series.

www.ingramcontent.com/pod-product-compliance
Lightning Source LLC
Chambersburg PA
CBHW030529190726
48283CB00006B/1837